MOONLIT THORNS

MIDNIGHT MANOR

P. RAYNE

Cover Designer: Regina Wamba

Line Editor: Joy Editing

Proofreader: My Brother's Editor

About Moonlit Thorns

No one knows what happens up at Midnight Manor.

The home of the Voss brothers sits like a sentinel looking down on our small town, remaining a mystery. The four brooding billionaires rarely leave the confines of the iron gates, fueling rumors that have existed for decades.

When my father dies, all the security I've known is ripped away, forcing me to come face to face with the eldest brother, Asher Voss. His outward beauty is just as I'd heard —it belies a predatory nature, irresistibly drawing me in.

A bargain is made, and I have no choice but to live in the shadowy confines of his gothic manor to save my family. As time passes, it becomes harder and harder to deny our attraction.

Asher Voss might be too old for me, and he's definitely cursed by his own demons, but an inferno of passion between us threatens to either consume or destroy us both.

MOONLIT THORNS is a dark contemporary romance Beauty and the Beast retelling.

the Midnight Manor series

MOONLIT THORNS

P. RAYNE

TRIGGER WARNINGS

Trigger warnings can be found on our website if you want to check them out.

WARNING: These trigger warnings contain MAJOR spoilers.

Playlist

Here's a list of songs that inspired us while we were writing the Midnight Manor series. You can follow the playlist (and us) on Spotify using the QR code below.

CHAPTER
ONE

ANABELLE

I rip down the paper pinned to the front door of my family estate. The paper shakes in my hands as my eyes scan the printed words. At first, I'm confused, but then it registers, and my stomach pitches, my heart stutters, and my knees wobble.

NOTICE TO QUIT FOR NON-PAYMENT

I KEEP READING, glancing over the words for the pertinent details.

...WE HAVE NOT RECEIVED your payment...

...your account is in arrears...

...you are hereby given ten days to vacate the property...

WHAT THE HELL? This must be a mistake. Oak Haven Estate has been in my family for over a century. There's no mortgage on the property and no bank to make payments to, so how could we possibly be in arrears?

My assumption is that when all the paperwork to settle my father's estate was being done months ago, something got messed up, and this has been sent here in error.

The thought of my beloved father sends a pang through my chest, and I look at the column on my left, my favorite place to hide behind when I was young, and we'd play hide and seek. He'd pretend he couldn't find me as I circled around it, trying to avoid detection.

I cut off those memories. There's no time to wallow in grief right now. I've had no time to grieve since I got the phone call that he'd been found dead, attacked by some animal on an adjoining estate.

Swallowing hard at the image that haunts me, I scan the remainder of the notice, which is filled with legal bullshit, until I reach the end and see who it's signed by. A chill rushes over me, causing the hair on my neck to prickle. My mother always said that means someone is walking over your grave, but a quick glance at the family plot off in the distance tells me no one is over there.

I try to shake off the ominous feeling, but when I look at the name printed in the deepest black ink against the starkest of white paper, the feeling washes over me a second time.

. . .

ASHER VOSS, CEO of Voss Enterprises

FEELING LESS certain now that this is a mistake, I push open the door and head inside, panic taking hold. *Don't freak out, this may still be a mistake.*

Even though I'm sure the Voss family rarely makes mistakes.

My fist squeezes so hard the paper crumples in my palm.

Everyone is situated in the dining room having breakfast as expected. Grandma Boudreaux, my father's mother, with her perfectly curled short hair, is dressed with a minimal amount of makeup. Seated to her right at the head of the table is my mother, Frances. Her face is drawn, the same dark circles under her eyes she's had every day since my father's untimely death. But at least she's out of bed today. That's a win.

I hate to think of what this will do to her if the paper I'm holding in my hand is true. She's been walking a tightrope between despair and sanity, and on any day, I'm unsure which side she might fall on.

It's the only reason I'm still in my hometown of Magnolia Bend after three months and haven't returned to Nashville, where I intern at a small publishing house. Thankfully, being an intern is the only reason they gave me such a long leave of absence. They aren't paying me anyway. Since I graduated, I've been surviving on a monthly stipend I receive from my family. A stipend I'm now thinking is drained.

Luke, my younger brother by two years, sits next to my mom. Now, at only twenty years old, he has to take over running the ranch, including the cotton and soybean farming and the bourbon distillery my father started a few years ago.

My grandmother notices me in the doorway. "What were you doing out so early?"

I want to tell her that doesn't matter, but I would never disrespect my grandmother, the matriarch of our family—especially now with my mom being so checked out. "I went for a run before breakfast."

I went for a run first thing this morning to listen to my audiobook. My book was getting to a good part—my favorite part in any book—when the hero is about to proclaim his love for the heroine. Though I hate running, I love listening to audiobooks, and I find that pairing something I hate with something I love allows me to listen while I exercise.

I need something to help me stay sane while I'm back home. Though I grew up here, I've always been anxious about what lies outside the village limits. For as long as I can remember, I wanted to leave here to explore the world. College gave me the excuse I needed, and though I always want to return home to visit my family and spend time on the estate, there is still a part of me that wants to explore more of what the world has to offer.

I swallow hard before stepping into the dining room, tempering my panic, not wanting to alarm my mother if this is some big misunderstanding. However, the more I think about it, the more doubtful I am. "There was something posted on the front door when I returned."

Luke sits taller in his seat, reading my energy.

"What is it, dear?" my grandmother asks.

My mom is listlessly moving her eggs around her plate. I don't know if she's even registering the conversation right now.

I pass my grandmother the crumpled notice, and her age-spotted hands with swollen knuckles smooth the paper out on the table next to her plate. She holds it at arm's length because she doesn't have her reading glasses. She must be at the part that says we have to vacate the premises because she glances at me, unable to disguise her alarm. When she finishes reading, she puts a hand to her chest and sets the crumpled paper on the table saying nothing.

"What is it?" Luke asks. When neither of us answers, he pushes his chair out and leans across the table to grab the paper.

"It's a mistake, right?" I ask my grandmother while Luke reads. Even though I'm sure the Voss family doesn't make errors, especially the eldest of the four Voss brothers.

"I can't be sure." Her voice is smaller than I've ever heard.

"What the fuck!" The paper slips from Luke's grip, dropping to the table.

"Watch your mouth," my grandmother says, regaining some of her elegant composure.

"Apologies." He lets his head dip. "Anabelle's right, this is just some mix-up or a prank."

"The Voss family aren't known for being pranksters," my grandmother says.

That's putting it mildly. The four brothers who live high on the hill in Midnight Manor are known for a lot of things—being billionaires and untouchable, mysterious deaths, the vast number of unmarked vehicles that roll onto their property once a month—but definitely not their sense of humor.

"It *has* to be a mistake. This property has been in our family for well over a hundred years. There's no way Dad would have taken a loan and risked Oak Haven, especially with the Vosses no less."

"Frances," my grandmother says gently.

For once, my mom acknowledges her name. "Yes?"

"When the lawyer gave you everything for the estate, did you see anything about the Voss family?"

My mother's eyes gloss over. "Do you know when Heath will be home?"

A pained sound, similar to a wounded animal, escapes my throat.

This isn't the first time since my father's death she's asked about him as though he's still among the living. I don't know whether she's losing her mind entirely or if her confusion is a by-product of the medication her doctor put her on after my father's death to help her through the process.

"Safe to say she's not going to be any help," my brother sneers.

I glare at my brother. He's taken my mother's new mindset personally. I understand his anger. Our mother was always alive and vivacious, so full of love for her family. I'm sure it's horrible trying to carry on without our father, but she has to try.

My grandmother pushes away from the table. "I'll get the papers from the lawyer and see what I can find."

I snatch the paper off the table. "I'm not waiting. I'm going directly to the source."

My brother's chair legs screech along the floor, and he stomps around the table until he's standing in front of me. He places his hands on my shoulders and dips his head so we're at eye level. "You're not going to Midnight Manor, Belle."

My chest squeezes from him using the nickname my dad had for me. "It's the fastest way to get answers, and if this is true, it's the only way to find out what we can do to keep the estate."

Luke shakes his head. "No way. We can figure something else out. That place..."

He doesn't finish his sentence. He doesn't have to. Midnight Manor is where our father died.

"I have to. If there's any chance of us losing our ancestral home, I have to see if there's a way to stop it. It's what Dad would have wanted."

His lips press into a thin line, and his jaw clenches because we both know I'm right. "Then I'll go."

"Not happening, little brother. You stay here and help Grandmother search through the lawyer's papers. Look after Mom."

He looks relieved, and I can't blame him. Midnight Manor is not a place I want to go either, but this is too important to wait.

Luke nods. "Be careful."

"I will. Now I have to go shower and change before I head out." There's no way I'm showing up at that place looking like roadkill.

Grandmother walks over and places her hand on the small of my back. "You get in and out of there and tread lightly with Asher Voss. You don't want to anger him."

The band around my chest tightens. "I know."

Without another word, paper in hand, I leave the dining room and head to the staircase, my ire growing with every step.

Being faced with the prospect of never being able to return to Oak Haven Estate, I realize how important my childhood home is in my life. I want to be out in the world exploring, yes, but I also want to know that I can return to the safety of my childhood home and a place that holds so many warm memories. Memories of my beloved father and the last place I saw him alive.

Luke has been groomed his entire life to run this place. He has no other qualifications, and if he found something else, who would take care of my mother and grandmother? If Voss has anything to do with this, he's mistaken if he thinks

Oak Haven Estate can be ripped away from us as easily as tearing a sheet of paper in half.

Oak Haven Estate will remain in the Boudreaux family.

It has to.

And I'm going to do whatever I need to in order to ensure that happens.

CHAPTER
TWO

ANABELLE

I take one last critical look in the mirror, surveying myself in the same way I'm sure Asher Voss will.

I've only seen Asher Voss in person a handful of times, but his reputation precedes him. He's not someone to be fucked with. None of the Voss brothers are.

My brown hair hangs in loose waves, and I add a subtle amount of eyeshadow and mascara around my matching brown eyes. My blue sundress with cap sleeves has little white flowers in the pattern and ends just above my knees. The dress makes me feel a little childish and cute, but it's the best I've got here at the estate.

If I had my way, I'd wear a designer power suit to meet with Asher Voss, but I left all those back in Nashville since I didn't plan to be in Magnolia Bend this long.

It's just a reminder that at some point, I'm either going to have to accept that there's nothing I can do to help my mother and head back to Nashville, or I'm going to have to accept that I have to officially move back to Magnolia Bend for however long and get my things packed up and shipped here.

"That is a problem for another day," I tell myself in the mirror.

Satisfied that I look put together enough to try to see Asher Voss, I grab the eviction notice off my dresser and shove it into my purse. A knock sounds on my door, and when I swing it open, Luke stands there.

"You're not coming with me," I say.

"I came to tell you that Galen is here."

My shoulders slump. Dealing with my narcissistic ex is the last thing I need right now. "Send him away."

"I tried. You know how he is. He insists he won't leave until he sees you. I managed to make him wait outside on the porch."

With a sigh, I swing my purse over my head so the strap rests on one shoulder. "Suppose I'm going to deal with two jerks today then." I make my way toward the stairs.

"He doesn't know how to take no for an answer, does he?" Luke says, trailing behind me.

"Never did. I can't believe I ever dated him." I reach the bottom of the stairs, and I turn to face my brother.

"You were a teenager. Teenagers always do stupid shit." My brother does know how to make me feel better.

Galen is three years older than me, so I didn't date him until I was a senior in high school. At first, I thought he'd be an exciting man to date, but I quickly learned that what he is, is obnoxious and self-involved. We broke up before the end of the year, so at least I don't have to look at pictures of him as my prom date for all eternity.

Since I returned home, Galen's made it clear he's ready to settle down, and he's chosen me to do it with. I honestly don't know why he's so fixated on me. He's the sheriff and an attractive man as well. He could take his pick of most women in Magnolia Bend. When we did go out, it was embarrassing how many women hit on him right in front of me.

I step toward the door, but Luke whirls me around and draws me into a hug. "You sure you can do this?"

I know what he means, he doesn't have to tell me. Visiting the place where my father was killed is bound to be painful, but not as painful as losing his legacy. "I can. It will be... difficult, but I'll manage. I have to."

Luke pulls away and looks at me, hands still on my shoulders. "You be careful up there. If anything feels... wrong, you leave. Immediately."

After swallowing hard, I nod. "Trust me, I don't want to be in that place any longer than I have to."

He gives me a sharp nod, then turns to go to the back of the house. He's already behind with everything that needs to be done at Oak Haven this morning.

With a sigh of resignation, I head out the front door. I catch sight of Galen at my left on the porch waiting for me, but I don't stop, heading down the front steps.

"Good morning, Sheriff LeBlanc."

His deep chuckle echoes behind me. "C'mon now, Anabelle, we know each other better than formal pleasantries."

I continue toward my car, the May sun already high in the sky and beating down on my neck. "I'm sorry, but I don't have time to talk right now."

"What could be more important than catching up with me?"

As I reach my car, I whirl around to face him, meeting his gaze. "Almost anything else."

Galen smiles at me, black hair slicked back and blue eyes twinkling with amusement.

He never could take a hint, and he's impossible to insult. It's almost as if he can't fathom someone saying something negative about him.

He puts his hand on the top of my car, caging me against it, leaning into me. "I've decided we should be married."

I cough, choking on my own saliva. "Excuse me? We're not even dating, Galen."

"We have in the past, and you haven't dated anyone better. I haven't dated anyone nearly as great as you. Why not just get back together?"

I don't even have words for the nonsense he's spewing. "I'm not marrying you."

"C'mon, Anabelle. Just think of how good we could be together." He raises his other hand and skims the back of his knuckles down my face, and I cringe and lean away from him until the back of my head hits my vehicle. "Our children would be knockouts. You could give up that job you got in Nashville and move in with me here. Then after we start our family, you could help at the school and on the parent committee. I'd coach our sons in football. It'd be a perfect life."

"Sounds like you have it all figured out."

"You agree then?" He arches a dark eyebrow.

"Absolutely not. I'm not staying in Magnolia Bend. I've told you that."

The corners of his lips tip down. "That was before you had something to stick around for." He pushes away from the car and puffs out his chest as though he's a peacock showing off his colors.

I can't do this anymore. The piece of paper in my purse feels as if it's burning a hole against my hip. "I really can't discuss this anymore, Galen. Suffice to say, we won't be getting married, but I wish you luck on your search for a Mrs. LeBlanc."

Without a backward glance, I climb into my car and roll down the windows as soon as the engine starts for relief from the suffocating heat.

"I'm not giving up on you, Anabelle Boudreaux," Galen yells.

"I wish you would!" I call out, driving away.

Once I'm headed down the long drive from the main house, I roll the windows back up and turn the air conditioning to full blast. The last thing I want is to look as though I've been windsurfing when I arrive at Midnight Manor.

My stomach pitches with the thought of where I'm headed.

I've never been inside Midnight Manor before. Almost no one in Magnolia Bend has. I realize for the first time since I came up with my plan that there's a good chance I'll be denied access to the property. I'm likely to be turned away at the gates and never even get to see, let alone talk to, Asher Voss.

My hands tighten on the steering wheel when I drive over the small bridge that stands over the river winding between our two properties and acts like a natural barrier between them.

No way. One way or another, I am going to talk to Asher Voss today and ensure our family home will be passed down through many more Boudreaux generations.

If not for my mother and brother, then for my father. It's what he would have wanted.

CHAPTER
THREE

ANABELLE

I stop at the iron gates that separate the sprawling estate from the road, and my heart rate picks up as if I'm still on my jog from this morning.

Midnight Manor is surrounded by mystery and folklore and has been since it was built almost two hundred years ago. Like my family's much more modest estate, Midnight Manor has been in the Voss family since it was erected.

But unlike Oak Haven, it wasn't built in the classic Antebellum style of most of the landowners at the time. Midnight Manor appears more like a Gothic palace in both size and scale and sits high on a hill with the town of Magnolia Bend far below in the distance.

With one deep breath, I roll down the window, then gather the strength to press the button. Once I do, a man's voice comes through the speaker.

"Can I help you?"

"I'm here to see Mr. Voss." I grip the steering wheel tighter to keep my hands from shaking.

"Which one?" the voice from the speaker snaps.

Right. Four Mr. Vosses live here. "Asher Voss."

"Do you have an appointment?" I can hear the condemnation in his voice.

"No, but it's imperative that I speak with him."

"You need to leave if you don't have an appointment."

My mouth forms a thin line. "I'm not leaving here until I see Asher Voss. Please tell him it's Anabelle Boudreaux."

The man in the speaker says nothing for a few beats, and my heart sinks with the thought he's just disregarding me now. Then finally, "Wait there."

Nothing happens for almost five minutes, and the tension coils tighter inside me with every second that passes. I debate hitting the button again but decide that I'm more likely to gain entry if I follow his instructions. So I sit in the car, becoming more and more nervous. What will I do if I'm denied the opportunity to speak with Asher Voss?

A loud buzz startles me, and the iron gates slowly part. I quickly shift my vehicle into drive and roll past the gates, holding my breath.

This is the first time I've been on the property of Midnight Manor.

As kids, we were always warned not to cross the small river that separates our properties, or we'd face dire consequences. Which makes my father's death even more puzzling—what was he doing on the other side of the river the day he was killed?

I continue down the long drive flanked by bald cypress trees. Though it's only late morning, it's dimmer here than when I drove through the gates. Almost as though the sunlight is being filtered through black gauze. When I come to the end of the drive, the cypress trees fall away, and the manor rises up to greet me. My breath catches in my throat.

Midnight Manor is even more intimidating than I imagined. The structure is built from dark gray stone, and two wings lead in an angle off the main part of the house. At the end of each wing is a tower with a spire that reaches toward the heavens.

I park my car in the circular drive and inhale a deep, calming breath before grabbing my purse and stepping out of the vehicle. The air here feels heavier, as if it's dense and eats up the sound of my sandals on the stone.

Perched along the top of the manor are stone gargoyles. An ominous feeling of being watched makes all the hair on my arms stand at attention like soldiers. Towering over the front door is a large stained-glass rose window, and before I have a chance to knock, the door appears to open all by itself.

I step back when a tall thin man steps out from behind the door. His warm smile puts me slightly at ease. My best guess would put him to be in his fifties as there's gray sprinkled in his brown hair.

"Mademoiselle." He bows, and I'm unsure what to make of the gesture. This is not the welcome I expected.

"Um... hi."

"I am Marcel Lacour. Pleasure to meet you."

Despite his very French name, he doesn't have an accent of any kind.

The breeding my mother drilled into me kicks in, and I do my best to smile at him despite my nerves. "Anabelle Boudreaux."

His eyebrows raise. "Ah, from the adjoining estate."

I nod. "Yes. I'm here to see Mr. Voss... Asher Voss, that is."

He claps his hands in front of himself, startling me. "Of course. Right this way. Mr. Voss is in his office."

Marcel waits for me to step into the house before he closes the door and leads me through the house. It's no surprise to me that Midnight Manor is big, but I didn't realize how enormous it was until I follow Marcel through room after room.

The only other people I see are servants.

Though there are many arched windows throughout the property, even in the middle of the day it's still dim. Shadows encompass every corner of the rooms, except the ones with all the lights on. And even then, it feels darker than it should be this time of day.

When Marcel leads me down a long hallway with a soaring ceiling displaying ribbed vaulting, I realize that we're moving away from the central part of the house into one of the other wings. I'm so turned around that I have no idea whether it's one of the two I saw from outside or a different one entirely.

Eventually, we stop in front of a dark wood door, and Marcel turns to me. "If he's a little... *difficult* today, please forgive him. It's already been a day, and it's not even lunch."

My eyes flare wide. Wonderful. I've chosen to visit a man rumored to be a predator when he's having a *bad* day.

Marcel doesn't wait for me to respond. He spins quickly on his heel and knocks on the door before swinging it open a couple of feet. "A Miss Anabelle Boudreaux to see you, sir."

Marcel pushes the door open the rest of the way and retreats down the hallway, leaving me staring at a man who exudes power and dominance. Even with his attention on some papers on the large wooden desk in front of him, it's obvious this man is harmful.

I'm frozen where I stand. My legs won't work, won't move when I command them to. I'm standing in the center of the house that fueled the urban myths and nightmares of my childhood. Not only that, but I'm under the scrutiny of the biggest and baddest of them all.

"Did you come here to stare at me all day, or is there an actual purpose to your unscheduled visit? Be quick about it, Miss Boudreaux. I have things to do." His voice is deep and menacing, and when he raises his head to look at me, my breath lodges in my throat.

It's not as though I've never seen a picture of Asher Voss—though there are few of him online—but the few pictures don't do him justice. Sure, I've passed him on the street a handful of occasions, but even then, I couldn't take him in.

His deep blue eyes settle on me. The way his dark hair curls down toward his ears, some pieces falling forward onto his forehead, makes me want to reach across the expanse of the room and brush them away from his perfectly sculpted face.

He's perfect as if his beauty was created to draw you in.

I stand at the threshold of his office feeling like a rabbit caught in the sightline of a hunter, too afraid to scamper away for fear it will draw attention to me.

He continues to study me with measured patience. Finally, with resignation, I step into his office, close the door and walk toward his desk. The bored and irritated expression on his face does nothing for my confidence.

"Thank you for taking the time to see me." I clear my throat since my voice sounds squeaky to my own ears. "It's an urgent matter that couldn't wait."

"So I gathered." He motions to one of the chairs in front of his desk.

I slowly sink down, careful not to wrinkle my dress. I notice a tattoo of a lethal-looking bear on his hand. Its eyes are fierce, and its jaw is wide open in a ferocious roar, long sharp teeth on display.

Once I'm seated, I reach into my purse and pull out the paper, then set it on the desk in front of me, careful not to get too close. I'm not dumb enough to get within his grasp. "I think there's been some kind of mistake. This was pinned to our door this morning."

He gives the paper a cursory glance and leans back in his chair as though this entire conversation is a waste of time. "I assure you, there's been no mistake."

I blink a couple of times. I secretly hoped he was going to tell me there was an error of some kind. Maybe be rude and dismissive, annoyed that he had to deal with me, but the letter was not meant for us.

"How can that possibly be? Oak Haven has been in my family for centuries. There's no mortgage on the property, no liens."

"I'm afraid, Miss Boudreaux, your father needed money. I gave it to him, and in return, if he defaulted on payments, Oak Haven Estate was mine."

"Why would he ever come to you?" My voice comes out more forcefully and snippier than it probably should.

Asher Voss's eyes narrow like the beast he is. "Tread carefully, little girl. You're lucky I even allowed you to see me today. I did it as a courtesy because you've just lost your father and for no other reason. I'm just as apt to throw you out without giving you the information you want."

Daddy, what did you do? Why would you sign a deal with the devil? Tears sting the corners of my eyes, but I refuse to let them fall in front of this man.

"To answer your question, your father didn't have a choice. The banks would never lend a cent to your father. So he came to me because he knows I have money and was his last resort."

The idea of asking this man for information about my dead father, a man I thought I knew so well, stings, but the idea

25

of losing Oak Haven Estate is unfathomable. "Why did he need the money? Why wouldn't a bank give it to him?"

Asher Voss stares at me for a long moment, but there's judgment under his silence. His head tilts as if I'm a child. And I suppose to him, I probably am. Twenty-two to his thirty-six, according to Google.

"Did you really not know about your father's gambling addiction?"

Every muscle in my body tenses and anger fills my veins. "My father did not have a gambling addiction."

He chuckles low in his throat, the deep timbre reminding me of an animal's growl. "Apparently you didn't know your father as well as you thought."

I shoot out of my seat. "I knew my father! I loved him."

Asher Voss, slowly, like a predator readying to strike, stands from his chair and sets his palms on his desk, leaning toward me. If there weren't a desk between us, he would tower over me. "I'd gather there's a lot you don't know, Miss Boudreaux."

My hands fist at my sides at the censure in his eyes and the way he's talking to me as though I'm beneath him. "If what you say is true, I demand to see the paperwork my father signed. He'd never put Oak Haven Estate at risk. I don't believe you."

He pushes off his desk, standing to his full height, smoothing his tie down his chest. Although he's clothed, the way the suit has clearly been tailored for him shows off his broad shoulders and narrow waist. I assume under the suit is a magnificent body. "I'll have my assistant at headquarters have it couriered to you as soon as you leave. Which is now." He gestures toward the door behind me.

"That's it?" I don't know why I'm so stunned he's dismissing me so easily.

"That's all." He nods once. When I don't move, he stalks around his desk toward me, standing tall in front of me. His nostrils flare. "You need to leave. Now."

Something flashes in the depths of his blue eyes, but I can't decipher what. For a moment I think it might be panic, but would a man like him ever panic?

"I'm not leaving here until you tell me what I can do to keep the estate."

"There's nothing you can do. Now go." He grips my upper arm.

The feel of his large hand wrapped around the bare skin of my upper arm causes me to gasp. He, however, is unaffected as he drags me toward the door. But as he reaches for the handle of his door, I wrench my arm from his.

"There has to be something I can do." I look up at him with pleading eyes.

"There's nothing you can do. Not unless you have the funds to pay off the entire balance of the loan now that it's in arrears."

"How much is that?" Maybe I could sell my car... I only rent my place... maybe I could get a loan for the amount myself if I—

"Three million dollars."

My stomach bottoms out, and my legs shake, causing me to almost collapse. *My father gambled away three million dollars.*

As if he can read my mind, Asher says, "A lot of it he gambled. Some of it he had to use for the distillery and the farm because he was also a shit businessman."

My gaze whips up to meet his in outrage. Who is this man who can so callously speak about a man to his daughter after he was killed only months ago on his property?

I recall all the opulence as I walked through this mansion. The needless displays of generational wealth. Three million dollars is like pennies to a billionaire like Asher Voss, and yet it's as if he's taking pleasure in causing this pain. He could work something out with me if he wanted. It would make no difference to his bottom line.

"My father might have been a gambler and a poor business-man, but he was a thousand times the man you are!"

A patronizing chuckle ripples out of him. "Please stop trying to flatter me, Miss Boudreaux. It doesn't change the fact that in less than two weeks, I'll be the new owner of Oak Haven Estate."

Nausea coils in my stomach, but I refuse to throw up on his expensive leather shoes. We can't lose the only tie we still have to our father and his memory. My mother... I don't even want to know how she'd react if we were forced off the estate. She'd never recover.

"Tell me what I can do. There has to be something. I'll do anything, Mr. Voss, please." I'm a prideful woman, and I hate the desperation in my voice, but I am exactly that —desperate.

He studies me. It's almost impossible not to shrivel up within myself, but I hold my ground. Then he steps closer to me, and I step closer toward the door.

"Why should I do anything other than what the contract your father signed dictates? I did nothing underhanded. He knew what he was signing, and he didn't live up to his end of the deal. Therefore, I have every right to make Oak Haven Estate mine. Yet you're here looking at me like I'm the villain, rather than your precious father who put your family in this position in the first place."

It's not lost on me that his words ring true, but I don't care. He's the one who holds the loan. He can put a stop to this if he wants.

"I can't lose the estate. It's all I have left of my father. My brother is in charge of the farm and the distillery now. He can get things running more profitably, and we can work out a payment plan. Please." I put my hands in front of me in a prayer pose. "I'll do anything."

He shoves his hands in his pockets and is silent. I don't dare take a breath.

"Okay then... I'll make you a bargain."

My heart speeds up. "Anything."

Whatever interest rate he wants us to pay back the loan is going to be ridiculous, but it doesn't matter. It's worth it if we can keep the estate.

Without warning, his hand wraps around my wrists where they're still raised in front of me, and he wrenches them above my head, using the leverage to walk me back a couple of steps until my back is pressed against the door. My breath heaves in my lungs, and my eyes widen as fear seizes control of my limbs, leaving me frozen in place.

His gaze dips down between us before his blue eyes meet mine again. "You come to work for me for a year, and I'll consider the debt paid. You can keep your precious estate."

I blink at him in confusion. He wants me to *work* for him? "Wh... what would I be doing?"

He takes a long, leisurely look down at my body before our eyes meet again. "Whatever I want."

Something about the way he says that sounds inherently sexual, but there's no way that can be what he means. He'll probably have me filing paperwork for eight hours a day or fetching him coffee.

Gathering my courage, I raise my chin, even though it's more than obvious that he has the advantage of me pressed up against the door. "Do you always work from your home office?" Will I have to relocate to work from Voss Enterprises' head office?

"I don't. But you will work from here. In fact, you'll live here." He sounds as if he's coming up with these rules as we stand here chest to chest, so close I can smell the mint on his breath.

"Here? At Midnight Manor?"

He arches a dark eyebrow. "Afraid all those urban legends are true?"

I remember all the stories I've heard over the years. How the manor is haunted, cursed even. How more than one person has died suspiciously on these grounds—my father included. How no one knows much about the Voss brothers. How one Saturday night a month, expensive vehicles with blacked-out windows make their way through town and up the hill to Midnight Manor.

How can I possibly live here for a year?

But how can I not?

Thoughts of my family and memories at Oak Haven Estate take over all the fearful questions about Midnight Manor. To work here, I'll have to give up my internship in Nashville. But I can start over trying to get a foothold in publishing once the year is up, and I know for certain that Oak Haven Estate will remain in the possession of my family.

"I want it in writing that we're free and clear if I come to work for you for a year."

"You don't trust me?"

"Not even a little."

He smirks and releases my hands but stays only inches away from me. "You're not as naïve as I thought."

"I'm under no illusion that you're going to make anything easy for me."

"Smart girl. You can bet I'll make it very hard and unpleasant."

My neck cranes to stare up at him. The predatory gleam in his eyes mixed with the sexual innuendo has my nipples pebbling in my dress. *What kind of reaction is that for me to have?*

"Good." I nod, and he backs up a few steps, allowing me to finally breathe normally. "When do I start?"

"Be here at eight tomorrow morning." He turns and walks back to his desk, his tone dismissive.

"Your lawyers or whoever can get something together that fast? I'm not starting until I have a contract."

He doesn't bother to even glance in my direction as he sits at his desk, picking up the papers he was reading before I arrived. "I pay people generously to make sure I get whatever I want, whenever I want it, Miss Boudreaux. Marcel will see you out now."

The door behind me swings open, and I whip around, meeting Marcel's patient smile.

Without another word from Asher Voss, I walk out of his office. Only as I'm following Marcel through the manor do I question why Asher Voss would even want me to work for him. Surely whatever kind of work I'm doing for him isn't worth a three-million-dollar salary. But who am I to question a man like Asher Voss? He must have his reasons.

All that matters is Oak Haven Estate stays in the family.

CHAPTER
FOUR

ASHER

The morning after Anabelle Boudreaux's visit, I finish up my swim and join my brothers in the dining room for breakfast as usual. Nero and Kol are already there, but Sid is absent.

"How was your swim?" Nero asks, pouring himself a coffee.

"Fine." I sit beside him and slide my cup his way for him to fill it. I take a sip and set it down to put some eggs and toast on my plate, along with berries.

"You swam longer than usual. You're usually the first one here in the morning," Kol says.

"What is this, an interrogation?" I stab my eggs with my fork.

The truth is that I did swim longer than normal. I've been agitated and filled with restless energy since yesterday and wanted to burn it off with the hopes of a more productive day.

Kol chuckles as if he's in on some inside joke, but I ignore his childish antics.

"Anyone know where Sid is? I need to ask him about that EPA bullshit going on over in Delaware."

Voss Enterprises purchased some land to develop into a high-end oceanside resort, and the EPA's been on our ass about displacing some fucking birds that nest there every year.

"Don't know where he's at," Nero says.

We eat in silence before I decide to give them the heads-up they need regarding our new employee who will be starting today. I've been somewhat dreading it, knowing they'll likely read something into the arrangement I made, but they shouldn't.

"You two should know that I've hired Anabelle Boudreaux from Oak Haven Estate to work for me. She'll be living here for the next year."

Kol's fork slips from his grip, clanking against the plate. "Why the fuck would you do that?" He glares.

"For my own amusement." I reach for my cup of coffee.

"Maybe if you ever left this fucking place, you wouldn't have to drag in strays to keep yourself amused." Kol pushes his chair back and leaves the room, sliding past Sid as he finally graces us with his presence.

"What's his problem this morning?" Sid asks as he sits beside the chair Kol just exited, reaching for one of Mrs. Potter's freshly made scones.

"He's pissed that our big brother hired the Boudreaux girl to work for him *and* live here for a year," Nero says before popping a grape into his mouth.

Sid pauses from ripping apart his scone and eyes me across the table with an arched brow.

"Her father owed me money and defaulted on the loan, and I was set to take their estate. She begged me, said she'd do anything to keep it. Making her life miserable for the next twelve months felt like it would be entertaining." I shrug, playing off my own confusion as to why I decided on this avenue for her to repay the debt instead of a more customary agreement with a higher interest rate.

I'm still not sure what possessed me to make the offer. Yesterday when she was in my office, sitting in the same chair as her father had two years before, begging and sniveling like the piece of shit he was for me to grant him a loan, all I noted was the difference between them. Whereas he'd disgusted me with his display of weakness, Anabelle had put on a strong and tough front. Oh, she'd been pissed, there was no doubt about it, but she was equal parts afraid. Still, she put on a good show, and it sparked something in me—the need to keep pushing her to see how much she'd take before she broke.

Sid rips the scone the rest of the way apart and pulls the fresh cream and jam toward him. "What are you going to do about—"

"I'll handle it." My voice is sharp.

The idea that he thinks I'd let an outsider discover anything they could use against us is insulting.

He nods. "What's she like?" Nero asks.

I turn to my left and look at my youngest brother. The one we all tried to protect from the horrors that were inflicted in this place. "I have no idea what she's like, Nero. Nor do I care."

"Is she hot?" Sid asks.

My head whips in his direction. "Don't even think about it. She's not here to serve anyone but me. I don't need her riding any Voss dick that comes her way, thinking that gives her a free pass to skirt her duty to me."

"Interesting..."

I scowl at Sid. "What?"

He shoves a large bite of his scone into his mouth and gives me an innocent look. Well about as innocent as he can manage.

"She's practically a child compared to me. You'd do well to remember that too."

"Speaking of women, I started dating one I think might have promise," Nero says, changing the subject before Sid and I get into it.

At thirty, it wouldn't be unheard of for Nero to want to settle down with someone, maybe start a family, but my protective instincts flare to life. Even before our father left this earth eighteen years ago, it always felt like my duty to protect my brothers. Nero especially.

"Who is it? What do you know about her?" I ask, spreading honey on my toast.

"Uh-oh, you've switched on Ash's overbearing big brother mode," Sid says and shoves another chunk of scone into his mouth when I glare at him.

"Her name is Maude Johnson, and she lives a few counties away. Before you say anything, we met unexpectedly when her tire blew out on one of the county roads, and I stopped to see if I could help."

"Such a Prince Charming," Sid says with no small amount of sarcasm.

"How do you know she didn't target you?" I ask before taking a bite of my toast.

Nero rolls his eyes, always thinking the best of people.

I'm right to ask though. When you grow up a billionaire's son, you spend your entire life vetting whether women want you for your money and power or just for your dick. Which is part of the reason I stick to fucking women now, not dating them.

"She didn't target me. Did you hear what I said? She had a flat tire."

When he says shit like that, I wonder if maybe the three of us sheltered Nero too much.

"Just be careful," I say, knowing I'll be ordering a background check on this woman at some point today.

The sound of a throat clearing has me looking across the room. Marcel stands straight as a ruler, hands behind his back. "Miss Boudreaux is here for you, sir."

39

"Put her in my office. I'll be there shortly." My fingers tingle with anticipation. It's been a long, long time since there's been anyone new in Midnight Manor.

I take my time finishing my honey toast and getting the latest update from Sid with regard to the EPA situation. He's the lawyer in the family and assures me that the team of lawyers at Voss Enterprises are on it.

"Let me know if and when Kol needs to get involved." I glance at Sid from under my brows, and he nods.

Suffice to say, those cocksuckers at the EPA don't want Kol involved.

I push away from the table, discarding my napkin beside my plate.

"Have fun with your new pet." Sid chuckles. It would probably sound good-natured to anyone else, but I hear the cutting edge under the surface.

I grin at my brothers. "Oh, I plan to."

Poor Anabelle Boudreaux isn't prepared for the likes of me. Gone is the cushy life provided to her by her father with borrowed money. She's about to wish she could give me the estate and call off our deal, but once she's signed on the dotted line... she's mine.

FIVE

ANABELLE

My leg bounces as I sit in Asher Voss's office, waiting for him to come in.

I don't know how long I've been sitting here, but the longer I sit, the more my nerves set in. I didn't even eat this morning because of my roiling stomach—which got worse from the way my brother and grandmother were looking at me as I stood next to my vehicle saying goodbye. My mother didn't even deem my departure worthy of getting out of bed. I push back my anger at her. She might not be aware of what I'm doing.

When I arrived home yesterday and explained the situation, my brother and grandmother were adamant I didn't agree, but it's the only way. Giving up one year of my life to play secretary or whatever to Asher Voss is worth keeping the estate in our family, and when I put it that way, neither of them could disagree, no matter how much they don't like the idea.

The more time that passes as I sit alone in this cavernous room, the more nervous I become. I wouldn't put it past my new boss to leave me here on my own this long just to make me nervous. Seems like something he would do. Not that I know the man, but he and his brothers are certainly infamous.

I use the time to see if I can get a better sense of the man who sits behind the desk. Dark, ornate wooden bookcases line the wall behind the desk and are filled with tomes that appear to be as old as this manor. I'm too far away to read the spines, but the bookworm in me would love to see what he has on his shelves. I don't dare get up and make my way over, though. Instinct says that Asher Voss wouldn't take kindly to someone snooping around his office.

His laptop is on his desk, placed in front of the deep brown leather chair. The large desk, though covered in files and papers and such, is neatly arranged so that everything is at his fingertips.

A giant Persian rug sits under my feet and covers most of the room, including the area behind me that has a sofa and two chairs set opposite a large dark stone fireplace.

When footsteps sound through the open door, outside the office farther down the hallway, I draw in a long breath and smooth my black dress down my stomach, sitting up taller in the chair. I don't bother to turn when the footsteps enter the room and the door closes behind the person, but the hair rises on the back of my neck. Seconds later, the footsteps are muffled by the rug.

"Good morning, Miss Boudreaux," Asher says from behind me.

"Can you please call me Anabelle? I keep thinking my mother or grandmother is here every time you refer to me that way."

He stops on the opposite side of the desk as me, wearing a navy blue silk suit that's perfectly tailored to his large frame. "I see our first order of business is to make it clear that *you* work for *me*. I'll refer to you however I so choose. Understood?" He arches one of his perfect eyebrows at me, and though I want to tell him to go to hell, that could result in him ending this deal before it even starts.

"Fine," I spit out between gritted teeth. "And what should I call you?"

"Mr. Voss is fine. Unless you prefer sir?"

My eyes widen. I'm sure it's not intentional, but the way he says the last sentence sounds sexual, and I hate the way my stomach whooshes with the thought of something sexual between us.

Of course, how could it not? A man as appealing as Asher Voss could probably make anything sound sexual, including reading the instruction manual on how to put a cabinet together.

"I'll stick with Mr. Voss." There. I think I managed to inject some steel into my voice.

He sits at his desk and takes a large envelope off the pile of papers to his right, then slides whatever is inside onto his desk. "This is the contract to solidify our arrangement. My lawyer has drawn it up, and while you're welcome to have your attorney look it over, I will not be changing any of the terms. It's an as-is contract. Take it or leave it."

"You're not going to let me negotiate the contract?" I hadn't even considered the possibility that I wouldn't get a say and be able to have some influence over my life for the next year.

He delivers me a patronizing look, and I suddenly feel every bit of the fourteen-year difference in our ages. I must appear so naïve to a man like Asher Voss. God, I hate that.

"There's no negotiation here. You agree, or you don't." When I don't say anything, he continues, sliding the papers over to me. "Allow me to explain the gist of it... you will work directly for me for the next 365 days. Your duties will consist of whatever I deem them to be—no questions asked. I'll pay you minimum wage and you will live on the premises so that you are always available to me. You will give up your phone as of today and not get it back until your contract is fulfilled. Anything you see, hear, or do here will be covered by an NDA included in this contract, and if you breach it—in any way—I will sue you so fast that not only will the estate be mine, but so will your firstborn. Understood?"

I nod, hands in my lap and meeting his narrowed gaze, pretending this doesn't scare me.

He nods in return and carries on. "You will only be permitted to leave Midnight Manor on Saturday evenings."

My mouth drops open. Part of how I rationalized making it through this next year was that as soon as I was done working for the day, I'd spend the evenings with my family.

"Do I have a curfew too?" The words slip from my mouth before I can stop them.

"Would you like one?" he growls.

I look at my clenched hands in my lap, loosening them to rid the white knuckles before he notices. "No, sir."

The sir just comes out of my mouth, and when he doesn't say anything, I raise my head. He's looking at me with what I think might be surprise and... need? But before I can really be sure, the mask he always wears slips over his face, and he speaks again. "In return for following all those rules, you will be allowed to keep your estate free and clear, plus I will pay you a small salary to live off of."

He seems to be finished, so I pick up one copy of the contract and scan the first page. I decide I'm going to read over every single word of this contract—twice. I know it's an effort to prove I'm not as childish and naïve as he assumes I am, and I don't know why I care. If I'm honest, I'm also hoping it annoys him. He has all the power here, and it's apparent he likes it that way.

I find that the contract says everything the way he explained it. No surprises that I can tell.

"Are you just about done? I need to get on with my day." He looks down at his Patek Philippe watch.

"I can't exactly take your word for what's in here before I sign."

He chuckles, but there's no humor to it. "Be honest with yourself, Miss Boudreaux—you'd sign it no matter what was printed on that paper. That's how desperate you are."

I have to grind my teeth to keep myself from saying something. Lowering my head, I go back to reading. "It says here that if I break any of these rules, you decide the consequences."

"That's right."

I stare at him. "What will the consequences be? It doesn't spell it out here."

"I'd suggest you don't break any rules, and you won't have to find out."

Sick of this back and forth, I hold out my hand. "Fine. Give me a pen so I can sign."

He does so without saying a word.

A chill sweeps over the room as I take the pen and put it to paper, signing and dating the document. The air in here grows thick now that I've committed my life to this man for the next year.

"You may use the communal parts of the property as you see fit while you're here. Stay out of the north, south, and east wings unless you're specifically instructed to go there for reasons that have to do with your job. Those are my brothers' wings, and if you wander in there without my knowledge, you may find that I'm the nice brother. Do not venture into my area, the west wing, unless I specifically direct you to. And you are under no circumstances permitted below the main level. Am I clear?" He pins me with an intense stare.

"Crystal."

He takes the pen and signs both copies of the contract, then looks up and over my shoulder. "Come sign these, Marcel. You can be our witness."

I startle and look over my shoulder. I hadn't even heard the door open.

Marcel strides across the room with what appears to be folded clothes in his hands. He sets them on the corner of the desk and walks around so that he's standing beside Mr. Voss, bending at the waist and signing the contract.

"Is that Miss Boudreaux's uniform?" Mr. Voss nods toward the pile of folded clothes.

"It is." Marcel gives him a quick nod, standing straight with his hands behind his back now. He reminds me of a soldier standing at attention.

Mr. Voss nods. Marcel seems to know that means he's been dismissed, and he leaves the room. This time I do hear the door shut.

"I think you'll find this will work fine for your duties this week."

I lean forward and take the pile of clothes off the desk, looking through it. It's a housekeeper's uniform and not the sexy kind. The mundane black dress has short sleeves folded back to reveal a band of white, a white collar, and buttons up the front. It also comes with a white apron and black shoes that look orthopedic.

My head whips up. "What is all this?"

"Your job for at least the next week. Though if I had to guess, much longer. You don't seem like the sort who will catch on easily. The stubbornness you've already displayed will likely cause you to put up a decent fight before you submit." The gleam in his blue eyes tells me he likes the idea of me being insubordinate, though I'm unsure whether it's the fight or the submission.

"I thought I was going to be working for you?"

"You are. Now go get changed."

"But I thought I'd be, like, your secretary or something."

He heaves a long sigh, face tightening. "Like I said, stubborn." He stands from his desk. "Marcel should be waiting in the hall for you. He'll show you to the outbuilding that houses the staff and show you to your room where you can change into that." His gaze drops down to my lap. "Unless you'd rather forfeit your end of the deal now and get this over with?"

I bolt up out of my seat. "Never. Oak Haven Estate is mine. You won't break me no matter how hard you try." *Shit.* That stubbornness he spoke of got the best of me.

A slow, predatory grin shows him baring his teeth. "Challenge accepted."

CHAPTER
SIX

ANABELLE

Marcel shows me to a room in a building that's about a ten-minute walk over the property from the main house. It's out of view of the manor but has much the same vibe.

My room is sparse with only a twin-size bed, a small dresser, and desk, and no other adornments. It's the only room available, though, so there's no point in complaining.

When Mr. Voss said I'd be living on the property, I pictured myself staying in a room in the manor. It didn't even dawn on me that I might be put with the rest of the staff.

I'm self-aware enough to know it's because of how I was raised. We didn't have the same level of wealth as the Voss family, but we still had housekeepers and nannies. Gardeners and other people kept things running on the property. I didn't make a meal for myself until I moved away to college and was on my own.

I suppose I never thought I'd be on the other side of things. The thought makes me feel ashamed. I've never thought myself better than anyone else because I was born into affluent circumstances, but clearly, I'm more biased than I thought.

That point is driven home after I've changed into my new uniform. Not because it denotes I'll be doing manual labor, but because I don't look or feel like *me* in it. Which I'm sure is the point.

The skirt goes down to the bottom of my knees, and the shoes make me feel like a grandmother. The whole thing chafes, and I know for certain that this was done on purpose. I caught a glimpse of the other staff when Marcel was showing me through the house, and those women wore more fitted, professional, and tailored uniforms than the one Asher gave me.

Whatever. It doesn't matter what I look like, just that I put in my time. Asher Voss can dress me up in a hot dog costume every day and tell me to scrub toilets. I don't care. He's not going to run me off and break our deal.

Marcel meets me at the entrance to the building to walk me back to the estate.

"I'm sorry if you're going to be forced to lead me around all day."

I don't mind Marcel. He might work for an asshole, but he doesn't appear to be one himself.

He huffs. "It's no trouble at all. Besides, you're giving me an excuse to see Finn." His smile grows wider.

"Who's Finn?"

Marcel diverts us to the right when the path comes to a fork. Damn it, I was sure we had to go left there. I'm really going to have to pay attention if I want to make sure that I stay out of the areas of the manor I was warned about.

"Finn is my boyfriend. He's the head of housekeeping, so I don't normally get to see him during the day. So worry not, *you're* doing me a favor." He winks.

I welcome the idea of having a light conversation about normal things. "Oooh, do tell. What's Finn like? How long have you been together?"

He grins as we make our way past a pond on our left. "It sounds cheesy, but he's dreamy as hell. You'll see when you meet him. Beyond that, he's about a decade younger than me, but I'm not complaining."

We both laugh.

"It's not against the rules to be involved with someone else who works here?" Seems as though that wouldn't be tolerated here. Too many secrets that could be shared.

He moves his head back and forth. "It's not exactly forbidden, but it's not encouraged. We keep our antics out of the main house, so it doesn't become an issue."

I nod. "I'm surprised. Mr. Voss seems like the type who would be against that sort of thing. You know, anything that brings joy to people."

Marcel's jaw tightens.

"I'm sorry, I shouldn't have said that. I don't want to get you in trouble or anything if I'm caught complaining about him."

"I know Mr. Voss can be... difficult sometimes. Best to stay on his good side. But he's not as terrible as he might appear. He and his brothers..."

I'm quiet, waiting for Marcel to finish that sentence, but he doesn't. "Well, I'll have to take your word for it. I haven't seen any evidence to the contrary."

We're quiet as we walk near a long row of hedges. I didn't pay it much attention the first time past, but now I realize it seems to form a huge square.

"What's that?" I ask.

Marcel glances at the hedges that must be ten or twelve feet in height. "That's the maze. Don't go in there unless you don't want to get out."

"Is it really that hard to find your way out?"

His eyes fill with what I think is sadness. "Best just to heed my word on that."

A minute later, we're back inside the manor. The air is definitely thicker in here. Marcel leads us, and it only takes me about a minute before I lose my bearings again. Great.

He leads me down one of the smaller hallways and knocks on a partially open door. A man sitting at a desk with his back to us and typing on a computer, spins around in his seat. When he spots Marcel, a huge smile instantly transforms his handsome face. The moment Finn sees me, he schools his expression and stands.

I'd guess he's probably in his early forties with cropped blond hair and blue eyes. He's tall and on the slender side, and there's a deep dimple in his cheek when he smiles. There's a boyish quality about him.

"I see what you meant about being dreamy," I say under my breath so only Marcel can hear me.

"Told you," he says back, pride filling his voice. "Finn, this is Anabelle. Asher has brought her on to work for him, but he wants her in housekeeping until he says different."

It sounds weird to hear him refer to the eldest Voss as Asher, though I suppose with there being four brothers, simply saying Mr. Voss wouldn't do.

"Pleasure to meet you." Finn steps forward with his hand out, and I shake it. "Do you have any experience in house-keeping?"

My cheeks heat. I'm starting to think I probably won't have any experience in anything I'm going to do here. "No, sorry."

He lets my hand go and glances at Marcel. "That's okay. We can always use an extra set of hands. I'm happy to show you how to do things."

"I appreciate that." A little of my anxiety eases. Asher Voss might be a prick, but so far everyone who works here isn't.

"I'll leave you two to it. If you need anything, Anabelle, let me know." Marcel gives Finn a long, heated look before leaving.

Finn stares after him for a beat before shaking his head and returning his attention to me. "Just let me respond to a few things in my email, then we'll get started."

I nod and sit in a cushioned chair in the corner of the some-what messy office. This is not what I want to be doing with my life.

But that doesn't matter. I just have to make it fifty-two weeks.

Three hundred sixty-five days.

Eight thousand, seven hundred, sixty hours.

I can do this.

CHAPTER
SEVEN

ANABELLE

The first three weeks pass in a blur and are filled with scrubbing, wiping, mopping, and every other sort of domestic labor. By the end of each day, I'm exhausted and want nothing more than the barren room and uncomfortable bed I've been assigned.

I always thought I was in decent shape, but it's clear to me that jogging and the occasional gym visit haven't prepared me for ten-to-twelve-hour days of hard, physical work.

The fatigue has been a blessing, though. It doesn't give me much time at night to dwell on all I'm missing outside these walls. I'm not lying awake wondering if my mother is all right, thinking about how my brother is coping with running the estate on his own.

Every Saturday evening, though, as soon as I'm finished with work, I rush home to check on everyone. So far, nothing has changed with my mother. My grandmother is

61

still as uneasy with the arrangement as she was in the first place, and my brother is keeping a good handle on things with the estate.

As of this week, I've been moved to work under Mrs. Potter, who is in charge of the kitchens and the serving staff. She's a delightful, no-nonsense Englishwoman I'm guessing is in her midfifties, and her husband works for the Voss family on the estate grounds. Her hair is graying at the temples, and she's round around the middle. Though she can be stern at times, I take an immediate liking to her, the way I did with Marcel.

My first couple of days are spent in the kitchen, learning some of what they do and helping to prepare the meals. Mostly prep work, but I prefer it over the work I was doing for the past few weeks.

When I walk into the kitchen today, I head over to the hooks on one wall where the aprons hang and take one down, pulling the loop over my head. "Morning, everyone."

"You won't need that today, love," Mrs. Potter says.

My forehead wrinkles. "Am I going back to work under Finn?"

She shakes her head and walks up to me, taking the apron from me when I pull it back over my head. "Mr. Voss has requested that you prepare his green drink for him this morning and serve it to him after his swim."

I tense at the mention of Asher Voss. At least I'm assuming that's the Mr. Voss she's referring to. I've been lucky and only run into him a handful of times these past weeks. He does the same thing every single time—pretends I don't exist. He doesn't look my way nor address me.

I can't help but watch him whenever he's near. I tell myself it's because anyone would keep an eye on an obvious threat, but I fear that it's more than that.

"His swim?"

She hooks the apron back on the rack and motions for me to follow her. "Swims every morning. Then he has his smoothie out by the pool, comes in and showers, changes, and takes breakfast in the dining room with his brothers before he goes to his office. Creature of habit that one."

"And he asked me to make it and deliver it to him?" I swallow back my nerves. I'm sure this is some kind of test.

Of course it is. The asshole probably waited until I'd grown somewhat comfortable in my new role here, then decided to spring this to put me off-kilter.

"He did." She pats my arm as we reach the end of one of the long counters. "Now don't look so worried—it's just a drink. Let me teach you how to do it in case this becomes a daily thing."

I swallow, hoping that won't be the case. The last thing I want is to have to come into contact with him first thing every morning. Talk about a bad start to the day. I liked it a lot better when I did my thing without any interference from him.

Mrs. Potter shows me where all the ingredients are and measures how much of everything to put into the high-speed blender. When I'm done and pouring it into the tall glass, I can't help but cringe. There's no doubt it's healthy, but it looks and smells disgusting.

Mrs. Potter passes me a small silver tray. "Now take this out with the glass on top and wait at the end of the pool until he's finished. You don't need to announce your presence. He knows you'll be there and waiting."

"I don't know where the pool is," I admit. I still haven't gotten used to how big this place is, and I get easily turned around.

She gives me a patient smile and turns to one of the younger guys who acts as a sous chef in the kitchen. "Chris, can you show Anabelle to the pool please?"

He nods and sets down the onion he was about to chop before motioning for me to follow him. I do so with the tray in one hand and the glass in the other. No way am I risking walking through this manor with the drink on the tray. I'm likely to dump it all over some priceless rug or piece of furniture.

"Just through those double doors." He motions ahead. "Here, let me get it for you." Chris opens one of the doors for me, and I walk through.

"Thanks." I glance around when I get outside. I've never been on this side of the house before.

I'm standing under a large portico that looks out over a stone patio with some iron furnishings. Past that is the large pool, gleaming in the early morning sun.

I swallow hard and place the tall glass on the silver tray, saying a small prayer that I'm able to balance it so that it doesn't slide right off. Carefully and slowly, I make my way over to the end of the pool, and Asher Voss comes into view.

He slices through the water like a ship gliding through the ocean, not stopping for a break as he reaches one end then turns and pushes off to continue back down the long length of the pool. The muscles in his arms and back bunch and clench as he swims. It's impossible not to appreciate the sheer strength and power of his body.

I stand still, balancing the drink on the tray, trying hard to not move. He's paying me no attention, but after a certain amount of time, it's awkward. The sun warms the back of my neck, and though it's early in the day, I get warm under my uniform. Sweat beads at my temple, and my hand shakes as I continue to hold the tray out in front of me.

Finally, after what seems like time moving through molasses, he stops at the edge of the pool in front of me. There's no expression on his face as he pulls off the goggles and tosses them to the side, then uses his arms to hoist himself out of the pool.

Water slides down his body onto the stone. If drinking the disgusting concoction I prepared for him is doing *that* for his body, I can understand exactly why he forces it down his throat every morning.

Because his body is utter perfection.

Perfectly muscled and honed the way you'd expect from a swimmer, except he's bigger. The wide expanse of his chest would swallow me up if I was ever tucked into it.

Jesus, why am I even thinking like that?

But I know why. Because his olive skin glistens in the sun, and I want to lick every one of the water droplets off of him. I want to run my fingers through the small patch of hair between his pecs. I want to brush back the dark hair that falls to his forehead. Examining the man standing before me makes me realize that I've only ever dated boys, and Asher Voss is all *man*.

The sound of his voice draws me from my thoughts, and I blink at him, not registering his words.

"I'm sorry?" My cheeks heat from having to ask him to repeat himself, knowing he's not going to be pleased.

"I asked if you were going to offer me my drink or just stand there openly gawking at my body like you're hoping I'll sit you on the edge of the pool and feast between your thighs."

All the air rushes from my lungs.

Was I that obvious? Oh, god. Even if I was, why is he saying that to me?

But I already know why. He does it to make me uncomfortable and embarrassed. I won't give him the satisfaction.

Raising my chin a touch, I hold the tray farther out from me, offering it to him. "I can assure you, that's the last thing I'd want to happen."

If only because I wouldn't be satisfied by only his mouth. No, I'd want his hips grinding into me.

I manage to keep my face blank at my errant thought.

His eyes flash with anger, but he says nothing as he grabs the glass off the tray. I let my hand fall to my side, still holding the tray, and my muscles thank me for the relief.

He brings the glass to his lips as he turns to walk away from me, and I get my first look at his ass in his tight black Speedo. I didn't dare look below his waist when he was facing me. Never in my life did I think I would find a Speedo attractive on a man, but I now see the error of my ways. Because the fabric stretches perfectly over the tight globes of his ass.

There's no time for the inappropriateness of that thought because he spins back around, scowling. "This tastes like shit. Make it again." He shoves the glass toward me, and I take it from him. Then he walks over to a lounger, picks up the black towel, and dries himself. "I'll wait here. Don't take long. I need to start my day."

Asher Voss sits and stretches his long legs out in front of him and leans back, eyes closed as though he hasn't a care in the world.

I frown and make my way back to the house, biting back my irritation. Mrs. Potter oversaw everything I put in, and I made it exactly how she told me to. Did I do something wrong? Did she forget an ingredient?

Thankfully, I remember my way back to the kitchen, and I explain to Mrs. Potter what happened. She doesn't look pleased, but she doesn't say anything untoward against Mr. Voss, just sets about showing me how to make it again.

When it's ready, I head back through the house to the doors that lead to the pool, shoving the tray under one arm and holding the glass in my hand so I can use my free hand to swing the door open.

Setting the drink back on the tray, I walk over to where Mr. Voss sits on the lounger in the same position as I left him.

67

When he doesn't react at all to my presence, I clear my throat. He opens his eyes, and his gaze finds mine. I refuse to wither under his intense stare.

"I remade it like you asked. Mrs. Potter once again oversaw everything, so you should find it meets your standards." I give him a saccharine smile.

He doesn't say a word as he pulls the glass off the tray, bringing it to his lips. After one swallow, he cringes and sets it back down on the tray with more force than necessary. So much so that I almost drop the tray.

"Do it again. Something is wrong."

My jaw clenches, but I manage to keep myself in check as I turn and go back toward the house.

What an asshole. He's doing this to get under my skin. And the worst part is that it's working.

I stomp through the manor back to the kitchen and don't bother to enlist the help of Mrs. Potter this time. She has better things to do than to be involved in this power play. Every ingredient is added methodically until I'm certain it's exactly how it's supposed to be, then I head back out to the pool.

Asher is exactly where he was when I left, reclined on the lounger, eyes closed, the picture of relaxed sophistication. Jerk.

"Here you go, Goldilocks," I mutter under my breath, not bothering with pleasantries this time. I stand beside him and shove the tray toward him.

His eyes open and narrow at my insolence. But screw him. The contract never said anything about having to be pleasant while I did his bidding. I've already lost the battle of pretending he's not getting to me.

Rather than reaching for the glass, he nods at it as if I'm supposed to pass it to him. With a huff, I clench my teeth and do as he requests.

He eyes me up and down in a way that makes me feel as though he's sizing me up somehow, and he brings the glass to his lips once more. I wish watching him swallow wasn't so sexy. Since when is swallowing sexy?

I'm still pissed, but my nipples pebble at the same time. I bite my bottom lip until it hurts to distract myself. I don't want to be attracted to this man. He's a total asshole, and he's way too old for me.

When he pulls the glass away from his lips, he licks them, gaze still on me. "If you keep looking at me like that, you won't like the consequences." His voice is clipped and restrained.

Irritation rises to the surface. "The contract didn't stipulate that I had to perform all my duties with a smile on my face."

"You're not looking at me like you're irritated, Miss Boudreaux."

My forehead wrinkles. "What are you talking about?"

"You're looking at me like you want me to fuck you." He motions to his lap.

For the first time, I allow my gaze to drop below the front of his waist and suck in a breath. His hard, thick, rigid length is pointed in the direction of his hip and straining against the fabric.

"There are always consequences, Miss Boudreaux. I learned that early in life. It's time you did too."

I sputter for a moment, nothing intelligible coming out of my mouth.

"The next time you look at me like that, I might take you up on your offer. Remember that." He sets the glass on the small table beside the lounger. "Now get back to work."

I don't wait for him to say anything else. I turn around and rush back inside the house, unsure what I'm more embarrassed about—the fact that he noticed what I was thinking or that I had those thoughts for a man like Asher Voss in the first place.

CHAPTER
EIGHT

ANABELLE

The next few days are more of the same. First thing in the morning, I bring Mr. Voss his disgusting green drink, and he sends me back at least two times to remake it.

I manage to somehow keep my temper in check—maybe because I know what to expect from him now. But on Friday morning, Mrs. Potter tells me that I'll be serving breakfast to the Voss brothers in the dining room.

My eyes widen, and I still at her words.

"C'mon now, don't be frightened. Their bark is worse than their bite for the most part."

It doesn't escape me the way a few of the kitchen staff look at her with disbelief when she says that.

It's been almost a month since I got here, and I have yet to see any of the Voss brothers other than Asher. He's enough to deal with. I can't imagine being relegated to the abuse of four of them at once.

Mrs. Potter instructs me how to properly serve everyone and in which order everything should come out. She tells me where to place what on the table based on what each of the men prefers for breakfast. Then she explains where I'm to stand in the room in case they need anything, and she makes it clear that I am not to react to anything I see or hear. I am to be invisible.

When I enter the dining room to put out the coffee, cream, and sugar, the room is empty of people. I'm thankful, since it allows me to get the lay of the land without their intimidating presences.

The dining room, like all the rest in this house, is huge and has a large, ornate crystal chandelier hanging over the middle of the dark wood table. Each side must have eight or ten chairs. The walls are painted a deep royal blue that almost looks black depending on where the dim light hits it. Paintings in intricate gold frames dot the walls, and a large mirror hangs over the huge fireplace.

I set the coffee service on the end of the table closest to the oversized picture of a pretty woman with long, flowing dark hair and deep blue eyes, as Mrs. Potter told me to.

When I return with the eggs and scones, there are two men there seated side by side. I've seen one in town before, so I know that the one with his dark hair cut shorter on the sides and slicked back on top is Obsidian Voss.

"Morning." I stand on the opposite side of the table and place the items in front of them.

The one I'm not sure about looks up at me with malice, and my heart stutters. "You must be Ash's new plaything."

My eyes widen. I'm not sure what to say to that, but I'm saved from having to respond as I straighten up because Obsidian speaks.

"You'll have to forgive my brother. He's not used to having new people at Midnight Manor. I'm Sid, the best-looking Voss brother, which you're probably figuring out now, and this is Kol."

"Stop flirting with the help." Asher's voice startles me.

"You're frightening the poor girl, Ash. Ease up," Sid, as I now know him, says.

I feel Asher's presence behind me, and I'm afraid of what I'll find, but I raise my chin and turn around. It's been hard to look at him without thinking about the size of his dick since that day I saw the magnificent outline in his Speedo.

Our eyes meet and neither of us says a word for a moment, until his expression becomes more lethal. "You're standing in front of my seat."

Embarrassment floods me like water rushing past a broken dam, and my cheeks heat. Here I thought we were locked in some power play when really the man wanted to sit and eat his breakfast. "Oh."

I sidestep and hurry from the dining room to bring in the rest of breakfast. For the most part, the three brothers ignore me as I come in and out, continuing with their conversation. Once I've brought everything in, I go stand in the spot where Mrs. Potter said I should.

Things are going well, and after a couple of minutes, I don't find it so difficult to stand with my hands behind my back, facing forward and pretending I don't even exist. I prefer it to the alternative of being the center of attention in this room.

But then the dick Asher Voss says, "Where's my honey?"

Shit. I picture the small bowl of honey where I left it on the counter. I must have forgotten to put it on the tray and bring it in. "I'll go grab it."

"Is it really that hard to remember I need honey every morning? I'm sure Mrs. Potter would have told you."

"I'm sorry. I'll go get it."

Before I can turn, he reaches for me. I look down at the ferocious bear tattoo on the top of his hand as his fingers easily wrap around my wrist. His hands are so large compared to mine that they're like bear paws.

"Is this going to be another smoothie incident?" He arches a brow.

My body tenses and is on high alert, but damned if I know whether that's because I'm afraid or if it's because his skin is touching mine. I shake my head. "No, sir."

There's a snicker from the other side of the table, but I don't dare look away from Asher Voss.

He nods and releases me. I twist around and leave the room, trying to look as if I'm not running away like a scared little rabbit.

When I return with the honey, Asher doesn't thank me or acknowledge my presence, and it's then I realize that the energy in the room shifted in my short absence. I don't know what was said, but it feels heightened in here now.

"Where's Nero?" Asher asks his brothers once I've returned to my spot in the corner where I will hopefully be forgotten.

"Probably with that girl he's been seeing," Sid says.

"Can't seem to pull his dick from her pussy long enough to come up for air," Kol grumbles.

My eyes widen, and I resist the urge to look at them.

Asher doesn't say anything, but there must be something on his face because Sid says, "What, you don't approve?"

"He needs to be careful, that's all."

I chance a quick glance at Asher. He's seated facing my direction. His jaw is set, then he shoves a piece of his toast into his mouth. When he glances over and catches my gaze, I stiffen and look straight ahead.

"He will be. He knows the drill," Sid says. "Maybe we need to get you laid, lighten you up a bit."

I wonder how a man like Asher Voss gets laid. Because there's no doubt he has to be getting laid somewhere. He's too hot and too full of sexual charisma not to be. But from what I know, he rarely leaves the house. Does he have women brought in for him? Does he have a girlfriend? I'm guessing no, from what Sid just said. Jesus, why do I care?

"I think we all know that's not a problem for me." Asher's voice is smug.

"Have you fucked your new pet yet?" Kol says with such distaste, I stiffen.

"I don't fuck the help," Asher says, as though I'm not standing here listening.

"Maybe I will then," Kol says, and Sid chuckles under his breath.

The sound of cutlery being dropped onto a plate sounds, but I don't dare look anywhere except straight ahead, my breathing picking up and sounding loud in my own ears.

"Ash's plaything, come on over here." It's Kol's voice.

I don't move my head, but I do let my gaze flicker over to Asher Voss's. His jaw is set, his expression is thunderous.

"Don't look at him for permission," Kol spits out. "You work at Midnight Manor, do you not? I'm just as much a part of it as he is."

I walk over to Kol. He slides his chair out at an angle and motions for me to stand between him and Sid, across from their eldest brother.

"Pour me some more coffee."

It sounds like an easy enough task, but I can't help but feel as if there's some kind of catch to his request. Regardless, I lean forward to grab the coffee in the tall silver pot, and I pour it into his empty cup.

A hand skims up my leg past my knee. I falter and spill on the tablecloth. A sound comes out of the back of my throat, and I hastily set down the pot to clean up my mess.

"I-I'm sorry."

"Cut the shit, Kol," Asher says with malice.

I straighten, ignoring the mess for now.

"What? I'm just getting to know your pet better. If you're not going to make use of her obvious assets, why can't I? Don't tell me you haven't already thought about what those full lips of hers would feel like wrapped around the base of your cock."

I suck in a gasp.

"That's enough!" Asher stands so quickly, his chair falls back onto the carpeted floor. He sets his hands on the table and leans in our direction. "Get over here *now*, Miss Boudreaux."

I do as he says, happy to be away from Kol, and rush to his side of the table.

"Miss Boudreaux is not here to become one of your playthings, Kol. She works for me. Don't forget it again." Though Asher's not shouting anymore, there's an eerie sort of calm about the way he delivers his words that makes them sound even more lethal.

It's apparent Kol wants to say something back. His jaw is set like stone, and his hands are in fists on the table, knuckles a stark white against his olive skin.

Asher Voss turns to me with a look of putrid disgust. "As for you, come with me."

He latches his hand around my upper arm and drags me out of the dining room and down the hall. He's holding me tightly, but not so tightly that he'll leave any marks. He seems to be barely holding it together, so I don't say anything as he drags me to his office.

With every step, I grow more and more enraged at the way he's manhandling me. Once he closes the office door, I rip my arm from his grasp and whirl on him, but my words die on my tongue from the fury on his face.

"What the fuck was that?" he seethes.

"What was what?" I step back, but he matches it with a step forward.

"That shit you pulled with my brother?"

"I didn't pull any shit with your brother. He was being an asshole. That's not my fault."

His hands fist at his sides. "I told you to stay away from him."

My hands fly up at my sides. "I was in there doing the job you assigned me. If you didn't want me near him, then you shouldn't have told Mrs. Potter I was to serve breakfast."

"Are you blaming me for the way you were flaunting yourself in there?"

I open my mouth, close it, and open it once more. "Are you serious? Flaunting? I couldn't even if I tried. I'm wearing something fit for a senior citizen, thanks to you."

"And that's how it will stay since I obviously can't trust you not to fuck one of my brothers to get in their good graces. Believe me, if you sleep with any of them, it will only make me more determined to make your life a living hell."

He's delusional, and I've had enough of this. I step forward. "And why exactly is it that you want to make my life a living hell when you don't even know me?"

He doesn't say anything, just glares down at me, teeth bared.

At some point in our stand-off, our breathing falls into sync, and I go from agitated and enraged to feeling as if my skin is stretched taut over my body. I'm hyperaware of every place where my uniform touches me, of the way his breath fans over the top of my head, of the musky scent of his expensive cologne.

The small amount of space between us feels fraught with things that neither of us should be feeling—until he speaks again.

"You can shovel shit out of the stables today as a consequence of your actions."

I open my mouth to argue but think better of it. I've embarrassed myself enough here. I'm sure my desire was plain as day on my face, and clearly, I was making things up in my head as far as what he was feeling.

He'll probably laugh about it with his brothers later—the silly little girl lusting after the older man.

Without another word, I push past Asher and whip the heavy door of his office open without a backward glance, but I feel his eyes on me the entire time I walk down the hallway.

CHAPTER
NINE

ANABELLE

I find myself in the stables, working alongside Mr. Potter. I have a feeling he's here with me at the behest of his wife since I'm sure he has better things to do—given that he's in charge of all the grounds and all the people who work on it.

By late afternoon, my arms feel like Jell-O from shoveling shit and hay all day.

"You want to come help me brush some of the horses?"

I spin around toward where Mr. Potter stands at the entrance to the stable. "Sure thing, Mr. Potter. Just let me finish up here."

"What did I tell you about the Mr. Potter thing? It's Jack."

I chuckle. "Okay, Jack. I'll be right there."

He seems like a nice man, and I understand how he and Mrs. Potter got together. They're alike in that way.

Once I've finished, I leave the stables and head to where Jack stands with a mahogany-colored horse in one of the paddocks, brushing it. Off to his right is a black horse with a gleaming coat.

"Wow, he's beautiful." I approach the huge beast slowly.

Jack chuckles. "That he is. This here is Poe. You can brush him, just take it slow and let him get used to you first."

I've been around horses before. We used to have some on the estate when I was growing up, but I never got that into them, so when I was in my early teens, my dad sold them. The thought that perhaps my dad sold them to pay off a gambling debt taints the memory now, and I press my lips together.

"I've never seen a horse with a coat like this." It almost looks metallic.

"That's because he's an Akhal-Teke. They're the only breed in the world with a coat like that."

I slowly reach out a hand, and when the horse doesn't give me any indication that I shouldn't touch him, I press it gently on his neck and run my hand down. "You sure are handsome, aren't you?"

Poe nickers as if he understands me.

"Why Poe? Does it have anything to do with Edgar Allen Poe?" It's the first thing that came to mind when I heard the stallion's name. I bend down to pick up the brush.

Jack shrugs and keeps on brushing the other horse. "Not sure, you'd have to ask Asher."

I still. "This is his horse?"

"Yup. Been his horse for a while now."

I straighten up and start brushing, not saying another word about Asher Voss.

We're quiet as we rhythmically brush out both horses. I don't want to be impressed by Asher Voss's horse, but it proves impossible. He's a gorgeous creature—massive and beautiful and a little dangerous, just like his owner.

"He likes you."

Jack's voice startles me from my thoughts. "I'm sorry?"

"Poe likes you."

I don't know why Asher was the first thing to come to mind. Of course he meant the horse.

"He's not usually this amenable with new people," he continues.

I smile at the black beauty as I work the brush over his coat.

The silence stretches between us again until I realize that Jack probably knows whoever found my father's body on the Voss property, or he may have even found him himself. He could have seen my father's body before the authorities arrived.

I don't want to put Jack on the spot, but I feel like I need to know. It feels like the thing between us that isn't being said.

"Can I ask you something, Jack?" I let my arm drop from brushing Poe, cringing at the pain in my shoulder.

It's like Jack senses what I'm about to ask, because he stops working on his horse and turns to me, eyes full of remorse. "Of course."

"Did you... were you the one who found my father?" My chest feels as if a hole is burning through it.

Jack gives his head a small shake and frowns. "No, that was Don, who works for me. But I got the call from Don and went out there."

I don't know what I was hoping that information would give me, but all it does is bring back the image I've had in my head since the day I got the phone call—my father's ravaged body lying in blood-soaked grass. We had to have a closed casket because the funeral home told my grandmother that the injuries were too great for an open casket.

I squeeze my eyes shut against the unshed tears that burn my eyes, then suck in a breath and look at Jack. "Do you think... he suffered?"

Jack softens his expression as though he wants to wrap me in a hug as if I'm a little girl who needs consoling after a bad dream. But this is my new reality. My father is dead, and my mother has essentially checked out. I lost both my parents in one fell slash of the Grim Reaper's scythe.

"I don't think so. I think as far as these things go, it was a pretty clean death for him."

I don't know whether he's saying that to try to make me feel better or whether he believes that, but I choose to take him at his word.

The official cause of death for my father was listed as an animal attack, though there didn't seem to be any agreement over what kind of animal. A bear? Wolf? Something else? Not that I suppose it matters either way.

We go back to brushing the horses in silence until the words I probably shouldn't say slip from my mouth. "My father isn't the only person who has died at Midnight Manor."

Jack stills, glancing over his shoulder at me. "We don't talk about such things around here, Anabelle. If you're smart, you won't either."

It's obvious from the look on his face that this is the end of any conversation between us, and I continue brushing the stallion while loneliness settles in around me, threatening to suffocate me.

I have to work hard to regulate my breathing as the grief of losing my father hits me all at once. Since the funeral, I've been pushing against it, erecting a wall in my mind to keep it away. The household needed running, and my mother's recovery felt more important. I'd already lost one parent. I didn't want to lose another.

But being away from the estate where my family lives has left me more time with my thoughts, and those walls I'd so perfectly built are crumbling into ruins.

Now, being alone in this enormous estate, under the thumb of a man who disdains me, I feel as though I have no one in the world. That I'm truly on my own.

I cry myself to sleep that night while despair covers me like a weighted blanket, holding me down.

CHAPTER
TEN

ANABELLE

By the time Saturday night comes, I can't wait to get off Midnight Manor's grounds. Normally I would head home to see my family, but I can't handle the idea of seeing zero improvement in my mother this week.

Ever since my conversation with Jack yesterday, I keep seeing flashes of my father's dead body in my head, so instead of driving home, I ask one of the workers who is leaving until the morning if he would mind dropping me off at the Black Magic Bar. My only mission for tonight is to drink so much that the image of my father's dead body leaves my head. I'll worry about how I'll get back to Midnight Manor later.

I push past the rickety door of the bar and glance around inside. There's no one here that I know right now besides the bartender, which is preferable. I'm not up for making chitchat with anyone.

"Hey, Sawyer." I take a seat on one of the wooden barstools along the bar.

The place hasn't changed since high school. We're a small town, and the Black Magic Bar has never been huge on making sure you're of age to drink. The owner is a strange woman—in her late fifties now, I'd guess—and there are always rumors that she's a witch or something. I think it's just because of the bar name, but there's no doubt she's a little out there.

An exposed brick wall holds the shelving where all the bottles of liquor are lined up like soldiers. Interspersed between them are various knick-knacks—voodoo dolls, portraits of tarot cards, half-burned candles of different colors, crystals, skulls. Those themes repeat throughout the small bar in the wall décor and the things hanging from the ceiling. I've always likened it to a creepy dive bar.

"What can I get you, Anabelle?" Sawyer asks.

He was a few years ahead of me in school and never went anywhere after graduation. I can't imagine why.

"A shot to start, pick whatever. Then a whiskey sour."

His eyebrows raise. Probably because I'm usually a beer girl. "Long week?"

"You could say that, yeah."

He nods, knowing enough not to ask anything further. People in these parts are good about minding their business. At least in front of you. Magnolia Bend keeps the gossiping behind your back.

I pull the book I'm reading from my bag. I'll read until I'm drunk enough that the words start to blur.

Sawyer slides a shot glass down the bar to me. I lift it and toss it back, coughing a bit when the taste of tequila hits the back of my throat.

"Lime?" he asks, hand on the bowl of limes in the middle section of the bar.

I shake my head and wave him off, picking up the whiskey sour he set in front of me to chase down the shot. It's a good start, but I'll need more if I want to push away all my intrusive thoughts. It seems as if the more time I spend isolated at Midnight Manor, the harder it's becoming to turn away from the demons that chase me.

I sip on my drink as I read. The book I'm reading is a small-town romance about a large family who lives in Alaska. It feels worlds away from where I am, which is exactly what I need right now.

When I'm on my third drink within an hour, I hear my brother's voice behind me, and I stiffen.

"Figured I'd find you here."

It's not that I don't want to see Luke. It's just that seeing him makes me think of the rest of my family, and not thinking about my father or my mother was the goal tonight.

I put the bookmark in my book and turn on my barstool to face him. "Hey."

He frowns, probably either because he can tell I'm already half drunk or because he can see the sadness flooding from all the cracks in my armor.

"How come you didn't come to the house tonight? Grandmother was worried."

I shrug. "Didn't have it in me to see Momma tonight. It's been a long week."

His forehead wrinkles, and he takes a couple of steps closer. "Are they forcing you to do something you don't want to up there?"

I shake my head. "Nothing like that. It's just a bad week, that's all."

His shoulders fall. "Well, I'm glad you're here instead of up there, even if you're not at home. The fleet was moving through town when I came in here."

I rush over to the window and watch as a stream of expensive cars with blacked-out windows make their way through town as they do on the last Saturday of every month. No one has to wonder where they're going because we all know—Midnight Manor.

I'd forgotten that tonight was the night for whatever weird shit goes on at Midnight Manor. It dawns on me that this is probably exactly why Asher Voss gave me Saturday nights off.

"Any idea what that's about now that you're on the inside?" my brother asks me on my left.

"None. The people who work there are nice, but they aren't exactly forthcoming about anything to do with the Voss brothers." A huge part of me wants to know why these mysterious strangers arrive at the manor once a month, but it's not something I'm going to figure out tonight. "C'mon. I'll buy you a drink."

Luke follows me back to the bar, and I order us each a shot and a drink. I should be feeling *really* good after I finish these.

I chat with my brother about how things are going with him running the estate. He seems to have a pretty good handle on things but tells me that the coffers are pretty lean, and he needs to have a good year in order to keep things in the black.

"If anyone can do it, you can, little brother."

He chuckles. "I appreciate the confidence, but I think you're probably just drunk."

I laugh and lean into him. "Maybe, but that doesn't make it any less true."

He smiles at me, and the way he does reminds me of before. Before my father died, before my mother fell apart, before I was beholden to a man I'm drawn to but know without a doubt could ruin me.

"What's wrong? Why did your expression just change?" Luke asks.

"What? Nothing, I'm fine."

He takes my hand. "If it's horrible, whatever you're having to do for Asher Voss, you can leave. We'll figure something else out."

I know he believes that, and I know he wouldn't judge me if I did break my deal with Asher, but he's wrong. The only way out from under the crippling debt my father accumulated, the only way to keep our family's estate, is for me to do this. At least there's an end date.

"I'll be fine. Don't worry about me."

He squeezes my hand. "You know I'm going to until you're out from under his thumb."

I give him a sad smile. "I can handle it." *I think.* "I'm going to use the restroom. Be right back." I slip off the stool a little too quickly but catch myself on the bar.

"Maybe you should slow down on the drinks," Luke says.

"Little late for that." I stick my tongue out at him and half stumble, half walk to the bathroom.

When I come out, I stop, almost falling over. Galen stands beside my stool, the book I'd left on the bar in his hand. He isn't in his sheriff's uniform, so he must be off duty tonight.

The bar is full of people by now, and I don't want to make a scene, but I stomp toward him and rip the book from his hand anyway, bending to shove it into the bag I have resting against the bar. Luke has to rest his hand on my back when I pop back up so I don't stumble.

"Why do you bother with that shit?" Galen asks me in a condescending tone.

"Reading?" I arch an eyebrow and cross my arms.

"That crap is totally unrealistic." He laughs and looks at my brother as if waiting for Luke to back him up.

But Luke shakes his head and sips his drink.

"It's not unrealistic to think that a man can fulfill a woman emotionally and physically," I say. "Just because you haven't had any experience with it doesn't mean it's not possible."

Galen smiles as though I didn't just insult him. "Why would you need to be reading about fictional men when you can have me?" He puffs out his chest and flexes his bicep. Just when I thought it couldn't get any worse.

I slide back onto my stool. "I already told you that's never going to happen."

He blows out a breath and shakes his head as though I'm too cute for words. "You don't have to pretend anymore, Anabelle. I feel the same for you."

I lift what's left of my drink and down it in one big gulp. "I'm not pretending anything, Galen. In fact, I think I've been pretty clear about how I feel about you."

Luke chuckles to my right, staying out of it.

"Went by the estate a few times over the past couple weeks. You're never there."

"Maybe you should take that as a sign." I give him a saccharine smile.

Galen waves me off, still unable to take an insult.

Luke, my grandmother, and I all agreed not to tell anyone where I was. The last thing we want is the townsfolk gossiping about our involvement with the Vosses or my father's apparent gambling problem. It's not unlikely that some of them would stop doing business with the farm or the distillery if they thought we were somehow tied to the Voss family.

Thankfully, the other staff at Midnight Manor seems to be keeping my presence there quiet. I imagine they had to sign the same kind of NDA Asher included in my contract.

"I'm ready to leave." I turn to my brother. "Can you drive me home?"

"Sure thing." Luke gets up off the stool and bends to pick up my bag for me. "See ya around, LeBlanc."

I walk toward the door. "Hopefully I won't see you, LeBlanc."

I use his last name rather than his first, hoping it will piss him off, but I don't think it works because Galen just laughs as I step into the warm night air and look to my right. Midnight Manor is all lit up at the top of the hill.

Although I was eager to leave the grounds earlier tonight, now I feel its pull like a siren's call. What the hell?

CHAPTER
ELEVEN

ANABELLE

The next morning, I wake up with a fuzzy feeling in my head that's accompanied by a headache. Last night, I forced myself to drink my weight in water after my brother dropped me off at the gates of Midnight Manor. Otherwise, my head would likely be pounding, and I wouldn't be able to leave my bed.

The last thing I want to do is go for a run, which is exactly why I force myself out of bed and into my sports bra and leggings. The vision of my mother spending days in bed, staring aimlessly at nothing haunts my mind. I refuse to let my grief turn me into her.

Though we're well into spring and approaching summer, a dense fog covers the property when I step outside. The sun is likely just beginning to crest over the horizon, but it's not visible yet. It should burn off most of this mist once it makes its appearance though.

Thankfully, Marcel went to bat for me with Mr. Voss after I complained to him about not having my phone to listen to my audiobooks when I run. He agreed, but first removed the SIM card and forbade Marcel to tell me the wifi password so I'm limited to what I already have downloaded. At least it's something though.

I put my AirPods in my ears and hit Play on the mafia romance audiobook I'm listening to, then I slide my phone into the side pocket of my leggings. After a few stretches, I start on the path.

No one is out. It's too early on a Sunday morning for anyone to be hanging around the grounds or working yet, and I have to shove away the feeling of trepidation when I set off.

Being unable to see any farther ahead than about ten feet because of the fog is weird, but if I stay on the path, I should be fine. As long as I don't get lost. I still don't have the layout of this place cemented in my mind, and without being able to see any points of reference in the distance, I could quickly lose track of where I am.

I start at an easy jog to warm up and get my body back into the idea of running. Once my limbs are limber, and I'm in my groove, I pick up my pace until I'm running, sweat dripping from my hairline down my neck. My lungs burn, but the punishment to my body feels good. It keeps all the horrible thoughts from my mind until I'm only focused on the here and now.

My legs burn, and I realize that I don't even know where I am anymore, but I also don't care. I just keep running as if to outrun the demons themselves.

A figure appears in the mist ahead of me. I try to slow down to a stop before I hit them, but I can't. I plow into the body with a grunt and almost fall back until two hands grip my upper arms. I blink and realize I'm staring into the deep blue eyes of Asher Voss. Tired eyes. Eyes that look as if they've seen things no man ever should.

Neither of us says a word until I sputter out, "I... sorry, I was going so fast..."

He's still holding onto me, staring at me impassively. Gone is his usual aggression and predatory ways. Right now, he reminds me of a defeated man. I don't know what to do with that, nor do I know why I care at all.

"I'm okay now, you can let me go." I nod in the direction of where one of his giant paw-like hands is wrapped around my arm.

He blinks, seeming to come out of a haze, and his hands drop. "What are you doing here?" His voice is a little gruff, but nowhere near his usual ornery tone.

It dawns on me that I can hear him because one of my AirPods has fallen out of my ear. "Going for a run. What does it look like?"

It's then that his gaze skirts over my body, which is clad in tight black exercise wear. His gaze feels like a caress even though I'm sure he doesn't mean it to be.

When he doesn't say anything, I ask, "Why are you out here so early?"

He's dressed in black dress pants and a white shirt, no tie, with the top few buttons undone. The sleeves of his dress shirt are rolled up, and rather than his clothing looking perfectly pressed, it's rumpled. Even his hair isn't in its usually coiffed style. Some of it has curled over his forehead.

If I had to guess, I'd say he's been in this outfit all night and never went to bed.

When I arrived back at the manor last night, nothing seemed to be amiss, and there was no sign of anything untoward going on. In fact, there was no sign of the people who had funneled through town up to the manor, besides their empty vehicles. Maybe that was the sign that something was amiss.

Asher doesn't say anything, just pushes his hands in his pockets and turns so I'm looking at his profile. He heaves out a sigh, and his shoulders drop, giving him a world-weary sort of look.

I turn my head to see what he's looking at, and my stomach feels as if it's been scooped out when I realize we're standing beside the Voss family plot. An iron fence surrounds the graves of generations of Voss family members. The fog prohibits me from seeing how far back the plot goes.

My grief rises to the surface, and I hate the empathy I feel toward the man at my side. I know what it is to miss someone you love.

Finally, Asher says, "Yesterday was the anniversary of my dad's death."

I'm shocked he's telling me this bit of personal information —not that it's not publicly available if I cared to search it out. I can't help but wonder if this has something to do with why he was so hard on me this week.

I swallow, unsure what to say, so I say the only thing that comes to mind. "I haven't been able to go visit my father's grave on our estate yet. Not since the day we buried him."

He doesn't say anything. When I glance at Asher, there's sorrow and desolation in his deep blue eyes.

"Do you miss him?" I ask.

His head dips in my direction and meets my gaze. "The day he was murdered was the best day of my life."

My eyes widen.

Everyone knows that Ramsey Voss was murdered, but it was never proven by whom. All four brothers were suspects at one point or another, from what I've been told, but there was never enough evidence on any of them to lay charges.

Could Asher have murdered his father?

What kind of monster does a father have to be to have been murdered by his own child?

What kind of beast does a child have to be to murder his father?

I don't know what drives the impulse to open up to him. It might be how forlorn he looks and what a contrast that is to his usual self, but I can't help the truth coming from my lips. "I'm sorry. I don't know why you feel that way, but I know what it feels like to have the love of a good man... even if my father was hiding things from me. I'm sorry you didn't get to experience the same."

I don't dare ask why he feels the way he does. I guarantee he wouldn't tell me the truth anyway.

His expression is a mixture of confusion and disbelief, but it's almost as though he doesn't see me. He's looking through me. "It's all changing. It's changing, and it's going to come crashing down."

I frown. "What's changing?"

He shakes his head as though he's back from wherever his mind was. His attention goes to my ear that still has the AirPod in it, and before I register what he's doing, he crouches and retrieves the one on the path.

"What are you listening to?" he asks as he straightens.

He brings the AirPod to his ear. The audiobook I'm listening to automatically starts playing again in my ear, as well in the one he's holding. My face heats as the words reverberate through my skull.

"Let me see that tongue, bella."

She opens her mouth, sticking out her tongue. Still fisting the base of my cock, I step close enough that her tongue is on the underside of my balls. Without me having to tell her, she licks and worships them, pulling one into her mouth and sucking gently, then the other. It feels phenomenal.

I decide to reward her for her efforts and bring the vibrator to the juncture of her thighs. She jolts from the surprise, moaning instantly. Her back arches, and her head twists, so I pull the vibrator away.

Instead of lunging for the AirPod, I'm frozen to my spot. His lids become heavy as the book continues.

Aria makes a disappointed sound. "Please don't stop."

"You stop, and I stop, understood?"

"Yes." The word is desperate and breathy.

"I'm going to tuck this in your underwear, between your pussy lips. Do you think that will feel good, cara?"

"Oh god, yes." She moans as though she can already feel it.

"And then I'm going to fuck this mouth. And if you stop, it stops, got it?"

His blue eyes don't leave mine as we listen to the characters in the book play out the scene. They don't leave mine as he pulls the AirPod from his ear. And they don't leave mine as he asks, "You enjoy that, do you?"

Part of me wants to deny it, pretend that I could take it or leave it, that it doesn't get me hot, but I refuse to cower in front of him again. Not anymore. "I do," I say with confidence.

His nostrils flare, and his entire body goes taut before he takes a small step toward me, closing the distance between us to mere inches. I arch my head back to look at him.

"What do you like most about it?"

I swallow. Admitting I like to listen to steamy romance novels is one thing, but admitting to this man what turns me on sexually is another. He'll most likely use the information against me somehow at a later date.

Asher takes my hand, moving his thumb back and forth over the inside of my wrist. It's such a small thing, but I swear he might as well be running his thumb over my clit for the way my body reacts.

An electric current races up my arm and settles between my thighs. My nipples pebble in my sports bra. His eyes dip as he notices.

Asher licks his lips like an animal ready to devour me. "Don't make me ask again."

My breath is shallow, and I struggle to suck in enough oxygen to keep me upright. "I like that he's in control. That he's telling her what to do."

He closes his eyes, and his head rocks back as though he's savoring my answer. I don't know what to make of his reaction. Then he chuckles and straightens his head, his eyes once again open and on me. Embarrassment floods my body. Why must he be so cruel?

I yank my hand from his grip. "I knew I shouldn't have told you."

"I'm laughing because you're perfect. Of course you would be."

Perfect for what? What is he even talking about?

But before I ask, his large hand rests on the edge of my jaw, his thumb stroking my cheek, and his fingers push into my sweaty hair that's pulled back into a ponytail. I don't dare move except for my chest heaving up and down to keep breathing. It's not as though Asher Voss has never touched me before, but this is different. This is a new level.

His gaze roams my face, and that invisible string between us grows taut, dragging both of us forward. There's no time to question what we're doing or whether this is smart or not. A man like Asher Voss could easily chew me up and spit me out. I'd be left like roadkill on the other side of his wrought-iron gates.

Our lips touch, and he retracts, a rush of air leaving him before he places his lips on mine again, and his tongue glides along the seam of my mouth. I part my lips for him, eager for more. I could never deny this man, as messed up as that is.

He tastes like expensive whiskey, and I realize he's drunk. Hence the reason he's kissing me and all the strange things he's said to me.

It dawns on me that I should probably push him away. But if this is the one time I'm going to know what it feels like to be kissed by a real man, a man like Asher Voss, then I'm going to take it for all it's worth. The consequences will be the same at this point anyway.

I sink into the kiss. His other arm wraps around me until I'm cocooned by his large body, and his hand splays across my lower back. He dominates the kiss, setting the pace and using the hand along my cheek to direct me.

No one has ever kissed me like this. As if I were their possession, and they'd die if they didn't have me.

When a low moan works its way up my throat, it sparks something feral in him, and our kiss turns frantic, animalistic. The hand on my back dips lower, fingers spreading over my ass. He squeezes, pulling me into him until I'm pressed against his hardness at my stomach. The memory of exactly how thick his length looked in his bathing suit causes me to grind against him.

As I willingly give myself to him, I'm thrust away from his body. I stumble back, and he looks at me in horror. When he wipes the taste of me from his mouth with the back of his hand, it feels like a swipe across my face from a set of claws.

"What the fuck do you think you're doing?" he roars.

My head rears back. "You kissed me!"

He stalks forward then stops and takes two steps back, increasing the distance between us. "You kissed me back!" He clenches and unclenches his hands at his sides.

I guffaw. "Isn't that what someone does when they're kissed?"

He pushes both hands through his already disheveled hair. "I don't know what game you're playing, but it ends now. Even if I were to fuck you, it wouldn't mean anything. It wouldn't change the situation you're in. You owe me a year, and a year is what I'll get. Not even a taste of your cunt will change that."

I gape at him, and he whips around and stalks off.

As he strides away, disappearing into the mist, I have one disturbing thought... I hate that man as much as I want him. Which is a bad position to be in.

CHAPTER
TWELVE

ANABELLE

I haven't seen Asher for five days.

Five long days.

A huge part of me doesn't want to see him ever again. He comes onto me and then makes me feel cheap and stupid for going along with it? Asshole.

But there's also a part of me that's dying for a glimpse of him.

Our kiss has played on repeat in my mind since Sunday morning. I remind myself what a dick he was afterward, but my body doesn't care.

I'm back to doing housekeeping in the manor, which suits me fine. I don't ever run into Asher's brothers—they must stay in their wings of the house, and I'm not permitted there.

After the disaster that was me serving them all that one time, if I'm lucky, I'll never have to see them again. Dealing with one Voss is enough.

Finn assigns me to polish some of the wood paneling in one of the massive rooms in the main part of the house. By late afternoon, my arms are limp from applying lemon oil. It's simple but physical work, and it gives my mind time to wander. Something I don't appreciate.

Finn checked on me about a half hour ago, and I haven't seen anyone since then. Not that I'm surprised. There must be hundreds of rooms in this place.

I shift the stepladder I'm using to my left and climb back up and scrub the cloth over the paneling. Sweat drips down my neck. It's not yet sweltering outside, but it's nice enough, and there's no air conditioning in a property this old. Some of the individual rooms may have wall units installed, but none of the main rooms do.

I'm concentrating on what I'm doing when a cool breeze wafts by me. The hairs on the back of my neck rise, and I get the distinct sensation of being watched. Slowly, I turn, careful to stay centered on the stepladder, but there's no one there. The room is somewhat dim, as it always is in this place, but there's certainly enough light that I could see if anyone were standing in the shadows.

With a frown, I turn back toward the wall and get back to what I was doing.

A few minutes later, the opening sounds of a classical song plays in the distance, and I pause with the cloth against the wood. Then operatic voices join in, singing over the music. I step off the stepladder and look around again.

"Hello?" I call, but no one answers.

The music continues. It feels like a pull in my chest, every word a tug on some rope inside me, and I move out of the room toward the sound. It's powerful and ethereal all at once, emotional and atmospheric. My feet move of their own accord. The music stops for a moment, then starts back up from the beginning.

I find myself in a long hallway with a high, pointed-arch ceiling. To my left are large archways with stained glass in them. Most of them don't depict anything in particular, but the center arch depicts a large beast, a bear standing on its hind legs, claws and teeth bared in a ferocious roar.

A shiver runs through me. I want to stay to study it, something about it appealing to me, but the music drives me forward until I find myself in a section of the house I've never been to.

I grow closer to the music until it feels like a living, breathing thing inside me. And then the final tug on my chest comes as I approach an ornate door. My hand runs over the roses carved into the wood. I can *feel* the music on the other side pulsing into my palm through the wood.

I push the door open, and the music immediately stops.

It's a huge library with soaring ceilings and two levels of dark wood shelves filled with books. Transfixed, I step into the space, looking all around. There are just so many books. Pure, unadulterated joy fills me at the sight of them all. All the stories and secrets they probably house. The adventures and love and loss detailed on their pages. I can barely contain my excitement at finding this treasure.

It doesn't appear that anyone is using the library. No books are lying out except one. I step over to the lone table in the room and examine the book. It's old. Very old. It's Edgar Allen Poe's *The Raven and Other Poems*.

Never having seen such an old book in person, and certainly not one that appears to be an original based on the "1845" on the spine. I brush my fingers over the top then freeze when I hear someone breathing behind me. Slowly, as if I've caught the scent of a predator, I turn around. I relax a little when I realize it's Asher, but stiffen again from the wrath in his gaze.

His eyes narrow, full of pure malice. "What are you doing in here?"

I've seen him lose his temper on several occasions, but somehow, the way his voice is so lethally quiet feels scarier.

When I open my mouth to respond, nothing comes out.

"Did I not tell you to stay out of the west wing? This is my private area." He bares his teeth and steps forward until his breath is on my face as he looks down at me.

"I'm sorry. I didn't mean to come here—"

"Yet here you are. Looking for secrets? Something you can use against me to perhaps try to get out of our deal?"

My fear gives way to agitation because never once have I tried to get out of our deal, but he continues to insist that I am. "Of course not. I came here because—"

"Let me guess." His gaze roams my face then lowers for a beat. "You came here hoping for round two of what happened on Sunday morning?" Asher arches a dark brow.

"That's never going to happen. I was still drunk from the night before, and I don't make it a practice to fuck around with needy little girls like yourself."

I don't know why I care what this man thinks, but my chest cracks open a bit at the way he describes me, the way he sees me. The impulse to strike out and hurt him as much as he's hurt me is too great to ignore. "You didn't seem to feel that way when you forced your lips onto mine, and your hard cock was pressing into my stomach."

Whoa, it felt good to let out my frustration on him.

"You want to be used, little girl, is that it?" He clenches my chin hard in his hand with the bear tattoo on it. "You want me to take what I want from you and toss you aside?"

"I'm not a little girl," I manage to say, barely able to move my jaw.

"You're not nearly the woman you seem to think you are. Now get out of my sight." His hand drops from my chin, and he steps back, wiping his hand on his pants as though I'm diseased.

The corners of my eyes burn, but this man will never know he's gotten to me. I step around him at a steady pace, not willing to let myself run from here in tears as I want to do.

"Don't let me find you in here again!" he roars behind me, and I pick up my pace.

Tears pool in my eyes as I rush down the long hallway with the stained glass. When I pass the stained glass bear, it's impossible not to think of Asher Voss and the parallels he has to the beast.

It isn't until I manage to find the room I was working in that I realize I still don't know where the music came from in the first place.

CHAPTER
THIRTEEN

ANABELLE

A couple of nights later, I set my book on my lap. My eyelids are heavy, and I don't think I can read anymore. I'm in the communal area of the building my room is in. I don't often spend time down here, but being alone in my room is starting to feel more and more isolating.

"I think I'm going to turn in. I'll see you guys tomorrow."

Finn and Marcel are on the opposite couch, watching television. They both glance over.

"I'll see you bright and early," Finn says.

With a smile and a wave, I leave them there. I don't know that I'd consider them friends per se—their loyalty definitely lies with the Vosses. But they're the closest people I have here at Midnight Manor.

When I reach my room, I hear it before I see it—the distinct sound of dripping water. And when I look across the room, there's a giant wet spot on the ceiling that's bulging, looking as if it's about to unleash a tropical storm in the middle of my bedroom.

"Shit." I rush back downstairs.

Finn and Marcel look over at me when I enter the room.

"Change your mind?" Marcel asks.

"There's a big leak in my room. It looks like the ceiling is going to cave in."

They bolt up off the couch.

"Get Jenkins to Anabelle's room right away," Marcel says to Finn as he makes his way to me. "Let's go have a look."

I don't know who Jenkins is, though if I had to guess, I'd assume he must be a maintenance guy or something.

I lead Marcel to my room.

"*Merde*," he says.

"What do you think happened?" I ask.

He shakes his head. "Probably a pipe or something would be my guess since it hasn't rained." He looks around the room. "You should gather your things before that blows. You're obviously not sleeping here tonight."

Before I can ask him where I'm going to sleep, Finn and the man I assume is Jenkins push past us into the room.

The older man puts his hands on his hips and looks at the bulge that's grown larger in the last few minutes. "Gotta be a busted pipe or something." Then he turns to me. "You can't sleep in here."

I nod. "We were just talking about that. I'm going to gather my things and get out of your way."

Heading over to the corner, I grab my suitcase, then I empty most of the contents of my small dresser into it. When I turn back to face Marcel and Finn, they're whispering conspiratorially, glancing over at me.

"Where am I going to sleep tonight? Is there another room somewhere in the building?" I walk past Jenkins, who's still studying the ceiling with his hands on his hips as though he can stop it with his mind alone.

Marcel turns to face me. "There are no more rooms in the building, but we have an idea."

A HALF HOUR LATER, I'm in one of the guest rooms inside Midnight Manor.

"I don't think this is a good idea. Mr. Voss won't like this." I don't have to say which Mr. Voss I'm referring to. We all know.

Marcel waves away my concern at the doorway. "Nonsense, he'll be fine with it."

"Does he know?" I arch an eyebrow, hand still on the handle of my suitcase.

"I called him, and he didn't answer, so I left a message. He won't even know you're here. This is a huge house."

I shift in place, uneasy about this. But what am I supposed to do? I have to sleep somewhere, and he'd probably freak out more if I left the property entirely and went home for the night.

"Okay... if you're sure." I'll just sleep here tonight and figure something else out tomorrow. Or make sure that Marcel has gotten Asher's okay before I spend another night in the manor.

"That's the spirit." He claps his hands in front of himself. "Do you need anything else?" He glances around the room. "Everything is always kept stocked, so you should have everything you need in the adjoining bathroom, but if anything is missing, please let me know. You might even know where to find it." He chuckles, but he's not wrong.

"Thanks for coming to my rescue, Marcel."

He gives me a dramatic bow before leaving, closing the door.

I take a moment to examine the space. The room is large, which is no surprise. It's probably ten times the size of my original room. One wall has an arched window typical of the manor, and the large fireplace on another wall has an ornate mantel and surround. The furniture is all dark wood and matches the age of the property. There's a couch with a pair of black fabric ottomans opposite it on the far side of the room, and the chandelier hanging in the middle of the room casts a dim light over everything.

I roll my suitcase over to the long bench at the end of the bed and heft it onto it. Since I only plan to spend one night here, there's no point in unpacking, so I only pull out my pajamas.

Once I've changed, I take my face wash into the adjoining bathroom and wash my face, then apply my moisturizer. I turn on the bedside lamp before making my way to the wall near the door where Marcel turned on the chandelier lights.

When I switch it off, the room is even more dim. I make my way back to the bed, walking quickly and feeling exposed. I'm not sure why. It must be the size of this new room when I'm used to something much more modest.

I'm tugging down the covers on the bed when the door whips open, bouncing off the wall.

My eyes widen at the image of Asher Voss—black dress pants, black button-down shirt with the sleeves rolled up, hands flexing at his sides. "I thought I told you I didn't want you in the west wing."

I didn't even realize that's where I was, though it makes sense that of any of the brothers, Marcel would put me in Asher's wing. "There was a burst pipe or something in my bedroom, and there was nowhere else for me to stay tonight."

His voice is filled with fury. "So you decided to stay in the manor despite my making it very clear that you are not welcome here?" His chest heaves as though he can't pull enough air into his lungs.

"All the rooms in the staff quarters are full. Marcel said I should stay here. I only planned to stay tonight. I assumed we'd figure something else out in the morning."

He shakes his head. "What do you not understand about not being wanted? Have I not made it perfectly clear to you?"

"I thought I was doing the right thing! I thought this would be better than leaving the grounds for the night."

"This was my mother's room!" He grabs the small table set against the wall to his left and tosses it to the side.

Fear lashes inside me, so sharp and stinging it hits me like a whip, and I run. I run from the room and down the hall, the need to preserve my safety driving me. I need to get as far as I can from Asher Voss. He shouts my name behind me, but I don't slow.

I run until I find myself outside and in front of the hedge maze. Glancing behind me, I race into its depths to be swallowed up and hide from the beast.

CHAPTER
FOURTEEN

ANABELLE

t's a full moon, and I use its light to guide me through the maze. The hedges rise on either side of me, feeling as if they're curling in over me as I rush past them. The grass is cool on my feet with every step as I twist and turn deeper into the maze. Panic grips me when I hear Asher shout my name.

It's impossible to tell how close or far he might be, so I keep running, the image of his eyes when he said the room was his mother's seared into my brain for all eternity. There was so much rage, yes, but also grief and pain. All of it is overwhelming and echoes some of the emotions I've been trying desperately to push down inside myself.

Of all the rooms I could have taken in the manor, it was apparent then that I was in the worst possible one.

I don't stop running until my lungs burn, and I find myself in a clearing I assume must be the center of the maze. It's a large square, and in the middle is a bush of some kind. On all four sides are stone benches.

Still trying to catch my breath, I step closer to the plant and realize that it's a large rose bush, though it appears it's seen better days. There's significant dieback on some of the stems, and the few red roses appear withered and unhealthy. The petal of one falls and drifts down to the grass below.

"Anabelle."

I freeze at Asher's voice so close to me now. There's a hint of relief in it, presumably because he found me.

I face him, the instinct not to give my back to a predator strong. He steps forward, and I hold my hand out in front of me. "Please stay there."

His shoulders sag, and he bows his head, heaving a breath and pushing a hand through his unruly hair. It's no longer slicked back and styled to perfection, but a mess of waves on top of his head that hang down toward his ears. "I'm sorry if I scared you."

His words sound sincere, but what if it's a ploy to get me to let my guard down?

"Can we talk?" He gestures to one of the benches. When I hesitate, he adds, "Please?"

I nod and make my way over, being sure to sit at the far end. But the benches aren't huge, and with his size, when he sits, we're almost touching.

There's only remorse on his face.

"You scared me," I say in a small voice.

Asher's lips tip down. "I know." He shakes his head, and it comes off as disappointment in himself. "I'm sorry I lost my temper."

"I didn't know it was your mother's room. Marcel just put me there, but I had every intention to figure out something else for tomorrow night."

He leans forward and rests his elbows on his knees, hands clasped behind his neck while he stares at the ground.

"I never would have agreed to sleep there if I'd known it was your mother's room. I'm sorry."

"It hasn't been her room for a long, long time." There's so much anguish in that one sentence that I'm not sure how to unpack it.

I know what it feels like to lose a parent before you're ready. I don't know many details about his mother or how she died or when, and I find myself wanting to know more. I risk Asher pushing me away with my next words. "When did your mother pass away?"

His hands drop from the back of his neck, and he slowly turns his head to meet my gaze. "She was killed when I was twelve."

My chest squeezes. He was so young. It doesn't escape me that he said she was killed, not died. But I don't dare ask for any further details.

"That must have been very difficult. You were so young." I know that's putting it mildly, but I don't know what else to say.

He straightens up and nods. "Yeah... my mother was one of the only good things in my life, besides my brothers, so when she was killed, I felt... alone."

I know his dad was still around for six years after his mother died, but they obviously weren't close. It feels like there's a lot to unpack there, but not now.

A sad sort of chuckle slips out of him. "I don't know why I'm telling you all this."

The truth falls from my lips. "I'm glad you are."

Our gazes lock and hold for three breaths. I know because I count them.

"I don't have to stay in that room. I can sleep on the couch in staff quarters or something."

He shakes his head and glares at me before I even finish speaking. "You'll stay in that room. It's fine."

I don't argue with him. "You said it was your mom's room... not your parents'."

I'm digging. I know I am. But I want to know everything and anything about this man. Who knows how long this open dialogue between us will last?

Asher's jaw tightens. "My parents probably started out sharing a room. I have no idea. No recollection of that time. They didn't have a good marriage. My father... he was a difficult man."

I get the feeling that other words besides difficult might be more appropriate.

"As long as I can remember, they kept separate bedrooms."

I nod and look straight ahead at the rose bush, unable to continue looking into the depths of his eyes sparkling in the night.

"That was my mother's prized rose bush. The gardeners always took care of the rest of the property, but this bush was her pride and joy. She'd tend to it every day. It started dying a couple of years ago, and no matter how much the groundskeeper tends to it, it continues to die off."

I walk forward to get a better look. The thorns on the stems are highlighted by the full moon, and I resist the urge to touch one. "Do they know what's wrong with it?"

"No," he says from where he's still seated on the bench behind me. "I've flown in experts to look at it. They've tested the soil, inspected the plant, done everything they could think of, and none of them can see any reason why it's dying."

I frown and turn to face him. "I'm sorry."

I'm saying a lot of that tonight, but what else can I say? I don't know anything about rose bushes, and as he said, he's employed experts to try to help him to no avail.

"It feels like a bad omen. And in some weird way, it feels a little like I'm losing my mother again."

I don't know what possesses me, but all I want is to offer him comfort. Pain is etched into his face, pain I somehow know he carries with him every single day.

Not questioning whether it's wanted or not, I step between his legs, wrap my arms around him, and hug him. "I know firsthand that nothing I say is going to take away the pain from your loss. But I'm sorry. I keep saying that tonight, but it's true. I'm sorry your mother is no longer with you and that you had to grow up without her."

At first, he lets his palms remain pressed against the bench, but he slowly wraps his arms around me, returning the embrace. I'm supposed to be comforting him, but I can't help the way I feel comforted in return. We hold one another for a moment, soaking in the feel of each other.

"I'm sorry about your father." His words surprise me, and I pull back to look at him.

"Do you know what happened to him?" I hold my breath, waiting for his answer.

His eyes fill with regret, and he shakes his head. "No more than you. It was an animal attack."

It's not that I don't believe that—I do. I guess I just hoped that someone could tell me how or what animal, or the most difficult answer of all—why. But I suppose sometimes there's no answer to that last question. That's why it's the hardest one to live with.

I nod, looking down at my feet. A chill rolls over me, and I shiver. It's not cold out tonight, but I'm in sleep shorts with a matching tank.

Asher frowns and slides his hands from back around me, bringing them to the top button of his black shirt.

"What are you doing?" I ask in a panicked voice.

"You're cold. Put this on over what you're wearing."

It's on the tip of my tongue to tell him I'm fine, but then he spreads his shirt wide, and his chest comes into view. I haven't seen it since he stopped having me come to the pool, and it looks no less desirable in the moonlight than it did in the sunlight.

He pulls the lower part of his shirt from his dress pants and slides the fabric down his arms before helping me into it. It's still warm from his body heat, and I watch as he does the buttons up from top to bottom, the ink from his tattoo bending and flexing as though the bear is moving its jaw while he does.

"I would never hurt you. Never raise a hand to you. *Ever*." His words are quiet, barely audible. They don't startle me any less, though. "I know it probably doesn't seem that way given what happened this evening, but if you never believe a word out of my mouth, believe those."

His voice pleads, his gaze desperate, and I find that I do believe him.

"I believe you." I can't take my gaze away from his.

Once again, that pull to him—which is all kinds of wrong—appears. I don't know if it's because I'm surrounded by his scent, dressed in his oversized shirt, or it's the hunger in his eyes, but when he threads his fingers through my hair, drawing my face closer to his, I'm not thinking about the last time we kissed and how he pushed me away after.

I'm not thinking about how much it will hurt if he does it again.

And I'm definitely not thinking about the consequences of what might happen here tonight.

The only thing running through my brain at this moment is that if I don't get my lips on this man, I might die.

As soon as his lips touch mine, I feel as though I'm being brought back to life. Dragged from a haze into the clear, moonlit night where there is only him and me and this moment.

CHAPTER
FIFTEEN

ASHER

*W*hat the hell am I doing?

I already promised myself I'd stay away from this girl. For her sake as well as mine. Nothing good can come of me kissing her.

But she's a motherfucking flame, and I'm the moth who doesn't care if my wings get burned.

Her full lips touch mine, and all the shit that consumes my mind falls away. The years of abuse at my father's hands, the daily bullshit I have to deal with running Voss Enterprises, the grief from speaking of my mother tonight.

All there is is her, Anabelle Boudreaux. Anabelle with her long, silky brown hair that I've fantasized about wrapping around my fist while I drive into her. Anabelle with her sweet smile and sassy mouth. She does her best to stand up to me when not many people ever will.

Anabelle who is fourteen years younger than me.

"This isn't a good idea," I murmur against her lips. "You're practically a child compared to me."

She rips her lips away from mine, and I instantly regret the small bit of conscience I have left that made me voice those words.

"I'm not a child. I'm a woman." She scowls, and I can't help but think that she reminds me of what a bunny might look like baring its teeth.

But she's not wrong—she is a woman.

If I hadn't been so in my head about my mother, I probably would have pounced on her earlier. Seeing her in her skimpy shorts and tank, ready for bed was beat-off material for my brain. Now, here I am pressed against her generous curves, desperate for more than just a kiss.

But she isn't nearly as experienced as I am. Doesn't hold the same sexual appetite and affinity for the things I do. I'll ruin her, scandalize her, and then I'll be done with her. Normally that wouldn't bother me in the least... but with her... it matters for some reason.

"You are a woman. All woman." I slide my hands up under my shirt that hangs to her knees. My ego likes seeing her in my shirt. It wants to roar at the visual and the thought of covering her in my scent. "But we're not compatible."

"How do you know?" She pushes toward me, sure to connect with my cock that's straining against the confines of my pants. "We feel pretty compatible to me."

A growl rips through my chest.

Her big brown innocent eyes look at me. "Please... you're all I can think of since you kissed me."

My eyes close of their own volition, savoring her words. It proves how little she knows me that she'd give me that little bit of truth to manipulate her with.

Fuck, the idea of sinking into her, having my way with her, here, now, in the middle of the night is almost my undoing. But some small shred of decency I seem to have when it comes to her prevents me from doing so.

My eyes snap open and meet hers. "Have you ever had a man feast on your cunt?"

My blunt words hit their target, and she blinks, momentarily stunned by my crass question. That's nothing. If she only knew. "Um... yeah. A couple times in college."

I scoff. "I'm not talking about some little college shit who doesn't know what to do with his tongue. I'm talking about a man, a man who knows how to work your clit with his tongue like he's a maestro. Who knows how to curl his fingers when he fucks you with them so that you see stars. A man who will lap at you like he'll never be able to get enough of your taste. Who feels like he'll die if you don't come all over his face."

By the time I'm done talking, her pupils are practically blown out. Instead of scaring her off, I've done the opposite. I've turned us both on.

"I've never had that," she whispers. "But I want it." Her hands slip up under my shirt and she slides her shorts down until they land around her ankles on the grass. "Will you show me what that's like?"

Jesus Christ. How can she be so sweet and sexy all at once? It's a paradox I'm desperate to decode.

The scent of her arousal wafts toward me, and my cock twitches. I have to taste her. I have to. Fuck the consequences. Because there are always consequences.

But if she thinks she's in control here, she's wrong. I'm going to show her who owns her body.

I lift my dress shirt, getting my first look at her pussy. Her *bare* pussy. She's managed to surprise me. It's not what I expected, but I'm pleased.

She has a two-inch birthmark just above her left knee. I lean forward and kiss it, slowly making my way up her thigh.

"Hold the shirt up," I tell her, and she takes it from my grasp.

When I reach the juncture of her thighs, I breathe her in. Sweet and tangy with a hint of musk. I cannot wait to have her on my tongue.

Using my thumbs, I spread her pussy lips and run the pad of my tongue over her clit. A small keening sound leaves her lips. When I repeat the motion, a little harder this time, one of her hands lands on my head, gripping my hair.

I smile against her most sensitive skin. I've barely gotten started, and already she's close to losing it. I'm going to make this woman come so hard she'll be dripping down my face.

I dive back in, working her clit with my tongue. Her grip on my hair tightens, and it isn't until her legs are shaking, and I think she won't be able to hold herself up that I pull away.

"No!" she cries, desperate for me to finish her off.

"We're just getting started."

I stand and pick her up in one smooth motion, turning to lay her out across the bench. Her pale skin looks gorgeous covered in moonlight, like an offering from the gods. When I've positioned her at the edge of the bench, I fall to my knees before her. Anabelle watches my every move with rapt attention as I use my hands on her knees to spread her further.

Her arousal glistens in the night, like a beacon calling me home, a lighthouse in the dark stormy sea that draws me to shore. My face is between her thighs in seconds, unable to deny myself the temptation of her.

I fuck her entrance with my tongue, using my hands on her hips to keep her in place. Her hands explore her own body, coasting over the fabric of my shirt as I lap up her taste. It's like a fucking drug, and if given the chance, I'd have my head between her legs every day, all day.

I work my way back up to her clit, using the tip of my tongue to stimulate her enough to make her crazy but deny her climax. I commit the keening sound coming from her to memory and push in one finger, then two, stretching her. She's so tight that I imagine exactly the way she'd feel around my cock. That thought fuels me.

Anabelle cries out as I finger-fuck her cunt and vibrate my tongue on her clit at the same time. Her core clenches around my thick fingers. I curve them to hit her G-spot, sending her spiraling into bliss if the way she grinds her pussy against my face is any indication.

She comes seconds later, coating my fingers with her arousal. I force her to follow that orgasm with another right behind it, not letting up one bit until I've squeezed every drop out of her and swallowed it down like a savage.

I'm torn between wanting to suck on my fingers or wipe her arousal all over her as some kind of evidence of what I can do to her. In the end, I wipe my hands on the insides of her thighs as she lies there catching her breath, loving the way her pale skin glistens. I want her to think of me when she washes it from her body.

No.

What the fuck am I thinking?

The last thing I need is this young, relatively innocent girl getting hung up on me. I can never give her what she needs beyond the physical. I'm not built for anything more. Maybe I could have been, but my upbringing took care of destroying that.

Besides, there are so many secrets between us. One of which is the true nature of her father's death. I didn't know who I was protecting at the time I paid the medical examiner off to declare it an animal attack so there would be a closed casket, but now I'm glad I followed my instincts and didn't allow the family to know it was a suicide. At the time I wasn't even sure where the instinct to protect Heath Boudreaux's family from the truth came from. But I would never want Anabelle to know, to have to live with the pain of knowing he chose to leave her behind.

Suddenly, the urge to run from her, to leave her lying on a stone bench, exposed to the night rises inside me.

But I can't leave her to find her way out of the maze—there's no guarantee she would. Even though I've been in here hundreds of times, I find myself lost at odd times. It's as if the maze changes its layout, and the path you've always used no longer works.

So as much as I want to run from her, from the things she makes me feel, I can't.

"We should get back to the manor." I don't bother helping her up from the bench. Instead, I put some distance between us and my back to her, adjusting myself in my pants so that my erection isn't so obvious.

"Oh... okay."

The disappointment in her voice makes me want to go at her again. Spend all night in this maze fucking her in every corner, but sooner or later, it would end like it is now.

The sound of her stepping back onto the grass and sliding her shorts on stops, but I don't turn to face her. "Follow me."

She does so silently, and I escort her through the rows of hedges. I'm careful not to touch her, and I don't speak, not willing to risk saying something that might make her think that what happened between us can ever be anything other than what it was—a brief pleasure between adults.

But the way she keeps looking at me with her big brown eyes glistening in the moonlight as if I'm her savior, I realize it'll take more than one conversation to put her off.

143

Good thing I have no problem being the world's biggest prick.

CHAPTER
SIXTEEN

ANABELLE

I wake up sore between my legs, but not in a bad way. In a way that reminds me that last night was not a dream, not some fantasy I conjured up in my mind.

Last night... I don't even have words for it. I've never had an experience like that. It was unexpected, and exciting, and the orgasms Asher gave me were mind-blowing.

I'm not a virgin. I slept with enough guys through college, I have experience, but Asher Voss was next level. College boyfriends gave me oral sex, but I could never finish. I was always too concerned with what they were thinking while they were doing it. I couldn't get out of my head enough to relax and climax.

But I didn't wonder with Asher. He was like a man possessed, and he knew exactly what to do to my body to get the response he wanted. Knew how to string me along until I thought I might die if he didn't let me come, then rachet me even higher so that when I did, it felt as if a mini atomic bomb had gone off inside me.

There was no doubt in my mind that I wanted to do it again. Wanted to do more. What would it be like to fuck a man like him?

But he fell distant afterward. Not cold or cruel like before, but it was obvious that he was in his head about what had happened. Most likely, our age difference was playing havoc inside him, since he'd mentioned it more than once.

I hadn't wanted to push, thinking that might be the wrong approach. Maybe it was better to show him that it was no big deal. That I could handle an adult relationship without clearly defined boundaries. It wasn't as though I thought the man was going to fall in love with me—I don't think he's capable of such a thing.

But if I can spend the rest of my time here having amazing sex and not have him be so mean and dismissive of me? That seems like a far better alternative than my situation before last night. I could never fall for a man like him anyway—so hot and cold, so mean and hurtful at times. It's just our sexual chemistry that draws me to him.

There's a tinge of denial in my thoughts, but I ignore it. Just because Asher proved he was physically capable of apologizing doesn't mean that I don't see him for the deeply scarred man he is.

A knock on my door has me sitting up and clutching the blanket to my chest. *Is it Asher?*

"Come in," I call.

Marcel pokes his head in. "Good morning."

I smile at him. "Morning."

"I trust you had a good night?" He walks a few feet inside the room.

My brain flashes to images of Asher with his mouth between my legs, and I try to keep a blush from creeping up onto my face. "I did, yes."

"Excellent." He claps his hands in front of him. "Mr. Voss has asked that you be moved from under Finn to a different department."

I frown. I wonder why he would do that. "Okay... where am I going now?"

Marcel smiles wide. "You're going to assist him from now on. We're working on setting up a desk for you in his office."

Despite my earlier promise to myself, a seed of hope springs to life inside me, fed with sunlight and water by Asher's request that I work by his side.

"Doesn't he already have an assistant?" I ask.

He nods. "He does, but she works off site mostly. Mr. Voss plans to spend more days here working from home, and he wants you to act as his assistant when he's here."

"Okay." I smile. It sounds better than scrubbing toilets and endless hours of polishing wood.

"You're to meet him in his office in exactly one hour."

I glance at the clock on the bedside table and nod. "I can do that."

"Wonderful." Marcel turns around to leave but stops and looks over his shoulder at me. "No update on when your room will be ready, but Mr. Voss said you're welcome to stay here until it's completely repaired."

I blink rapid fire. "Really? He wasn't too pleased when he found me here last night. Did you get in trouble?" I bite on my bottom lip, hoping not.

"Nothing I can't handle." He winks.

Then he's gone, closing the door behind him. I spring out of bed and rush into the shower, wanting enough time to blow dry my hair and apply a little makeup. I want to look good the next time I see Asher, especially with what happened last night.

Once I've showered, dried and styled my hair, and applied a little makeup, I go over to my bag to see what I'm going to wear. I don't have many options suitable for being the assistant to a billionaire. My things arrived at Oak Haven from Nashville, though, so I'll have to make sure to go by and grab some of the outfits I wore for my interning job.

I settle on a black wrap romper with shorts. It's not exactly professional, but it's not casual either. I can make it work.

With ten minutes to spare, I rush from the room to head to Asher's office. I'm finally getting better at finding my way around Midnight Manor, so I arrive a few minutes early. He's not in his office, so I go inside to wait for him, spotting the new desk that has been set up in the far corner from his.

My nerves set in. I was too distracted getting ready for anxiety to be an issue earlier. But now I can't help but wonder how he'll greet me.

I'm assuming, just from the fact that he's brought me here to work with him, that he's not going to push me away, but I can't be certain. Maybe he wants me with him every day because he wants to do a little secretary/boss roleplaying. I don't hate the idea, I'll admit.

When footsteps enter the room, I turn with a smile on my face, but it falters when I see a beautiful blonde standing beside Asher.

I clear my throat. "Good morning." I put on my most professional voice and don't show that I'm disappointed he's not alone.

"Morning," Asher clips out. "Miss Boudreaux, this is Clarise, my assistant at the head office. I've brought her here this week to help you get acquainted with what I'll need from you while you're here."

Recovering, I step forward, hand held out. "Good to meet you, Clarise."

She takes my hand and shakes it, studying me for a beat.

I'd put her in her late twenties. She's taller than I am, with green eyes and a willowy frame that reminds me of a model. Dressed in her sophisticated office wear, she makes me feel like a child playing dress-up in my romper.

As if reading my mind, Asher says, "We'll have to get you more appropriate clothing if you're going to work for me now. I'll have some things left in your room."

I nod, trying my best to hide my embarrassment. "Thank you."

"I'll leave you two to get started." He doesn't say another word before he goes over to his desk and gets to work on his computer.

"Do you have any experience assisting a man like Mr. Voss?" Clarise asks me.

There's a challenge in her voice, and I wonder if it's because she's territorial about the man himself or her job. Maybe both.

"I was interning at a publishing company in Nashville before I... came here." I doubt she knows how or why I'm here, and Asher would probably prefer to keep it that way.

Clarise blows out a breath. "Well, we better get started then. I don't want to be away from my girlfriend any longer than I need to be."

Guess that answers my earlier question.

The week passes quickly, and as he said he would, Asher has some more appropriate clothing left in the closet in my room. I'm still staying inside the manor as the work to repair my original room continues.

When I ventured home on Saturday night, I picked up a few outfits from what had returned from Nashville. I had a nice visit with my family, and I was surprised to find my mom out of bed, hanging out downstairs with them when I arrived.

Luke told me it had been a good week for her. While she wasn't exactly talking while I was there, she at least seemed to be following the conversation. It gave me hope that soon she might be back to her old self.

I didn't get a moment alone with Asher last week, and I wondered if that was by design. Though I suppose Clarise was there the whole time to train me.

Today will be the first day she won't be here, and I can't help the giddy feeling that rises inside me. The anticipation of being alone with him again is all I could think of. Will he kiss me? Will we do more?

It's hard not to skip like a schoolgirl through the manor as I make my way to his office.

When I arrive, I'm disappointed to see that he isn't there yet. No matter, I'll get to work, and he'll be happy when he comes in.

But when I step over to my desk, I see a note in the middle of my desk.

I'll be out of town on business all week. Contact Clarise each morning for your list of tasks to be completed.

A

THAT'S ALL IT SAYS?

I flip it over to find the back blank. It's so... impersonal. Maybe he was afraid someone else who works for him would see it if they were in here cleaning or taking out the garbage?

With a frown, I sit at my desk and reach for the phone to find out from Clarise what I need to be working on. This week is not going to be what I hoped.

CHAPTER
SEVENTEEN

ANABELLE

By the time the following Monday rolls around, I'm nearly desperate to see Asher. It's been over a week since I've seen him and more than that since we've been alone together. It's as though our time in the maze has infected me, and the only relief I'll get from my craving for him is to be around him.

I make sure to arrive early for work this morning, and to my relief, he's already in his office, sitting at his desk.

Asher doesn't look up when I enter and walk over to my desk, so I say a tentative, "Good morning." Maybe he's just really into whatever he's working on and didn't hear me walk in.

"Morning." He doesn't glance up from whatever he's writing.

My heart sinks a little, and I sit at my desk to get to work. Are we really not going to talk about what happened that night?

An hour passes and then another. The longer we sit in silence, pretending that nothing happened, the more irritated and angrier I become. If he doesn't ever want a repeat or if he regrets what happened between us, that's fine, he can just say that. But to just act like it never happened stokes a fire inside me.

I can do this. I can be brave and confront him about it. Maybe he thinks I don't want to talk about it.

Pushing my chair away from my desk, I stand and walk over to stand in front of his desk.

"What can I help you with, Miss Boudreaux?" He keeps typing on his computer, not sparing me a glance.

"Are we really not going to talk about it?" I cross my arms.

He lets out a long-suffering sigh. "Talk about what exactly?"

"About how you made me come twice with your mouth two weeks ago, and you've been avoiding me since."

That gets his attention. I figured being brash might work.

He leans back in his chair, smoothing his black silk tie down his torso. God, he looks good in an expensive suit. He looks me up and down lazily, not appearing all that impressed with what he sees. "What is there to talk about?"

I don't know what to say to that exactly. His demeanor once again makes me feel too young, too inexperienced compared to him. Maybe he does this kind of thing all the time, and it's no big deal. He has fourteen years of experience that I don't have.

"I don't know. It just felt like we should talk about it." My hands drop to my sides.

He sighs again, and I want to throat punch him.

"It happened. It won't be happening again, especially now that you work as my right hand." He shrugs. "We're both adults, right? It shouldn't be that big a deal." He arches an eyebrow as if challenging me to disagree with him and prove to him I am the child he thought I was.

I breathe hard through my nose, forcing myself to relax. "Sure, no biggie. Just wanted to make sure we were on the same page." I give him a tight smile while my chest squeezes with disappointment.

"Perfect. Nothing more to discuss then." He looks away from me and returns his attention to his computer.

I spin on my heel and ignore the stinging in my eyes as I return to my desk. I'm about to get back to work when he calls my name.

"Miss Boudreaux."

One last tiny lick of a flame flares to life in the hopes that maybe he's changed his mind.

"Yes?" I turn to face him with a hopeful expression.

"I need you to call Madeline Ridgeway and let her know I'll pick her up at seven on Friday evening. Her contact information should be in the system Clarise trained you on."

My stomach bottoms out. He holds my gaze, not looking guilty or repentant.

I know who Madeline Ridgeway is. Everyone in the state knows. She's a gorgeous socialite who could have easily been a model and is often photographed on the arm of the most rich and powerful men in the country.

And now she's going on a date with Asher this Friday.

Tears prick the corners of my eyes. I hate that he can probably see them, but he doesn't react. Probably thinks I deserve them for being so stupid as to think there could ever be anything between us—even if it was purely sexual.

"I'll make sure she knows." My voice sounds hollow to my ears.

He nods then stands from his desk and leaves the office.

WE DON'T TALK MUCH the rest of the week, and when we do, it's strictly work-related. I've erected my own walls and am cold whenever I have to deal with him, but he either doesn't notice or doesn't care.

When he leaves the office an hour early on Friday, telling me he has to go get ready for his evening out, I want to stab him in his eye with my pen, but instead, I smile and tell him that I hope he has a good time.

Once he's left the room, I silently scream and fall back into my chair, defeated.

He knew. He knew if we messed around, I wouldn't be able to handle it, and I hate that he's right. Jealousy seethes inside me at the thought of him doing to Madeline Ridgeway what he did to me in the middle of that maze.

For the next hour, I do my best to focus on work and not on where Asher Voss might be sticking his dick tonight, but it's near impossible. When my workday is done, I can't get out of there fast enough. All I want is to go have a nice hot bath in my room and relax while I read my latest book. Escaping into a fictional happily ever after sounds perfect because I'm clearly not close to finding my own.

After I stand, I push my chair into my desk and stomp toward the door, whipping it open and plowing into a hard chest. I stumble back, blinking and looking up at Asher dressed in a tuxedo.

Damn it. I did not need this visual to add to my jealous musings this weekend. He might look better than I've ever seen him. His hair is slicked back, he smells divine, and he oozes power and sex appeal. Madeline is going to be all over him tonight, I have no doubt.

"I forgot my phone on my desk." His gravelly voice does something to my insides. But then I remember that *she'll* be the one hearing it tonight, not me.

"Better grab it then. Don't want to be late for your *date*." I push past him and out of the office.

Screw him. I won't allow Asher Voss to hurt me ever again.

CHAPTER
EIGHTEEN

ANABELLE

The moment I'm permitted to leave Midnight Manor, I do, driving past the iron gates as they slowly swing open.

I know that tonight is the night all the expensive cars stream through town and onto the manor grounds, and weeks ago, I had debated sticking around to see if I could suss out what was going on, but after everything that happened this week, I'm no longer interested. In fact, I've decided I don't give a shit what Asher Voss is up to. I don't even want to think about the man at all.

Tonight, I need some good news. I want to go home and see if my mother has made any progress in the past week. Maybe the shock of my father's death is finally wearing off, and she's ready to deal with her grief.

I pull up to the estate and rush inside, out of the June heat. It's not terrible yet, but I sigh when the cool air greets me.

"Hello?" I call.

"In here," Luke answers from the kitchen, which is weird because he's never been known to cook a meal in his life.

I find him sitting on the counter, sipping a beer by himself.

"Where is everyone?" I ask.

"Grandmother is visiting with a friend. She said to apologize that she missed you but that her friend is only in town for the weekend."

I wave him off. It's no big deal. I actually think it's good that she's getting out rather than being cooped up here all the time. Before my father passed, she was a social butterfly.

"And Mom?"

The change in his expression tells me all I need to know. "She's upstairs in bed."

Disappointment threatens to crush me. "She had a bad week?"

He nods. "Yeah, hasn't been out of bed since Monday."

My shoulders sag. "What happened? What changed?" That little sprig of hope that had begun to grow inside me has just been plucked out of the ground.

He shrugs then brings his beer to his lips and takes a pull. "Don't know. Nothing as far as I can tell."

"I'm going to go see her." I turn to leave the kitchen.

"She won't even know you're there, Belle. Save yourself the grief."

I look at him over my shoulder. "I have to at least try."

He doesn't say anything.

Making my way through the house, I head upstairs to her bedroom and knock gently on the closed door. When there's no answer, I push it open slowly, and I'm greeted by a dark room. I walk in and turn on a couple of the lamps so at least I'll be able to see her face when I speak to her.

Everything in here is the same as it was months ago when my father died. His expensive watch that he'd wear to social events sits on the highboy dresser, the faint scent of his cologne still in the air. His robe hangs on a hook by the closet, and their wedding picture, taken so many years ago, still adorns his bedside table.

"Mom?"

Her back is to me, so I can't tell if she's asleep, but she doesn't react to me saying her name. When I round the end of the bed so I can see her face, I realize she's not asleep. She's just curled up on her side, staring aimlessly out the window.

"Mom, it's Anabelle." I sit on the edge of the bed and take her hand.

She doesn't react.

With a sigh, I use my free hand to tuck her hair behind her ear. "Mom, you have to get out of bed. You can't spend all your time here."

I need my mom, I want to cry out! She always gives such good advice, and it's been a shit week. I could use her support tonight. Unshed tears sting my eyes as I look at the woman who is a shell of her former self. Her hair is dull and lifeless, she's lost weight, and she's almost catatonic at times.

I squeeze her hand. "Mom, we need you. Please…" My voice breaks.

She doesn't move her head. Her gaze flicks in my direction, but there's no recognition.

Still, it's something. I have to try again. "We love you, and we need you. There's so much going on with me, with the estate. I need my mother. Please."

I feel like a little girl again. I'm desperate for her comfort, for anyone's comfort. I've never felt so alone in all my life.

She just stares at me, unseeing almost, with no reaction to my words.

"We're all grieving the loss of Dad, and I know you miss him terribly, but he wouldn't want to see you this way."

At the mention of my father, she rolls over, giving me her back. My chest tightens, and a sob racks through my body before I can pull it back in. It feels like the ultimate betrayal, as though she's turning her back on her own daughter, and it takes me a moment to control my reaction. I breathe slowly in through my nose and out through my mouth until I have myself together enough to leave the room.

"I'll see you next weekend, Momma. Love you."

She doesn't say anything, not that I expected her to. I turn off all the lights I turned on and leave the room, closing the door behind me.

Luke's on the porch, working on another beer.

"Has the doctor been by to see her?" I sit next to him.

"He was here a couple of days ago. Said there's not much more he can do for her. Suggested that we might want to think about sending her somewhere for more specialized help."

I whip my head in his direction, my mouth hanging open. "Are you serious?"

He nods and takes a pull from his beer. "He's at a loss. Said there are people better equipped to help her."

I slouch into my seat. "I don't know that we could afford it even if we wanted to."

"Probably not," he says.

I'm quiet for a moment until a scream rips out of my throat, piercing the quiet night air. I let out a big sigh when I'm done. "That felt good."

Luke looks at me warily. "I was going to ask how things were going at Midnight Manor, but I guess I have my answer."

I roll my head along the back of the chair until I'm looking at him. "It was just a bad week. At least I don't have to do manual labor anymore. Now I'm working directly for Asher Voss as his assistant."

My brother sits straighter in his chair. "Is he doing something that makes you uncomfortable, Belle? Because if he is, you need to leave. We'll figure some other way to keep the estate in the family."

I blow out a breath. "There is no other way. And I'm fine. Or I will be. I just needed to come home and see some friendly faces is all. I miss you guys."

"Miss you too, sis." He looks like he doesn't believe me, but he lets it go.

I push up off the chair. "Now what I need is a few drinks and some fun."

"You heading to Black Magic?" He arches an eyebrow.

"Yup." I walk toward my car.

"I haven't heard of any of your friends returning to town," he calls.

"Don't care. My only mission is to get drunk and forget this entire week."

And maybe to get laid. I don't tell my brother that though. Maybe if I get under someone else, I'll get over Asher Voss and how he delivered the best two orgasms of my life then tossed me aside like trash.

CHAPTER
NINETEEN

ANABELLE

I walk into Black Magic and find that my brother was right, I don't recognize anyone here. There are two couples playing pool who I think were a few years ahead of me in high school and some lifers sitting at the bar, but that's about it.

I order a drink from Sawyer and head over to one of the tables, not feeling like chitchatting with anyone. Maybe after my first drink.

At the moment, there's no one here for me to go home with, but maybe someone else will come in later on. It's not as though there are an unlimited number of bachelors my age in Magnolia Bend. At least Galen's not here. I'm so desperate to escape my life tonight that I might have even considered going home with him.

I forgot my book in my car, so about halfway through my drink, I step outside to grab it. I walk around the side of the building and look to my left when the sound of an approaching vehicle reaches me. Two blacked-out high-end SUVs pass by, and I get that hollow feeling in my chest whenever my mind travels to Asher because I know they're headed to Midnight Manor.

Maybe I should have stayed at the manor tonight to try to get some answers.

I'm almost at my vehicle when a car stops in the dirt parking lot behind me. I turn and watch a man get out and walk toward the bar, but I can't tell what he looks like because of the headlights.

Once I turn away from the glaring lights, I get my book from my car and bring it back into the bar with me. I've just set the book on the table and am pulling out my chair when an attractive man comes out of the back hallway where the restrooms are.

His eyes take me in from head to toe, and I can tell that he likes what he sees. There's a gleam in his gaze that feels a little off-kilter, but I set my concerns aside. He's definitely older than me, though probably not as old as Asher. Maybe in his early thirties.

God, why am I comparing him to Asher? The whole point of tonight was not to think of him.

He's wearing expensive black dress pants and a short-sleeve black button-up shirt. His hair is cut close to his head, and I can tell by the way the light reflects off of it that if it was longer, it would probably land somewhere between light brown and dark blond.

He smiles and walks over, taking the back of my chair from me and pulling it out. "Allow me."

Maybe my night is looking up. I smile at him and take a seat. "Thank you."

"My pleasure." He walks around to stand at the opposite side of the table, then briefly glances at his expensive watch. "Would you mind if I joined you for a bit?"

"Of course not. Have a seat." I motion to the empty chair across from me.

He pulls out the chair in one smooth motion, smiling across the table at me. "What's your name?"

"Anabelle." I might want to hook up tonight, but I'm not going to give this guy any more information than he needs.

I had a one-night stand my second year in college, and the guy found me on socials because I'd given him my full name. He wouldn't stop messaging me for weeks before he took the hint that I didn't want anything more than our one night together.

"Preston. Pleasure." He holds his hand out over the table and I shake it. When I try to pull my hand away, he holds onto it. Our eyes catch and snag, and when the corner of his lips tip up, he finally releases my hand. "I'll go get us some fresh drinks. What would you like?"

I give him my order and watch as he walks over to the bar. I'm not sure about him. There's no doubt he's attractive, and he seems interested, but I hate this unsettled feeling when he looks at me.

That's probably just my Asher brain talking, because Preston doesn't make me want to strip my clothes off and do whatever he says upon seeing him. There's no harm in having one drink with him and feeling him out before I decide whether I want to go home with him or not.

Preston returns and sets my drink in front of me, seeming to opt for straight whiskey himself. "So, Anabelle. What is it that you do for a living?" He leans back in his seat, the picture of relaxed sophistication.

How to answer that? I'm not about to tell him about my deal with Asher, so instead I say, "I was interning at a small publisher in Nashville, but I had to return home to see to some family matters." I bring my drink to my lips and sip from it.

"Interning? How old are you?"

"Twenty-two."

"Good. Had to make sure you're legal." He winks and sips from his drink.

A nervous chuckle leaks out, and I take another sip.

"What publisher were you working at?" he asks.

When I tell him, he seems to know a little about them. We chat about what direction I'm hoping for my career to take once I've resolved my family issues, and he seems to know a little about publishing, but when I ask him what he does for a living, he's vague.

I finish my drink and lean my chin on my fist as I look across the table at him. At first, I wasn't sure about him, but

I think he might be a good guy. A good distraction at the very least.

"So, do you have a boyfriend, Anabelle?" He finishes his own drink and slides the glass to the middle of the table.

"Pfft. Not at all." I shake my head, still pressed against my fist, and have to close my eyes for a second when the sensation of my head swimming hits me.

He smiles wide. "You sound like a woman scorned."

I shrug as best I can. "Maybe. Maybe I'm just a dumb girl who fell for the wrong guy."

Preston pushes his chair back and stands from the table.

Wait, where is he going? He's supposed to be my distraction tonight.

But instead of leaving, he walks around the table and comes to my side. "I'm headed to a party that might be just what you need. Care to join me?"

I lift my hand from my fist and smile up at him. "Absolutely."

This is exactly what I need. A little bit of fun to get my mind off everything I don't want to think about.

He helps me stand, and I have to clutch him for a moment before I get my bearings and can stand on my own. "Oops, sorry."

"No worries." He wraps his arm around my waist, and we make our way to the door.

My limbs feel heavy when I walk, but I figure it must just be from the extra hard run I did this morning. I should have drunk more water.

He leads me to the vehicle I saw him get out of, and I realize it's one of the same types of blacked-out SUVs that travel up to Midnight Manor once a month. I debate asking where we're going, but I really don't care.

If Preston is going to some party at the manor, and Asher will be there, let him see me with Preston. I don't care. He could be there with Madeline Ridgeway or some other woman he deems worthy for all I know.

"Shoot, I left my book on the table."

I try to turn around, but Preston opens the back door of the SUV for me. "I'll go grab it. You hop in and wait for me."

I smile at him as he helps me in the back. "Thank you."

The driver doesn't say anything to me, so I quietly wait. But my eyelids grow heavy, and suddenly I'm so drowsy that I can't keep them open anymore, so I opt to lean my head back and close them, just until Preston returns.

I awake with a start, and it takes me a moment to figure out where I am, but when I turn to my side and see Preston, it all comes back to me.

"Have a good cat nap?" he asks, grinning.

"I'm so sorry." I try to sit up straight, but my limbs still feel as if I can't move them properly. Maybe I'm getting sick or something?

"Don't worry about it." He reaches across the seat and takes my hand.

Well, at least he's still interested.

I glance out the window and realize we're on the grounds of Midnight Manor. "This is where the party is?"

"You know it?" he asks.

"Everyone in town knows about Midnight Manor." It's kind of a lie by omission but not an outright lie.

Besides, I stand by what I thought earlier. Let Asher see me with this handsome, available man. He made it clear I was nothing to him.

But Preston said he was going to a party. Could that be all this is? Are the Voss brothers throwing a party once a month, and the rumor mill is wrong?

It wouldn't surprise me. The people in town have a knack for taking something small and making something big of it. It's not beyond the stretch of the imagination that they could have done the same with this.

The driver takes the SUV to the side of the house, in between the south and the west wing, and pulls to a stop.

"Ready?" Preston asks me.

"Yup." A nauseated feeling comes over me, though I'm sure that's because the nerves are hitting me now at the idea of seeing Asher, especially if he's with that Madeline woman. Imagining them together was bad enough, but actually having to see it would feel like torture.

The driver comes around and opens Preston's door, then Preston helps me get out of the back of the vehicle. Again, I have to cling to him when my feet hit the ground because I feel so woozy, but he doesn't seem to care.

The vehicles must all just drop and go, because I don't see any of them milling about.

Once again, Preston wraps his arm around my waist and helps me toward the house and a large, intricately carved wooden door.

Before we reach the door, he turns back to me. "It's a theme party, so you have to make sure you're in costume when we go in."

"Oh." I blink up at him, not sure what he expects me to do with this information. My brain is sluggish.

"We're all going to be dressed the same, and I have an extra, so we're good. Let me just put it on you."

I hadn't even realized he had anything in his other hand. I don't really understand, but I'm so tired that I don't think I could help him even if I wanted to. "Okay."

Preston pulls something around me, and I feel myself being surrounded by fabric as it brushes against my bare legs. Then he places some kind of mask on my face that covers my forehead down to my nose and cheeks. And finally, he pulls up a hood.

I'm not sure what I look like, and the idea of moving my limbs to try to see seems like too much effort right now. When Preston dons his costume, I know that I'm likely dressed in a dark red robe and black mask as he is.

"You just happened to have an extra one of these for me?" A slow chuckle leaves my lips.

"My date canceled on me."

"Guess she's missing out then." Did I just slur a bit?

"I'm starting to think I got lucky that she canceled." He kisses me, and it's all I can do to get my tongue to work properly and kiss him back. He pulls away, and though his face is covered in a mask, his eyes look at me seriously. "If anyone asks your name, you need to say it's Penelope, okay? This is a private party, and they don't like outsiders. No one will know you're not her covered like this anyway. Got it?"

I scrunch my forehead under the mask. "I guess."

He wraps his arm around my waist and walks me toward the large wooden door. "It's important. Don't talk to anyone unless you have to, and if you do, you're Penelope."

Unease creeps up my spine. As the door creaks open, and a man I've never seen before stands there eyeing us, I don't know what to do.

Preston lifts his mask to show his face. "Penelope's had a little too much fun already for the night, so I'm going to help her in."

"No problem, Mr. Wallace."

The large man steps to the side, and Preston helps me in past the threshold. We're standing on a large landing with a steep set of stairs ahead. It's dark at the bottom of the stairs, so I can't see what's down there, but I hear the thrumming bass of music.

Do the Vosses have a nightclub in their basement or something?

Preston helps me toward the stairs.

"I don't think I can make it down those." Okay, now I'm definitely slurring.

"I got you." Without warning, Preston picks me up and carries me down the staircase.

My head lolls back and forth because I can't seem to keep it up in this position. By the time he sets me on my feet at the bottom, I'm nauseated again. He straightens my mask and pulls my hood up farther so it conceals more of my face before wrapping his arm around my waist.

It's dark here, and as he moves us forward, we step through an archway into a cavernous room that looks as if it's been carved from stone. Music bleeds through the room, seeming to fill all the crevices and cracks in the stone above us. It overflows my senses with its pulsating, thrumming beat.

My eyes drift shut as I look down from the ceiling at the people surrounding us. They're all dressed in the same red cloaks, though the masks are different. Some are black, some red, some white—all with different designs.

They're all standing in a circle, but I can't see what they're looking at. Not until Preston clutches my side harder and leads me forward, pushing into the inner circle.

I blink several times to be sure I'm seeing things correctly.

There's a dais at the far end of the room and the circle starts there. On it is a man—he's shirtless, that's the only way I know—standing over a naked woman wearing a black mask who is lying across some kind of riser. Another man is standing off to the side, and he reaches forward with a knife in his hand and passes it to the man with the girl. That's when I see it—the bear tattoo on his hand.

Asher.

Asher is the man passing the knife on.

My heart rate picks up.

The man with the knife in his hand now brings it to her breast, pressing the tip there until blood pools around the indent. Her back arches, and she moans loudly enough that I hear her over the music. Is she enjoying this?

The man bends down to her breast and runs his tongue along the curve of it until he reaches the place where he cut her, then he laps up the blood with his tongue.

Preston said not to speak, but I can't help myself, and I turn my head in his direction. "Is this a cult?"

Oh my god, are they going to sacrifice her?

Before he can answer, my head swims, and I feel it loll forward. Then I fall limp to the side. Though Preston is trying his best to keep me upright, I can't move my limbs, and I'm just so tired all of a sudden.

Preston curses in my ear before the world goes black.

CHAPTER
TWENTY

ASHER

I watch from across the circle as Preston pushes his way into the fray with Penelope by his side. That idiot is always arriving late. I'd love nothing more than to have him never show up here again, but barring him entry would cause more problems than it's worth.

Something about Penelope has me glancing over at her several times as the ceremony starts. Normally she wouldn't command much attention from me. We've fucked a few times, but she's average at best.

It takes me a moment to figure out exactly what is catching my attention. She's leaning her weight on Preston, almost as though she's counting on him to keep her standing. That strikes me as strange. Penelope doesn't usually come to these things messed up, though she can get messy once she's here.

I turn my attention back to Sid pressing the tip of the knife into Emery's breast. He loves this shit, so he's often the one to perform the annual blood ritual. And I know for certain Emery was pleased when he picked her to participate with him.

Blood pools on her breast and Sid leans down and swipes his tongue over the cut, tasting her as part of the ritual.

There's some type of commotion across the circle, and I glance at Penelope falling until Preston heaves her up into his arms. Her cloak spreads open, revealing her legs, and Preston swings her around, telling the crowd to part so that he can move her out of there.

What the fuck is she thinking about coming here in that state? The three of us will be having words after the rite is complete.

Then, what I just saw registers in my head.

The birthmark above her knee.

Anabelle's birthmark above the knee.

Panic freezes me for a beat until rage takes hold, setting my blood on fire and unleashing the animal inside me. I turn to Kol. "Take over for me. I have to deal with something."

"You can't leave—"

But I ignore him, leaving the circle and pushing through everyone as their murmurs get louder and louder around me.

Where did that fucker go?

I leave the main room and head down the hall that leads to all the specialty rooms. Because everyone is in the main room, it's not that hard to locate Preston and Anabelle. They're in one of the private rooms, and when I whip the door open, Anabelle is passed out on the bed. Her cloak is splayed open, and Preston sits on the side of the bed, hand on her thigh.

The idea of another man tasting her, knowing how sweet she is, brings out the savage beast in me. I don't think, I just act, tearing inside the room and pulling him away from her by the shoulders.

He stumbles but gains his footing. "What the fuck, Voss?" He pulls his mask off and tosses it on the floor.

Good, tonight is the last time he'll be using it.

"Don't what the fuck me, asshole." I push him, so he stumbles back. "First you bring in someone who isn't a member here, endangering every one of us." I push him again. "Then you've drugged her, and she can't even stay conscious?"

"I don't know what the fuck you're talking about!" he shouts.

I push him again. This time, his back hits the wall. At this point, it feels a little like playing with my prey before I eat it, and I savor the feeling.

"You know exactly what I'm talking about. I know what you're into. And I'd bet my fortune on the fact that the woman lying unconscious is not a willing participant." I bare my teeth at him and practically growl.

"You don't know shit. Prove it."

"I don't need to." I swing and hit him square in the jaw. Blood bursts from his mouth as his head whips to the side. The bastard doesn't even try to defend himself as I level hit after hit on him until he slides down the wall.

I stare down at him, and it feels good to watch him bleed. He deserves it for what he's done.

"Jesus Christ, what the fuck, Ash?" Nero rushes past me to where Preston lies against the wall, barely conscious.

Then Sid and Kol join us, and Kol tells everyone the show is over, and the door closes with a slam. Nero checks Preston's pulse.

"I left him alive," I say.

"What the hell happened?" Kol asks.

Sid chuckles. "Told you Preston would eventually reach the end of Ash's patience."

Figures he'd think this was funny. There will be repercussions for what I've done here tonight, but ask me if I give a fuck.

"Pull the mask off her face." I motion to where Anabelle is still unconscious on the bed.

My brothers are the only ones I trust to touch her.

Kol pushes her hood back as far as it will go and pulls the mask off Anabelle's face. His head whips in my direction. "How did she get in here?"

"This piece of shit." I motion to where Preston lies, beaten to a pulp.

"Doesn't surprise me that Preston would pull this shit. He's always thought he was above the rules. How'd she get past security is the better question," Sid says.

"Pull the footage and find out, Nero."

He nods and stands from where he's crouching. "At least Preston's still alive. I thought maybe we'd have another situation like we did with..." My youngest brother trails off before he says the name. "I'll figure out how he got her in here and take care of it."

"He drugged her." My hands flex and squeeze at my sides. It's all I can do not to strangle the life out of Preston.

"You don't know that," Kol says.

I glare at him. "We all know what he's into." Then I look at Sid and hold his gaze.

"Maybe she consented," he says.

"Not a chance." I step over to the bed, pushing Kol out of the way and gently picking up Anabelle's prone body. "She'd never consent to that."

"What? All of a sudden you know her?" Sid mocks. "The woman you hired merely to torment her for your own enjoyment?" A caustic laugh leaves his lips.

"If you don't want to be next on my list, you'll shut the fuck up right now." I pin Sid with a glare, and I think he might say something more to me, but he presses his lips together. "I need to get the doctor here to look at her. You guys will take the trash out?" I nod in Preston's direction.

"Gladly," Kol says.

I meet all their eyes and nod, then turn toward the door. Nero comes over to open it for me, and I move as fast as I can the opposite way of the main room, toward the entrance that only my brothers and I use. Nero follows and takes his skeleton key out to unlock and open the door for me. Then I start up the stairs with her and head through the manor toward the west wing.

Anabelle has her own room not too far from mine, but tonight she'll be staying in my room whether she likes it or not. I need to know that she's okay.

I bend down and kiss the corner of her eyebrow. "I'm going to take care of you, don't you worry."

The words surprise me when they leave my mouth, but there's no denying that what just happened changes everything.

CHAPTER
TWENTY-ONE

ANABELLE

I wake with a pounding headache. My eyes flutter open, and I don't recognize where I am and I still.

What the hell?

I cast my mind back to the last thing I remember... robes and... masks? Asher's hand reaching out to pass a knife to another man.

Did I have some weird kind of dream?

I remember meeting that guy at the bar... what was his name? I can't remember, but I think it started with a P. A lot of last night is blurry.

None of that matters, though. The first thing I need to do is figure out where the hell I am. I try to sit up, but I have to squeeze my eyes shut from the way that makes my brain feel as if it's rattling around in my skull.

When I bring my hand up to my head, there's a tug on the back of my hand and a sharp stinging sensation. I open my eyes and see an IV in my hand, but I'm not in the hospital. I raise my head slowly to look at my surroundings and freeze when I see Asher sitting in a chair at the far side of the bed, staring at me.

He doesn't look as though he's slept. His hair isn't styled to perfection. Rather, it's falling down over his forehead and the sides of his head. His face is stubbled with dark hair, and his dark shirt is rumpled, along with his pants.

I'm not sure what to make from the look in his eyes. There's some type of emotion simmering beneath the surface, but I can't be sure what. As always, he's an enigma.

"What happened?" My voice comes out in a croak, and it's then I realize how dry my mouth is.

"There's water on the bedside table." Though he speaks, he doesn't move a muscle.

I slowly turn and reach for the water with my hand that doesn't have an IV in it, then bring the glass to my lips. It's so refreshing that I want to guzzle the entire thing, but I refrain. Once I've returned the water to the table, I turn to Asher and repeat my earlier question. "What happened? Where am I?"

"In my bedroom."

My eyes widen, and I do a quick mental inventory of my body. "Did we…" I don't feel like I had sex last night, but who knows?

He scowls. "Unconscious women aren't my thing."

Unconscious? "I remember being in the basement of the manor and some kind of ceremony going on... and that's it."

"You passed out."

"What? How? Why?" Is there something wrong with me?

He sighs. "What do you remember from last night?"

"I went and saw my mother. She wasn't doing well, which just added to my shitty week, so I decided to go to Black Magic." I don't tell him I intended to pick up someone to make me forget him. "There was this guy who stopped to use the bathroom, and we started talking. He invited me to a party... it's kind of blurry from there. I remember he took me to the manor, and then I just have this vision of a bunch of people in red cloaks and masks on and you..."

"Me what?" He arches an eyebrow.

"You were there... you passed a knife to someone who..."

"Did he buy you a drink?" he snarls.

It takes my brain a minute to catch up to the change of topic. "Yeah."

Asher's hands grip the armrests of the chair he's sitting in so hard that the white of his knuckles bleeds through his olive skin.

His reaction has me more worried than ever. "Are you going to tell me what happened?"

"You allowed yourself to be picked up by Preston Wallace."

That name doesn't mean anything to me. "Who's Preston Wallace?"

"A predator."

A chill runs through my body, and I shiver. Asher's gaze dips down to my chest where my nipples harden, and it's then that I look down and realize I'm not wearing what I was last night.

"Where are my clothes? How am I in my pajamas?" I'm wearing one of my shorts and tank sets that I wear to bed. I hoist the blanket up far enough to cover my chest.

"When the doctor came, I had the nurse change your clothes. You vomited on your other ones when I got you back to my room."

I blink a few times at him. "What doctor? Are you going to tell me what happened?" Panic flares, and I need to know exactly what happened last night.

He stands from the chair, and so slowly, he walks toward the bed while he speaks. "Preston drugged your drink and brought you to Midnight Manor to a private event that he knew you were not permitted to attend. When you passed out, he brought you into a back room to do God knows what. I intervened then brought you to my room and had the doctor come to make sure you'd be okay."

I don't know what to say to that, let alone how to feel about it. My brain is still sluggish, and it's a lot of information to take in.

He reaches the side of the bed. That's when I notice that the knuckles on his right hand, the one with the bear tattoo, are bloodied.

"What do you mean you intervened?"

"I beat him within an inch of his life." There's zero remorse in his voice.

Some man drugged me, and Asher was angry enough to assault him. It takes me a second to wrap my brain around that fact.

I look at him, overwhelmed with emotion—gratitude that he got me out of that situation before Preston could do whatever he was planning to, shock that Asher would be angry enough to attack him, and desire because apparently, my Freudian brain likes it when someone stands up for me like that.

"You saved me?"

He scowls. "I'm no hero, Anabelle."

"But you saved me. You did. Who knows what he would've done if you hadn't stopped him. Thank you." Tears prick the corners of my eyes because I realize how lucky I am that Asher stepped in.

I'm not an idiot. I know that anyone invited was someone powerful in their own right, especially if they were a part of whatever was going on in that basement.

I glance at his knuckles again. "Will you get in trouble for hurting him?"

His jaw sets in a hard line. "That's not your concern."

I clutch the blanket to my chest harder. "It is, though. If you get in trouble or arrested for assault because of me—"

Asher presses his hands on the mattress and leans in across the bed. "Let's get one thing clear, Anabelle—*he* is at fault, not you. *He* drugged your drink. *He* brought you somewhere you should never have been. He probably saw you, your beauty and your innocence, and wanted nothing more than to defile you."

My heart speeds up when he calls me beautiful. Not in a conventional way maybe, but if he says the words, he must think it, right?

"But I invited his attention. I wanted it even." My face heats with that admission, but it's true.

Asher stares at me for a beat, gaze intense. "I'm sure he was as charming as he always is." He hesitates, almost as though he doesn't want to ask the next question but can't help himself. "Why did you want to leave with him, or were you already messed up when he took you from the bar?"

"I might have been a little messed up, but I knew what I was doing when I left with him. I... I..."

"You what?" he snaps, causing me to snap.

He's going to judge me after what he did? I don't think so.

"I was pissed at you for going out with that socialite and rubbing it in my face after what happened between us. I wanted to forget you even existed, and I thought that maybe messing around with someone else might help."

He pushes off the mattress and throws his fingers through his hair, blowing out a breath and pacing away from the bed. "It was because of me."

I don't respond to that. I don't know what to say.

There's something I want to know though. "What goes on in the basement?"

He whips around to face me. "The doctor said you need to rest, get more fluids in you. We're not discussing that right now."

"I'm fine. I have a headache, but other than that, I'm okay. I want to know what happens down there. Is it some kind of cult?"

He walks toward the door without acknowledging my question. "I'll get the doctor so he can do something about your headache. I want him to have another look at you now that you're awake."

Then Asher is gone, the door closed behind him, before I can even process his words.

With a sigh, I let the blanket drop and fall back into the pillows behind me.

Will I ever get a straight answer from Asher Voss about anything?

CHAPTER
TWENTY-TWO

ANABELLE

After the doctor came to see me, Asher ordered me to stay in bed. When I told him I could return to my own room, he refused, though I had no real idea why because he never returned. I slept most of the day anyway.

Someone left me trays of food while I slept, and though I was pretty sure it wasn't Asher, I hoped it was. The last thing I wanted was for anyone to know that I was in Asher Voss's bed.

I wake up Monday morning and find myself still alone. Alone and wanting answers. When I climb out of bed, I do it slowly, testing that I won't be lightheaded. But when my feet hit the floor, and I push up off the mattress, I feel like my usual self.

I'm not sure if Asher disappeared because he wanted to avoid having me pry about the basement or if it's because he just couldn't be bothered with me, but it doesn't matter either way. I need to know what I walked into on Saturday night. I want answers, and I'm not going to back down this time.

But I can't see him like this—bedraggled and two days unwashed in my pajamas. So I head back to my room, proud of myself when I find my way there without getting lost and grateful that I don't run into any of the other staff.

I take a shower, dry and style my hair, and apply a bit of makeup before sliding on one of the dresses that was left in my closet after Asher deemed my wardrobe unsuitable for work. I choose a soot-colored dress that hits just above the knee and molds to all my curves. There's a V-neck in the front, but it doesn't dip low enough to really show anything, just hints at the cleavage underneath. Then I slide on a pair of black patent leather Louboutins.

My makeup is subtle, but at the last minute, I decide to add lipstick that matches the bottom of my shoes.

As I look at myself in the mirror, I feel ready to go up against the infamous Asher Voss until I get what I want. I won't be the innocent, cowering little girl he seems to expect. I'm going to be the woman who has been cocooned inside me, transforming over these past couple of months, waiting for her chance to break free.

There's a knock on the door, and I suck in a deep breath through my nose, preparing to confront Asher. "Come in."

The door swings open and Marcel pokes his head through. "Morning, how are you feeling?"

Disappointment squirms through my chest. He asked how I'm feeling, which means he knows that something went down at the very least.

"I'm fine, thank you." I push away the discomfort as he gives me a once-over.

"I brought your breakfast to Mr. Voss's room, and you were gone. Thought I might find you here."

I am hungry, but more than that, I want to get this show-down with Asher over with. "Where is he?"

Marcel walks farther into the room and sets the tray on the dresser. "Mr. Voss insisted that you eat some breakfast."

I have to rein in my irritation somewhat and remember that Marcel isn't at fault here. He's just doing his job, and Mr. Voss is his boss.

"Thank you, I appreciate you bringing me breakfast, and I will have some. *After* I speak to Asher."

Marcel's eyebrows shoot up near his hairline. Probably at my use of Asher's first name. Oops. "I can see that you're a woman on a mission right now, and may I say that you look dressed for the part. But if I may also say, you had quite the ordeal this weekend. I think you'd be wise to have a little something to eat before you go discuss whatever it is you want to discuss with Mr. Voss."

I sigh, my shoulders sagging. "Does everyone know?"

He steps toward me and takes my hands. "Just Mrs. Potter and me. Mr. Voss assumed you wouldn't want the rest of the staff to know anything was amiss, so he had Mrs. Potter prepare your food yesterday, and I brought it to you and checked on you."

I can begrudgingly admit that that was actually pretty thoughtful of Asher.

"Good. I—" I don't know what to say after that. There's a level of embarrassment and shame for sure, even if I didn't *ask* to be drugged and almost sexually assaulted.

Marcel squeezes my hands. "You don't need to say anything. We're just glad you're okay."

I nod. "So, where is Asher then? He and I need to speak."

Marcel sighs and drops my hands, stepping back. "What about breakfast?"

"I promise I'll eat after I've finished my conversation. There are things I need answers to." I give him a pointed look, and he nods.

I'm not sure how much Marcel knows about what goes on one Saturday a month here, but regardless, I don't want my answers from Marcel. I want them from Asher.

"He's in his office."

I nod and step around him, ready to go head-to-head with the most powerful man I've ever known until I get the answers I want.

I DON'T KNOCK when I reach his office door, just swing the large door open and step inside.

I come to a stop when I see that he's not alone.

All three of his brothers are here. The four of them are seated around the lounge area on the couches and chairs, and the tension is as thick as the humidity around here in July. The room seems dimmer than normal, as though the shadows are hovering like mist in the corners.

"Leave us," Asher says, locking eyes on me. The brother with the wolf tattoo on his neck narrows his eyes at me as though he wants to say something, but Asher speaks again, though it's more of a growl this time. "Leave."

The three of them get up without saying a word and walk around me toward the door. They're an intimidating group, but I keep my chin raised until the door closes behind me.

Then I stride toward Asher. "We need to talk."

He stands from the chair he's in, slides his hand down his tie, then turns and walks toward his desk. "I see you must be feeling better."

"I told you I was fine yesterday." I follow him, trying my best not to feel like a puppy following its master.

"Yes, that must be why you slept for sixteen hours straight." He rounds the corner of his desk and takes a seat.

I come to a stop in front of his desk, hands in fists at my sides. "I'm not leaving here until I get answers."

"And what answers exactly are you looking for, Miss Boudreaux?"

God, I'm so sick of his shit. He knows exactly why I'm here.

"What goes on in the basement?" I cross my arms and stare down at him.

"Are you sure you want to know the answer to that question?" He arches an eyebrow, his dark eyes studying me. "The answer may be dangerous. Even my brothers can't decide what to do with you."

A creeping sensation travels up my spine, like spider legs crawling over my skin, but I keep my composure. "What does that mean?"

Asher leans back in his seat. His body language is relaxed and subdued, but his eyes...his eyes are like a laser target on me. "Well, one of them questions whether you can be trusted to keep your mouth shut, one wants to make an example of you, and the other wants to kill you to ensure your silence. You knowing more than you already do might fare worse for you."

I swallow, questioning whether this is wise or not, but I don't care. So much has already gone unsaid between us, and I refuse to let this be another thing that gets pushed into the shadows. "Are you threatening me?"

"I'm merely educating you on what your curiosity could cost you."

I plant my hands on his desk and lean over it, the same way he did in his bedroom yesterday morning. "I want to know what I saw. Is it a cult?"

I hold my breath while he continues to hold my gaze, unflinching.

With a sigh, he says, "So be it." He gestures to the chair behind me, and I sit, if only because I think he might actually be about to tell me the truth. "It's not a cult, though it's amusing that you think so. It's called The Ritual Room, a sex club."

The air whooshes out of me. So more lies then.

I lean forward in my seat. "I know what I saw. People in robes with masks on, a man with a knife on a dais, cutting into a woman." When his nostrils flare, I add, "That's right, my memory is slowly coming back to me. There wasn't any sex going on."

"You asked for the truth, and I gave it to you," he bites out. "What you walked in on was the blood ritual. It's performed once a year. Think of it as a tradition of sorts."

I lean back in my seat. He seems as though he's telling the truth. It's not as if telling me it's a sex club wouldn't have consequences of its own if I ever told anyone—which I never would.

"So you and a bunch of your friends get together once a month to sleep with each other?" I try not to think too hard about who and what Asher may have done there over the years.

"There's more to it than that."

I scoff. "Like what? Isn't everyone there wealthier than God? Can you not all get laid the regular way?"

A deep chuckle reverberates through his chest. "Power. Influence. Secrets. Leverage—at least for my brothers and me."

His amusement irritates me as though I'm some child. "So when you said I shouldn't have been there..."

"I meant you are not permitted to be there. You're not a member. You haven't been vetted—though I assured my brothers I had already done that part before you came to work for me."

"And that's why they're so concerned about me knowing anything."

He nods.

"This has been going on a long time." For as long as I can remember, the cars have been rolling through town on the last Saturday of the month.

"My father founded it, and when he died, I took it over."

I frown. "But you were only eighteen when your father died." His gaze doesn't move from mine. He doesn't even blink. My hand goes to my stomach when it lurches. "Oh god."

Eighteen years he's been partaking in the Vosses' little secret. It isn't judgment that makes me feel sick—it's the idea that he's been sleeping with different women on a regular basis for eighteen years. I don't know how I know that he doesn't have a steady partner, but somehow, I know.

Jealousy claws at my insides, jealousy that I have no right to feel. Asher Voss isn't mine—he's made that perfectly clear. Still, I can't help being drawn to him, wanting to experience more with him.

"How does someone become a member?" I ask.

"That's the end of this conversation. You got what you came for. You now know what goes on in the basement. It goes without saying that if you tell anyone, there will be drastic consequences."

"How does someone become a member?"

He stands from his desk. "Don't push me, Miss Boudreaux. This conversation is finished."

He steps around his desk and continues through the office. I think maybe it's to go open his office door and insist I leave, or maybe he plans to leave himself.

I stand from the chair to face his back. "I want to become a member."

He stops, and his back rises and falls with a deep breath. Asher whips around to face me, eyes full of fury. "That will not be happening."

"Why?"

He turns fully around and stalks over to me. "First, because you don't belong there."

"Because I'm not rich?"

"Because you don't know what you're asking, and if you did, I doubt you'd feel the same. Do you want to fuck a bunch of strangers, Anabelle?"

My eyes flare when he says my first name. It so rarely happens, and I love the sound of my name coming from his lips. "No, I want to fuck you."

There. It's out there. No taking it back.

I want to sate the desire tormenting me for this man whenever I'm near him, and lately even when I'm not. I want to know what it feels like to be owned by him. To drive him so crazy with my body that he loses control of himself.

"Don't say that." He leans in closer.

I put on an unaffected air and shrug. "Why? It's the truth. You can't tell me you're not attracted to me."

"You don't have to be a member of the club to fuck me, Anabelle." He trails a finger down my jawline to the edge of the V-neck on my dress to the center point above my cleavage. "Just say the word."

I smack his hand away. "Stop playing games. We both know that every time something has happened between us, you react by pushing me away. Besides, I'm curious. I want some adventure. Why do you think I left Magnolia Bend in the first place? I'm stuck here for another ten months, so I might as well make the most of it." I smile at him in challenge.

"You'll have to find adventure some other way."

"Fine. Maybe I'll see if one of your brothers will nominate me." I move to pass him, but he grips my upper arm to stop me.

"You'll do no such thing."

I wrench my arm from his grasp and face him. "I want in, Asher, and if you won't make it happen, I'll find someone else who will."

His gaze roams my face for a moment before he lets his hand drop. "Jesus Christ, you're serious. You're not going to let this go, will you?"

"No, I won't."

His jaw hardens, and he motions to the nearby couch. "Have a seat. You need to know what you're getting into."

TWENTY-THREE

ASHER

Anabelle sits on the couch with a grin.

I'm not sure how much she'll be grinning after she hears everything I have to say. She might think joining just means that she's going to get to fuck me in private in one of the rooms like the one I found her and Preston in, but she's wrong.

"The first thing you need to know, which you've already figured out on your own, is that you cannot speak to anyone about anything that goes on down there. Ever."

She nods and looks eager for me to continue. This girl's curiosity will be her downfall someday.

"You also need to know what the initiation involves. And don't even ask if you can skip it because there's no way around it. It's for everyone's protection."

She bites her lower lip. At least I know she has some sense of self-preservation.

"You must perform in front of all the members, and by perform, what I mean is this—whoever nominates you will make you act out whatever fantasy they want in front of the group. Unmasked and on video."

She shifts on the couch, gaze darting around the room for a moment.

Not so sure now, is she? Good.

"What happens to the video after?"

A slow smile spreads across my face. She's smart. "The video remains the property of my brothers and me, though in your case, I would be the only one with access to it." There's no chance I'm letting Nero get his kicks by playing back whatever might go down.

"And what will you do with it?"

Did her voice just get breathier?

"Nothing, if you never break any rules of the club. If you do, then it will be used as revenge or leverage. It's the same reason we keep the videos of all the members."

"Okay, is there anything else?"

Jesus. Why does she still sound so eager?

"Yes. Since I'm the one nominating you, it will be me getting you to do my bidding. And when I say you have to do anything, Anabelle, I mean it. I could ask you to shove a ten-inch dildo up your ass, and you'll have to do it. I might tell you to fuck every man or woman there that night, and you'd have to do it."

A slow grin creeps across her face. "But you wouldn't. So what would you do?"

Damn her for calling my bluff. "I'm a Dom, Anabelle. I like to dictate the scene, and you would be submissive to me and do whatever I tell you to. You'd relinquish all your control to me and trust that I'll take care of you."

She thinks about that for a moment and nods. "Will you hurt me?"

Her big, innocent eyes make me wish I could say no, but who knows how I'll feel once we're in a scene. "That depends. It's possible. But I wouldn't do it to be cruel or out of anger. In the end, it would be to bring both of us pleasure."

"Can I stop it if I want to?"

"You always have the option of ending a scene at any point. We'd have a safe word."

Damn it, my cock is growing in my pants from just talking about this with her. Thinking about how it would feel to control her pleasure.

"What else?" she asks.

This is the most important part. "You need to know that just because we're fucking, it doesn't mean anything to me. We will only be messing around on club nights, and it will not carry over into our daily lives. I won't fall for you. I won't fall in love with you. There is not going to be anything romantic between us."

My words are harsh, but they're for her own good. I can't be what she deserves, what she likely needs in a man. That fate was set in stone decades ago.

Hurt flashes across her face for a second before she covers it. "Sex only. Got it. But you do want me... sexually, right? I'm not trying to force you into something you don't want to do..."

The insecurity in her eyes guts me, but I can't tell her that. If she knew the truth—how she's become my obsession, how the idea of Preston laying one filthy finger on her makes me want to burn down the fucking world—it would give her too much power over me.

"You wouldn't be a pity fuck if that's what you mean."

She swallows hard again and nods.

"Consider all that. If you're okay with it, then we'll figure it out. But if you're not—and it's fine if you're not—then you can pretend you never stepped foot down there. Now, I have things to do. Take the day off, and I'll see you tomorrow. Give me your answer on Friday."

I stalk out of my office. Honestly, I'm not sure what answer I hope she'll give me—which just proves what a bastard I am.

THE NEXT MORNING OVER BREAKFAST, my brothers corner me in the dining room. I knew they would.

"What happened with Anabelle after we left yesterday?" Nero asks.

"You ready to admit she's a problem?" Kol practically growls before he shoves a forkful of eggs in his mouth.

I finish my sip of coffee and set the cup back on the table. "She wants to join the club."

They all stare at me for a beat.

Sid is the first to say anything, and he starts with a chuckle. "No shit. Who knew all that innocence was hiding a kinky side?"

I shoot him a scathing look. "She's young. And curious."

"What did you say?" Nero asks, refilling his coffee.

"I told her most of what she needs to know and told her to think about it and get back to me Friday." I pop a blueberry in my mouth.

"You're not seriously thinking of letting her join. She has nothing to lose. She can't be trusted," Kol says.

She's lost plenty already.

"If you want to fuck her, just do it, Ash. You don't have to have the club as an excuse," Sid says.

My hand fists on the table, the jaw of the bear tattoo stretching farther open. "This isn't about fucking her."

Isn't it though? If it weren't Anabelle, would I entertain letting anyone without stature and a shit-ton of money join? In truth, probably not. I'd likely just ask Kol to do whatever it takes to make them a non-issue.

"Oh, so we all get our turn with her then," Kol says with a sadistic laugh.

"None of you will lay a finger on her, do you understand me?" I look each and every one of my brothers in the eye until they nod their acceptance. "Whatever she decides, I'll deal with it. If she does join us, she knows what this is and what it isn't."

"Keep telling yourself that," Sid murmurs under his breath, but I don't bother responding.

We eat in silence for the next few minutes until Kol stands, tossing his napkin down beside his plate.

"I'll be out of town for a few days," he says.

My forehead wrinkles. I can't think of anything he has to leave town for. "Where are you going?"

"Got a lead on Rapsody I need to follow up on." He leaves the room without a backward glance.

"You'd think he'd have given up on that by now," Sid says.

I sigh. "I don't think he's going to give up until he's dragged her back here."

Lord help us when he does.

I finish my breakfast and walk to my office, ready to lose myself in work and stop fucking daydreaming about what it would be like to have Anabelle at my mercy. What I might do to her. What I might make her do to me.

When I swing open my office door, I pause. She's already there, sitting on the chair by the fireplace, waiting for me. Like yesterday, she came dressed to do battle. She's wearing another form-hugging dress that hikes up to mid-thigh since she's sitting, and her hair is down and wavy, falling in front of one shoulder. Her makeup is heavier than normal, and like yesterday, her lips are painted red. A color I wouldn't mind seeing wrapped around the base of my cock while tears destroy her makeup and saliva slides down her chin.

I have to give my head a shake to loosen the image from my mind. I step into the room, closing the door. "Good morning, Miss Boudreaux."

She doesn't bother to return my greeting. "I want in. I don't need to think about it until Friday. I know what I want."

I sigh and set my hands on my hips. "Anabelle..."

She stands from the chair and stalks toward me. "Don't treat me like I'm a child, Asher. I don't need you to protect me. I might not be thirty-six." She rolls her eyes. "But I'm not a child. I'm an adult, and I can make my own decisions."

I take her in, head to toe, and yes, there might be quite the age difference, but she is indeed all woman. And I can see clearly that she's a woman who will not be swayed. "All right."

She blinks a couple of times. "All right? I thought you'd put up more of a fight."

So did I. Which just goes to show that I can't rely on my better judgment where this woman is concerned. I have none.

"It's obvious you're not going to back down. Maybe you will after your first experience."

She juts her chin higher. "Not likely."

I chuckle because I admire her bravado. "We'll see." Then I walk toward my desk.

She follows. "What happens now?"

"What happens is that you'll undergo a health check—everyone has to between parties. Are you on birth control?"

Her cheeks pinken, and she nods.

Jesus, if she can't even handle me asking her these questions, how is she going to handle putting on a show in front of everyone?

"Good. The theme for next month is leather and lace. I'll provide you with what you should wear."

She walks closer to the desk and sits in the chair across from me. "There are themes?"

There's still a lot I haven't told her about how things work down there. "Yes."

"Will you tell me what you plan to do to me ahead of time?" She bites her lower lip, something I've realized is a tell for when she's anxious.

"No. Though we will discuss a safe word ahead of time."

She sucks in a deep breath and nods.

"You sure you want to venture down this path? That you can handle it?" I arch an eyebrow in challenge.

"Oh, I can handle it, Mr. Voss. Can you?"

That's the three-million-dollar question, isn't it? Because if this woman burrows any deeper under my skin, I'll have no choice but to send her away, for both our sakes.

CHAPTER
TWENTY-FOUR

ANABELLE

T t's the night of the club, and I sit in one of the rooms, waiting for Asher to come get me. I was wearing a robe earlier as we made our way through the house to the private entrance. I'd been unconscious the last time he brought me through it, and it felt a little like walking through a cave after we reached the bottom of the stairs— like a tunnel dug out of earth with the odd sconce on the wall to light the way.

My heart beats so fast that I hear it in my ears. My stomach refuses to stop flipping around like an acrobat. Still, I've never been more sure that I want something.

I want adventure. I want to experience some of the things I've read in my books. Since that night with Asher in the maze, I've felt a constant yearning to repeat it, to do more, and this is my opportunity. I'm just nervous about the other people watching, judging.

Pushing those thoughts from my head, I pace the room.

Asher brought what I was to wear tonight to my room earlier this evening. It's not even that revealing. I'm wearing a leather bustier that doesn't really show anything other than an insane amount of cleavage and a leather thong, along with black leather boots that go up over my knees. He instructed me to leave my hair down and put on no makeup except for my red lipstick.

I feel sexy and powerful in this outfit. Like I can do this.

Wait, no. Not like I can do this—I *am* doing this.

Immediately after Asher told me to think about it, I knew I wanted to do this. I'd regret it forever if I didn't take this experience. When would I ever get another chance? And to be with a man like Asher... I'll never get another chance at that.

I just have to make sure I don't do something stupid and fall for him.

The door creeps open behind me, and I spin around to find Asher. He comes in with no shirt on and leather pants that fit him perfectly. They aren't tight, but as he moves toward me, the leather showcases the strength in his thighs and the bulge in his pants.

On his face is a gold mask made to look like a bear, with two fangs protruding from the bottom of it. I see his deep blue eyes take me in.

"Are you ready?" His voice is low and sterner than I've heard it over the past few weeks since I made the decision to be here tonight. Maybe this is Dominant Asher.

"I am." I nod and let my hands fall to my sides from where I was fidgeting with them.

"You remember our safe word?" he asks.

We discussed it on the way through the manor earlier. When Asher asked me what I wanted it to be, his horse's name was the first thing that came to mind for some reason.

"Poe."

He nods. "Out there, you will only address me as sir. When I ask you something, every response you give me will end in sir. Understood?"

I can't tell behind his mask, but I have a feeling that if he weren't wearing it, I would see him arch one of his dark eyebrows as he does so often. "Understood."

He stares at me for a moment. The only sound in the room is the music that's pumping in here from the main room. A sexy, thrumming beat that winds its way around my body like a set of vines.

"Last chance to back out," he says.

"I'm not backing out, Asher. Let's go." I step around him and walk to the door—no easy feat in these boots.

He swings the door open and turns to look at me over his shoulder. "Follow me."

I step into the hallway behind him and follow him to the main room. As soon as everyone's gazes meet mine, the nerves set in. I'm so exposed. I might not have my nipples or my pussy on display, but the fact that everyone else wears masks and I'm the only one not wearing one makes me self-conscious.

They aren't in robes like the last time I saw them. Now they're dressed for the theme in leather and lace. Some women are already topless and have others in their vicinity playing with their breasts. They don't seem to mind—or notice for that matter. All their attention is on me.

Inhaling a deep breath, I concentrate on putting one foot in front of the other until we reach the dais at one end, on which stands a St. Andrew's Cross. I've read enough books to know what it is—a giant X with cuffs on the four ends for hands and feet. Beside it sits a table with a bunch of instruments on it—blindfolds, whips, crops, paddles, a ball gag. You name it, and it's here.

Asher helps me up onto the dais as I swallow hard.

I thought there might be some kind of speech or ceremony or something that had to happen before we begin, but as soon as I'm on the dais, Asher takes my hand and leads me to the large X. It's padded and covered in black vinyl-type fabric—for easy clean up, I guess. A blinking red dot in the corner of the room draws my eye, and I realize it's probably a camera. When I look over to the opposite corner, I see another.

Asher lifts my right arm and sets about doing up the restraint around it. My heart beats wildly, at odds with the steady, rolling cadence of the music. He puts the restraint on my left hand, then crouches behind me, dragging my left leg to the side and wrapping the restraint around it before repeating the action on my right leg.

I don't dare look behind me because I'm now fully aware that though I wear a thong, my ass is on display to the entire room. And I have to wonder if that's exactly why Asher has me facing this way, to spare me having to look at everyone.

As he stands from his crouch, he lets his hands slide up the backs of my thighs until they reach the globes of my ass, which he squeezes then spreads apart. Suddenly the cold metal of his mask is there, and I jerk in my restraints.

He continues to stand until his full height is towering behind me. "Last chance."

I look over my shoulder at him and find his eyes in the mask. "I'm not going anywhere."

His jaw tenses, and I hear him curse over the music before he steps away and over to the table. When he returns, he trails something up my leg slowly until it reaches my ass cheek, then he repeats the motion on the other side.

He does it a bunch of times, and I relax into the sensation, letting my head loll forward. Without warning, there's a stinging sensation against my right ass cheek, then my left. I moan, but no one hears it over the music. Again, he hits me on the ass. Slowly, the burning sensation turns into a pleasurable warmth, not only on my ass cheeks but between my thighs.

If I had to guess, he's using a flogger because while it's painful, it's not excruciating. He continues whipping me with the leather until my ass burns, then he moves his efforts to the backs of my thighs, which somehow feel more sensitive than my ass did.

Though my legs are spread, and I'm in restraints, the tingling between my legs intensifies, and I swivel my hips side to side, wanting what I don't know, just knowing I want *more*.

Asher leans in close and says in my ear, "You like that?"

I nod enthusiastically. "Yes, sir."

He groans low in his throat. I feel the heat from his bare chest radiating onto my back. "Do you need more?"

"Yes, sir."

One of his hands grazes over my ass cheek, and I automatically push my ass out, wanting more. I hear him chuckle low in my ear before he steps away. He continues with the flogger, and when he stops minutes later, I'm a panting, sweating mess. I've never felt this needy, this desperate for relief.

Asher first undoes my feet from the restraints, then my hands. I groan as I lower my hands, and the blood rushes back into them. Before I can even get my bearings, he whips me around to face the audience. I was so absorbed in what Asher was doing to me, I forgot they were even here.

But now I see all the masked faces pointed in our direction. Some people fondle each other, some are fondling themselves as they watch us. Rather than be creeped out, it gives me a boost of confidence.

"Are you ready to give everyone a show, pet?" Asher says it loudly enough that it can be heard over the music, and I suspect this is more for them than it is for me.

"Yes, sir."

He bands his arm across my chest and dips his hand down the front of my leather underwear. When his large finger crests over my clit, I nearly explode. My breathing grows labored the more he works me, and I squirm in his arms, unable to stay still. As I crest the mountain of my orgasm, he pulls his hand away.

He leans into my ear. "No one here is going to have the privilege of seeing you come except me."

He spins me again and uses one hand to apply pressure to my shoulder so that I end up on my knees in front of him. His hard length stretches the leather of his pants, and my tongue comes out of my mouth of its own accord, flitting across my bottom lip.

"Stay on your knees and place your palms on your thighs." I do as he says while he watches me through his mask with intense eyes. "Don't move your hands from where they are. Otherwise, you're going back on that cross, and I won't be as lenient the second time. Understand?"

I nod. "Yes, sir."

Gaze still on me, he brings his hands to his pants, undoes the button, and then slowly lowers the zipper until his cock is on display.

My first thought, stupid as it is, is that this is a real man's cock. It's thick and veined and perfect in its architecture— as if Michelangelo himself sculpted it. I glance at Asher's face and see the self-satisfied smirk on his lips.

His hands thread into the hair on either side of my head, and he pulls me forward until I'm millimeters from the end of his rigid length. "Put your tongue on it."

I inch forward and lick the base of his tip. His cock twitches. Because I like that reaction, I do it again, only this time I lean farther down and run my tongue from the base all the way up to the tip.

"Put it in your mouth. Just the tip."

I watch him as I wrap my lips around the end and suck gently.

His eyes close under his mask for a moment before they lock with mine. "Again."

I suck again. And again. The space between my thighs buzzes with arousal, and I wish more than anything that I could take care of myself while I do this.

"You like this, don't you?"

I pull my mouth off of him. "Yes, sir."

"Get ready to take all of it. Relax your throat, and don't fight me, do you understand?"

"Yes, sir."

He pulls my head forward with both hands, and I part my red lips. He slides into my mouth, and I have to stretch it to fit around his girth. There's no way I'm going to be able to fit all of him in my mouth.

But I do what he said and relax my throat so that when he pistons his hips and pushes in, he reaches the back of my throat. I gag but manage to keep my hands where he told me to keep them. He pulls out and rocks back in, holding my head in place while he fucks my mouth.

My jaw aches, but I ignore it. The satisfaction and pleasure of being the one to provide this outlet for him is too great to care about that. His eyes are hooded in pleasure behind his mask, and he looks down at me in wonder.

"Keep your eyes on mine."

I do.

Asher pumps into me over and over until he moves his hands from the side of my face. Using one hand on my chin and the other on the top of my head, he pushes himself as far into my mouth as I can take, curling his abdomen over me and holding me there.

My eyes water, and I panic because I can't breathe, but just when I think I'm going to have to move my hands and try to push away from him, he pulls out. I only have a moment to ready myself for his next assault. Again he pushes himself to the back of my throat and holds himself there, groaning. This time, he jostles my head a bit, and the tears from my eyes stream down my face.

When he pulls all the way out this time, I feel saliva drip down my chin onto my cleavage.

It's only when someone moans behind me that I remember we're in a room in front of a bunch of strangers. The same seems to be true of Asher because his head snaps up and whatever he sees there has him hauling me to my feet and throwing me up over his shoulder. He pops off the dais and strides through the room. I see the feet of people parting behind us like the wake left behind a boat.

I'm not sure where he's taking me or why, but I know enough not to ask and not to fight him. I hear the slam of a door and a lock click into place, then he bends down and sets me on my feet. I stumble back for a second, and he grips my forearm to steady me. We're in the room I was waiting in before.

"What are you doing? Did I do something wrong?"

I can't see his expression because of that golden mask on his beautiful face.

"Go open the top drawer of the table in the corner."

It's clear from the tone of his voice that we're still playing sub and dominant, so I do what he asks. I walk past the bed and open the drawer. All kinds of things are in there— vibrators, dildos, lube, condoms... a knife.

"Grab the knife."

CHAPTER
TWENTY-FIVE

ASHER

Anabelle stills in front of the drawer. Probably wondering if she should say the safe word or trust me. It only takes the space of a heartbeat for her to decide, and the moment she decides to trust me, her body relaxes, the tension melting away.

That's almost as big of a turn-on as when she had her red lips wrapped around me. I was about to blow and couldn't take it anymore, so I dragged her in here. I want to be inside her when I spill my seed, and there's no way any of the savages in that room are ever getting a look at her pussy. No, that's all for my viewing pleasure.

I'll probably hear about it from my brothers, but I didn't technically break any rules. There's enough on camera of Anabelle debasing herself to meet the initiation requirements.

She picks up the knife and walks it back over to me.

"Step closer."

She does as I say, and my dick twitches, still exposed in my splayed open pants. She's been so perfect tonight, so trusting, so obedient.

The corner of my lips tilts up slightly. "Don't move."

Before she can even respond, I dip a finger in between her cleavage and pull the fabric out and away from her body, then slice through the leather straps that weave in and out of the grommets, holding the bustier together. The knife and the garment drops to the floor in a silent thud because of the music.

She gasps, and it turns into a moan when my hands find the weight of her breasts. Her perfect fucking breasts that I've imagined when I jerked off more times than I care to admit. They're natural and the perfect size for the proportions of her body. Her nipples are a deep cherry color and puckered as though they're begging for my attention.

"I was too impatient to unravel all that," I say.

I pinch her nipples, and she arches her back at the sensation, and her mouth drops open.

"Go over to the chaise." I point to my left where the black leather piece of furniture is. One that's specifically designed for sex.

It's always reminded me of rolling waves, with the top curve on the one end coming up to a woman's stomach and the one at the far end about half as high as that with a dip in the middle.

She does as I say and walks over there, awaiting further instructions.

See? Perfect.

I slowly walk over, and I drop to my haunches, pulling the leather thong down her legs. The scent of her arousal hits me, and I briefly close my eyes behind the mask, taking it in. It reminds me of that night in the garden when I devoured her—something I plan to do again, but not tonight. Tonight, I need to feel her tight heat surrounding my cock while I own her pussy.

I discard the thong on the floor and stand. "We'll leave the boots on."

When I smirk, her chest heaves, an unconscious request for me to touch her. But rather than fondle her tits, I place a thumb and forefinger on her chin and force her to look at me.

"You look so pretty, red lipstick smeared all over your face from taking my cock. Tear tracks down your face."

Her dark eyes glitter in the dim light of the room. I can see the pride swell in her chest.

"You've made me very happy. As a reward, I'm going to let you come now with my cock inside you. Would you like that?"

She nods. "Yes, sir."

"Turn around and bend over the high end of the chaise."

She does as I say, and I leave her in that position to wonder when I might sink into her. For now, I'm content to look at her while I shed my pants and shoes. Once I'm naked and behind her, I gently run my hand over her ass cheek. There's still a red tinge to her skin from being hit with the flogger. I fist my dick in my hand, jerking while I enjoy the aftermath of my work.

Next time we'll try the paddle or a cane if I think she can handle it. I can't wait to get a spreader bar on her.

God, there's so much I want to do to this woman it's going to be hard to refrain from fucking around with her between club weekends. But it's necessary to put some parameters in place, otherwise I'd be inside her all day every day.

I run my finger through her already soaked folds, humming deep in my chest when I bring it to my mouth. My cock is so fucking hard right now that I can't deny myself any longer. I position myself at her entrance, then push slowly inside her, watching as her pussy surrounds my thick cock, pulling me in.

After a few strokes, I'm fully seated inside her. I spread her ass cheeks and watch as I pull out. There's not much she can do to move in this position because her upper body is pointing down, following the curve of the furniture. But I watch, as I drive into her again and again, as her hands search for anything to hang on to.

My cock is coated in her pleasure, glistening, and it drives me on. I smack her ass hard with my hand, watching as the handprint blooms to life on her pale skin. She moans into the leather beneath her, and I do it again on the other side.

Gripping her hips in my hands, I drive in and out of her, my cock harder than ever. When the tingling in the bottom of my spine starts, I pull all the way out, needing to see her pleasure before my own.

"Turn over."

I help her ease herself up, and I turn her hips in my hands, lifting her until she's seated on the end, then I gently push her until she's head down, her back on the curve of the chair. She's like a feast splayed out for my pleasure.

Using my hands on her knees, I splay her legs wide and sink into her. Anabelle moans, arching her back and cupping her breast with her hand. I hold her legs out as I take her again, enjoying being face to face.

She's in rapture, and I hook her legs around my waist and bring my thumb to her swollen clit. She cries out. I feel the first flutters of her orgasm around my cock, and I double down on my efforts, circling her clit with the pad of my thumb as I keep easing in and out of her.

Her back arches as much as allowed in this position, and her body tries to milk my cock. Through sheer force of will, I prevent that from happening. Because I'm not satisfied with just one orgasm. I want another.

I ease up on her clit as she comes down from her orgasm, but before she's finally down, I return my thumb to her pleasure point and snake my hand up her torso until I'm squeezing her tit. "Think you can take another one?"

Her head rocks side to side on the leather. "No, sir. No, sir, I can't."

"Have a little faith in yourself, pet." Then I send her flying again, twisting hard on her nipple.

She cries out, sounding near sobbing this time, and it's such a beautiful sight to see. So beautiful that I can't hold off anymore.

I push into her one final time and hold myself there as I spill inside her, not daring to pull out until every last drop of my seed is spent. Reluctantly, I pull out of her. Watching myself leak out of her, I stand and catch my breath. The vision will be seared in my brain for eternity. I have to fight the urge to reach out and shove my cum back inside her.

I walk over to the robe Anabelle was wearing earlier, then help her up. She's spent. I can tell by the way she's not saying anything.

Once I've wrapped her in the robe and pulled my pants back on, I pick her up. She doesn't protest, just leans her head against my chest and closes her eyes. It opens up some tender part of me I didn't know even existed until now, and suddenly all I want to do is take care of this woman.

ANABELLE FALLS asleep on the trek from the basement through the manor to my room. She doesn't even wake when I lay her on my bed to go ready a bath for her. I debate just bringing her to her room and letting her sleep, but I can't do it.

I went hard on her ass, and I need to make sure she's okay. The whole experience was unlike any I've had before. Not because I've never had great sex, but because I feel territorial over her.

Usually when I fuck women, in the basement or otherwise, I have no tether to them. I couldn't care less if I'm sharing her with someone or if she went and fucked someone else right after me. I don't care if everyone in the place is watching.

But with Anabelle, it was different. I hated that I had to do any of that with an audience. I want to keep her all to myself. The idea of someone else getting to see her come or see her naked makes me want to lose control.

Like that piece of shit Preston Wallace. We need to talk about that night again. As much as I don't want to upset Anabelle, I need to clear up a few things, to be sure.

Once the bath is drawn, I return to the bedroom and find Anabelle right where I left her, curled up on her side now. My mask is sitting on my dresser where it will stay until I return it to my safe, and I've ditched the leather pants for a pair of lounge pants.

I give her shoulder a shake. "Anabelle, wake up. It's time for a bath."

Her eyes flutter open, then her deep brown eyes, flecked with gold, look at me.

"C'mon. Let's get you in the bath."

She's groggy still, but she lets me sit her up so her legs hang off the edge of the bed. I get down on my haunches and slide the zipper at the back of one of her boots down then slide it off, then repeat the motion with the other.

Anabelle stands, and I loosen the tie around her waist until the robe falls open. I slide it off her shoulders, so it flutters to the floor. Her hand comes up to cover her breasts, and I pull it away.

"Why are you hiding from me?" I search her face for answers.

She shrugs, cheeks growing red. "I don't know."

I tilt her chin up with my thumb and forefinger. "I've seen it all." Despite myself, a smile forms on my face.

"It feels different here..." She looks around my room. "In this environment."

"You're beautiful in any environment. Now come on." I take her hand and lead her to the ensuite, not waiting to see what her reaction might be to the words that slipped out of my mouth and shouldn't have.

"You drew me a bath." She stops in front of it, looking down as if she's never seen a bath before.

"I told you that when I woke you. Did you not hear me?"

She shakes her head.

"It's my responsibility to take care of you once we've finished a scene." I don't bother mentioning that for the first time ever, I think it might actually give me pleasure to do it.

A slight frown mars her face. "Oh."

"Here." I hold out my hand to help her.

She takes it then steps in the bath, sinking down into the warm water. She closes her eyes and leans back. "This feels so good."

"There are some oils in there that should help. How are your ass and your thighs?"

She wiggles in place then looks at me. "Sore but not too bad."

"Good. When you get out, I'll spread some special cream I have over it."

Her gaze flicks down to the water where she's swirling her fingers under the surface. "You don't have to do that."

I tip her chin up—again. "I want to, and I will."

She holds my gaze for a beat, studying my now bare face, then nods.

I sit on the edge of the tub, studying her for any sense of what she's feeling after her first experience in the basement. She's quieter than normal. I don't know whether it's because she's tired, or she regrets what happened.

"You need to talk to me, Anabelle. A Dom/Sub relationship is all about communication."

"Is that what I am? Your sub?" I can't tell from her expression whether she's hoping I'll say yes or no.

I've had a few steady subs through the years, but no one who ever lasted long. There's never been anyone I wanted to form a long-term relationship with. But I can see myself saying yes to Anabelle. To practicing that kind of relationship with her outside of the confines of the sex club. Which is why I have to say no.

"When we're in the basement, yes. Otherwise, you work for me, just like I said when we negotiated this whole thing."

Disappointment is clear on her face, but she masks it quickly. "Right, I know that."

241

"You still haven't answered how you're feeling about what happened down there."

She sucks in a lungful of air, and it makes her breasts rise in the water just shy of her nipples. "I liked it."

I roll my eyes. "What did you like about it? Be more specific."

She thinks about it for a moment, running her hand back and forth in the water and studying the ripples that follow. Then she meets my gaze. "I liked that you were in control. That I felt safe even though I didn't know what to expect and hadn't done anything like that before. I... liked that I was the one to turn you on. When you talked to me and said... dirty things... I liked that."

I swallow as my dick twitches in my pants. It's all I can do not to haul her out of there and fuck her again in front of the mirror so that I can have a front-row view. "Does that mean you want to do it again next month?"

She nods immediately, and a chuckle escapes despite myself. Anabelle gives me a funny look.

"What?" I ask, frowning.

"I've just never seen you laugh like that before."

Uncomfortable with her insight and the truth of it, I stand, then reach down to drain the water. When I straighten, I offer her my hand. "Here."

With my help, she steps out onto the bath mat. I grab a towel from the hook and begin to dry her.

"I can do that," she says.

"I want to." Again, the truth escapes. It's as if this woman is my own version of a truth serum. It's unnerving to say the least.

Once she's dry, I don't bother wrapping the towel around her. Instead, I lead her into my room and over to my bed. I sit on the edge near the bedside table and grab the lotion I have ready for her.

"Come lay over my lap face down."

She blinks and hesitates for a moment, then does what I say. The heat of her body seeps into my legs, and my cock stirs again, which I'm sure she can feel in this position. Trying to ignore it, I take a good amount of the cream and spread it around her ass cheeks and the backs of her thighs.

It doesn't take long, but when I'm done, I don't want to remove my hand. As I draw my hand up from behind her knee to the juncture of her thighs, I think about how easy it would be to slide my fingers inside her. I repeat the motion over and over, and my cock grows harder underneath her. Anabelle's breath hitches, and a small moan escapes her.

My fingers hover between her thighs each time I bring my hand up, debating. But I can't do it. I can't. If I do, then next thing I know, I'll have her under my desk giving me head in the middle of the work day, and I'll want to take her in the pool in the oppressive summer humidity.

No. I have these boundaries for a reason, and I have to remember that.

I give her ass a light smack. "You're done. Grab your robe, and you can go back to your room."

I don't have to see her face to feel the disappointment wafting off of her.

She climbs off my lap, somewhat awkwardly, and looks around for her robe, quickly rushing over to put it on when she spots it.

"I'll see you bright and early Monday morning." It's an asshole-ish thing to say as far as parting words go after what happened tonight, but I need to make sure the lines between us are clear.

"Okay." Her shoulders sag, and she walks toward the door. With her hand on the handle, she turns and looks at me over her shoulder. "Did you like it? You never said."

Lie.

Lie.

Lie.

"I'll be counting the days until the next time."

A small smile blossoms on her lips before she leaves the room. Leaving me with nothing but regrets that I'm not the kind of man who could ever be with someone as sweet and innocent as Anabelle Boudreaux.

CHAPTER
TWENTY-SIX

ANABELLE

For the first week after our night together in the sex club, Asher barely speaks to me in the office. But now that we're in the middle of the week following, he seems to have unraveled some of the tension that wound him so tightly.

I wasn't lying when I told him I liked it. Hell, my only regret is that I have to wait two and a half more weeks before we can do it again.

Every time I look at him, I wish he'd order me around and tell me to do something. Make me his submissive. But he's been nothing but professional. Not cold per se, but not exactly warm either.

When he enters his office this morning, rather than heading over to his desk as he always does, he walks over to mine and stands on my right, leaning against the desk with his arms crossed. His eyes, the color of the deep blue ocean, take me in with what I think might be concern.

"Is everything okay?" I ask.

He sighs. "There's something I've been meaning to talk to you about, but I've refrained because I didn't want to upset you. It's about the night you met Preston."

Not exactly something I want to relive, but we haven't really spoken of it in much detail. In all honesty, there's been so much going on in my life that I've managed to push that night away into the recesses of my mind. I know at some point I'll have to deal with what almost happened, but I don't feel equipped at the moment. There's too much other stuff going on.

"What about it?" I move my hands away from the keyboard and lean back in my chair, my hands on the armrests.

"I always assumed, but didn't actually ask you, and now I need to be sure. Did you consent to Preston drugging you?"

I whip up from my chair, hands fisted at my sides. "Of course not!"

Asher frowns and nods.

"You believe me, right?" Tears prick my eyes, but I refuse to let them fall.

He clasps my shoulders. "Of course I do. I just needed to be sure. I know others who are into somnophilia. I assure you, you'll get no judgment from me if you are, but I needed to know if you had consented to that before Preston drugged you."

"Somno what?" My forehead wrinkles.

"There's no reason to be embarrassed if you are."

"Asher, I don't know what you're talking about."

He pushes his hand through his hair, dislodging some of his perfectly swept back waves. "It's when someone enjoys having sex with someone who is sleeping or unconscious. For some people, it's important that their partner wants to participate. Others... aren't as concerned about that."

The look of horror I give him is probably answer enough. "Well, that's not me."

"I didn't think so." His voice sounds grave.

"Why? Why are you asking me this?"

"Because I'm going to ruin him. And there will be repercussions for my family and my business."

That sounds... ominous. "Asher, you don't have to do anything. You already beat the shit out of him."

His hands drop from my shoulders, and he pushes up off the desk. "He's lucky I didn't bury him out back in the garden."

The viciousness in his voice says he's serious.

"Why would you put your company and your family at risk? I mean, we're not..." I'm not sure how to put it. We're not what? Boyfriend and girlfriend, lovers, friends? All of that is true, but at the same time, it doesn't feel wholly true either.

He ignores my question. "I spoke to Marcel this morning, and the repairs on your room in the staff building are complete."

"Oh, okay. I'll be sure to move my things out when I'm done working today."

I hate the twinge of pain in my chest at having to move farther away from him, which is stupid. It's not as if I spend any time with him in his bedroom, or him in mine. And sure, Midnight Manor is kind of creepy at the best of times, but especially at night. Still, I know I'll miss sleeping in the west wing.

"You're not going anywhere. I've already told Marcel that you are to stay right where you are."

"Why would you do that?" My voice is almost a whisper.

He levels me with his stare. "I think you know why, Anabelle." Then he leans in and brushes a soft kiss over my eyebrow before retreating to his desk.

It takes me a moment to move again, sinking back into my chair. I told myself I wouldn't develop feelings for Asher Voss, that this is just about sex and the pleasure he can give me during my time here. But something makes me think that maybe that promise is futile. Because the more layers of Asher I discover, the more I want to keep unraveling.

AT THE END of the workday, I head back to the staff housing to scrounge up something for dinner. After dinner, I plan to venture back into the maze until I find the center, where I'll finish the book I'm reading. It's getting really good. The hero has just broken the heroine's heart, but I know he'll put it back together. That's always my favorite part of any romance novel. The maze is a private space, and it reminds me of Asher and the night we first crossed the line. If I go in early enough, I have every expectation that I'll be able to find my way out before it's dark.

The humidity outside makes sweat slick my skin as I make my way along the path. It's always like that this time of year, even when it's overcast like today.

I turn when I hear my name called and see Marcel rushing toward me. I've been nervous about seeing the other staff members today now that Asher has told Marcel I'll be staying in the manor. It was one thing to be staying there when there was nowhere else to go, but it's another now that my old room has been repaired.

What will they think of me? Will they know I've had sex with Asher? Do they know about the sex club, and if so, will they somehow know I've been there with him?

I wait for Marcel to catch up and smile at him, hoping it looks natural.

"Where are you headed off to?" he asks.

"I was going to go make myself some dinner, same as I do every night. Why? Do you need my help with something?"

He laughs. "Not at all. I just wanted to make sure you weren't headed back to the staff quarters to take over your old room."

I shift in place. "About that—"

"I think it's marvelous." He throws his hands in the air as though it's a celebration.

"You do?"

"Of course." He loops his arm through mine, and we continue walking the path. "Mr. Voss obviously cares about you, otherwise he wouldn't have insisted. We all think that's a great thing."

I don't even know where to start with that statement. "We?"

"The rest of the staff. Well, not everyone knows of course, but eventually they all will."

I groan.

"What's that about?" He stops us, and I turn to look at him.

"I'm just thinking about what everyone else must think."

"They think the same as I do—that Mr. Voss finally has someone in his life he's opening up to, maybe even opening his heart to."

God, his words give me hope, but no. That will only lead to heartbreak.

I shake my head and walk again. "It's not like that."

He follows me. "Trust me, it is."

I whip around to face him. His words are only going to make it harder to keep my head in check, and I'll be the one who ends up hurt. "It's not. Asher doesn't care for me. Not like you're thinking."

Marcel shakes his head and gives me a sad sort of smile. "Did you know that Mr. Voss has never had a woman in the west wing? Ever. Because of how he was raised…"

I wait with bated breath for him to continue.

"Let's just say he has many walls he's fortified over the years, and it seems that you're the one who's figured out how to scale them. We're all hoping they'll eventually come crumbling down."

"How was he raised?" That's all I can focus on in his ridiculous statement.

Marcel frowns. "I shouldn't have said anything. It's not for me to say." He walks on, and now it's me chasing him down the path.

"You can't do that! You can't say something like that and not tell me the rest of it."

He glances at me. "If you keep down the path you're on, I'm sure you'll learn for yourself. I've already said too much. Now, let's go get something to eat, though you know you can eat in the manor now that you're staying there, right?"

Truth is, I wasn't sure. But I'm glad to hear him say it. It will be much easier to grab my breakfast and lunch at the main house.

"All right. Do you mind if I come for dinner down here most nights though? I wouldn't mind the company."

Living in the manor, closer to Asher is nice, but because he doesn't spend any time with me in the evenings, it's more isolating than when I stayed in the staff building.

"Of course not. You're always welcome."

At least I still sort of belong somewhere. At the moment, I'm straddling two worlds, and I don't feel as if I quite belong to either. There was the Anabelle who showed up here the first day, demanding to see Asher Voss, and the one who stands here now. I have a feeling by the time I leave, that Anabelle won't resemble either of her early incarnations.

CHAPTER
TWENTY-SEVEN

ASHER

Kol finally joins us in the dining room for breakfast and takes his seat.

Good. Now I can get this over with.

"There's something we need to discuss now that we're all here, but first I want to hear about what happened with you, Kol. Any news on Rapsody?"

The glare he shoots me across the table is probably answer enough. "No. It wasn't her. False lead. But I'm getting closer. I can feel it."

I have no idea whether he is or isn't—he has been at this for years to no avail. My other brothers and I have tried to talk him out of continuing to pursue this when he keeps coming to a dead end.

"Let us know if anything changes," I say.

"You have bad news. Just spill it," Sid says. He's always been the best at seeing past my façade. Probably because he's so well-versed at erecting his own.

"It's not bad news, per se. But something you need to be aware of."

"It involves that girl, doesn't it?" Kol practically spits out.

"Her name is Anabelle." My voice carries an edge that none of my brothers miss.

"I think it's good that Asher is spending time with her," Nero says. Of course, he's the only one around this table who would think so.

My brothers and I worked hard to protect him from the worst of what our father was capable of, and although Nero doesn't necessarily have a romantic view of the world, he's certainly not as jaded as the rest of us.

"I'm not spending time with her, I've fucked her. There's a difference." I pick up my coffee to take a sip.

"Is there?" Nero arches an eyebrow.

I sigh. "We're getting off-topic. I wanted you three to know that I'm going after Preston Wallace. I'm going to take him down."

"Jesus Christ." Sid shakes his head and looks at his breakfast plate.

"I fucking knew it. You're pussy-whipped by this woman," Kol spits out.

"He crossed the line, and we all know it." I jab my pointer finger into the table. "He brought a non-member into the club, and not only that, he drugged her and was going to rape her on our property." I shift my gaze to Sid, who has his mouth open in rebuttal, but I raise my hand. "And no. I talked to Anabelle to make sure. She didn't give her consent. So that's rape."

Sid simply nods. It's a touchy subject for him.

"What do you have planned?" Nero asks.

"I'm going to buy up all the shares of Wallace International under a bunch of shell companies. Once I have control, I'm going to oust him and his old man from the board. It will send a message."

"You sure that's the message you want to send?" Sid asks.

I nod. "I think that's the perfect message. Don't fuck with us."

Kol sighs. "They've been an ally of our family for years. We both know where each other's skeletons are buried. It won't be good for business."

"We were allies until that little prick Preston was born. He could never lead in his father's stead. Jessie Wallace should be thanking me." I reach for the honey and my knife to spread some on my toast.

"You sure this is a good idea?" Kol asks.

"I'm not asking permission. This is my prerogative, and I can do with my money what I want. I'm giving you the courtesy of informing you." I take a bite of my toast.

"It indirectly affects us," Sid says.

"You're willing to throw away tens, hell, hundreds of millions of dollars for this girl?" Kol asks.

I look him straight in the eye, shocked by my answer before I speak it. "Yes."

He shakes his head as though he's disappointed but says nothing more.

It's silent at the table for a blessed few minutes until Nero breaks it. "Well, since we're all sharing, I have an announcement too."

We all swing our heads toward Nero.

"I'm going to ask Maude to marry me."

"You can't be serious!" Kol shouts.

"Jesus, kid, why would you go and do that?" Sid asks.

"Nero, you just met the woman. What the hell are you talking about?" I slam my fist on the table, rattling all the dishes.

He shrugs. "I like her. A lot."

"So fuck her brains out until you get sick of her. Don't marry her," Sid says.

Nero frowns. "I'm not like you guys. I want to share my life with someone."

"Share *them* is more like it," Kol says under his breath, and Nero rolls his eyes.

"I'm serious. I think she could be the one."

It's not like I never thought Nero would get married. Of all my brothers, he'd be the most likely. But he's only been with this woman for a couple of months, not years. Who knows what her agenda is? We haven't even met her.

"Bring her to the charity masquerade ball so the three of us can meet her. *Do not* propose to her before then, understood?" I push away from the table and stand, no longer having an appetite.

"But that's not for another six weeks," Nero grumbles.

"I'm aware." I turn my attention to Kol. "In the meantime, you know what to do."

He nods, not saying a word. Kol will have a more thorough background check on my desk by this afternoon.

I stride from the dining room to head to my office, excited for two things today. The first is the beginning of my pursuit to ruin Preston Wallace's life. And the second is the surprise I have in store for Anabelle at lunch.

I spent my morning directing my investment manager on what to do and telling him to make it happen as quickly and under the radar as possible. I can't wait until I have Preston's balls in a vise so I can start squeezing.

It's a few minutes from the time Anabelle usually breaks for lunch when I stand from my desk and walk over to hers.

I told Marcel to keep me apprised of anything I need to know regarding Anabelle. He mentioned that he thought she might be feeling lonely because she's continuing to have her dinners down in the staff building, rather than in the main house.

The easy thing for me to do is to spend some time with her, but that would give her the wrong impression. Not only that, but it would make it even more difficult than it already is to resist temptation where she's concerned.

I'm already counting down the days until our next Saturday night together, planning what I want to do.

Even this little surprise I have planned for her has the potential of making her think there could be more between us, but I don't like the idea of her feeling all alone in this place. I know exactly how that feels from my childhood and the idea of Anabelle feeling the same... I can't take it.

"Ready to break for lunch?" I ask when I reach her desk.

She looks at me from where she's seated. As it always does when I see her from this angle, my brain makes the connection to when she kneeled in front of me with my cock in her mouth. But there will be none of that today.

"I guess it's time, isn't it? Do you need something before I go eat?" She tilts her head and looks at me a little quizzically.

Probably because I just usually mutter at her from my desk when she leaves for lunch.

"I don't need anything, but I do need you to come with me. I have a surprise for you."

Her forehead creases. "A surprise?"

"Yes, I'm sure you're familiar with the term. Now come on." I motion with my head toward the door and stride over, waiting at the threshold until she joins me.

"Where are we going?" she asks, wide-eyed.

"You'll have to come with me to see."

I lead her out of the office and through the common areas of Midnight Manor until we reach the hallway with the arches and stained glass that leads to the west wing. Although I want to lead her to my bedroom and spend the afternoon making her come, I don't. I need to stop thinking with my dick where Anabelle is concerned.

We continue past the stained-glass bear, and she doesn't say a word or inquire any further about where we might be headed. Maybe she's wishing we're going to my bedroom as much as I am.

When we reach the library doors, I pause, my hands gripping the handles. I don't know why I'm second-guessing myself. I've given this a lot of thought. But then again, that seems to be the effect Anabelle has on me—she makes me second-guess everything I thought I knew I wanted.

Pushing open the doors, I step inside the space that was once my mother's salvation. The place she'd go to escape the realities of her life and immerse herself in a different world.

"What are we doing here?" Anabelle asks from behind me.

I turn to face her. She appears hesitant, probably remembering the last time she was in here, and I chased her out.

"I want you to have this. It's yours to do what you want with—read what you want, arrange the books however you want, hang out in here as much as you want."

Her plump lips slowly part as her mouth drops open, and she glances around, wide-eyed. "What do you mean? I thought you didn't want me in here."

I step forward, fingers itching to cup her face, but I force myself to retract my hand. "This room is where my mother spent a lot of her time. She loved reading—she was like you in that way. I've already alluded to you that my parents' marriage wasn't a happy one, and this is where she found her solace. I want you to do the same. Use it as you see fit."

I know that I should tell her she can move back into her family estate, or that she can come and go as she pleases, give her phone back—but I can't bring myself to give her any of that.

If Anabelle knew how often I think of her, how I feel this pressing need to keep her hidden away from the world, safe, she'd probably run screaming from here.

But I can give her this. Something she'll appreciate and come to love.

She steps farther into the room, staring around, taking it all in. "Are you sure? I mean, I don't want to intrude."

I step up behind her, cupping her shoulders. I can't resist touching her. "You're not intruding. I want you to have this. Enjoy it."

She turns in my arms and wraps her arms around my neck, and I bend to let her because I'm weak where she's concerned. So weak for this woman.

"Thank you, Asher."

Allowing myself to wrap my arms around her, I get this strange sensation in my chest as our bodies press together. There's arousal there, yes. There's always an undercurrent of desire present whenever I'm with her. But this is something different, something foreign that I can't decipher.

Before I can no longer resist temptation, I straighten and unwind her hands from around my neck, then step back. "I'll have lunch brought to you in here so you can explore."

"That would be wonderful, thank you." The gold flecks in her big brown eyes sparkle with happiness, and I want to puff out my chest for being the cause for that look.

I merely nod and leave the room, disturbed by how her happiness fuels my own.

CHAPTER
TWENTY-EIGHT

ANABELLE

I've spent the past two nights in the library, exploring all it offers. There are more books than I can read in a lifetime, but it's such a thrill to go through them all and plan which I want to read first.

I even found an old gardening book about roses. There are notes in the margins in a feminine cursive I assume must be Asher's mother's. As soon as I saw them, a plan formed in my mind—I'm going to try to nurse the rose bush in the maze back to health as a thank you to Asher.

I'm still not exactly sure why he's given me free rein in the library, but I'm eternally grateful. It's almost overwhelming how many books are in there.

I have to force myself to put down the book I'm reading, turn out the bedside lamp, and go to sleep. I toss and turn for half an hour before I eventually drift off.

Hours later, I'm not sure what has awoken me until my brain fires up enough to recognize the sound of operatic music. It's the same song that originally drew me to the library the day Asher found me there.

I listen for a moment, fright turning my muscles to stone and making me unable to move. It's not coming from my room, but somewhere outside the door. Rolling over, I switch on the bedside lamp. It casts a golden glow over the room, not nearly full enough to prevent shadows from lurking in the corners.

"Hello?" I say into the darkness.

I'm relieved when there's no answer, though I don't know if it's good or bad.

The music continues, starting over from the beginning.

Could Asher be listening to music at... I glance at the bedside clock... three o'clock in the morning? Seems unlikely, but not impossible. His room is on the same level as mine.

Pushing off the blankets, I sit on the edge of the bed and set my feet on the lush area rug.

Midnight Manor is unnerving in the daytime, but even more so at night. I don't often wander through the house after dark, and the idea doesn't exactly appeal right now, but neither does lying here wondering where the music is coming from.

I walk across the room and crack open the door. The music is louder now, and the hallway is only dimly lit by flickering sconces. I creep down the hall, feeling the shadows at my back as though they're chasing me and urging me forward.

The long, wide hallway ahead of me feels never-ending as the darkness wraps around me.

Goose bumps prickle my skin, and that distinct sensation of being watched washes over me once more. I walk faster, panic rising and causing my shoulders to climb up toward my ears.

Just go back to your room. What are you doing?

I'm farther from my room now than I am from Asher's room, which is where the music seems to be coming from. The chorus of voices crescendos, and there's something deeply disturbing about the sound of them—male and female merging as one. They sound as though they're issuing a warning, but it's in a language I don't understand.

By the time I reach the doors of Asher's suite, the music is so loud that it surrounds me, fills me up, and becomes a part of me. There's something unearthly about it.

I stare at the doors for a heartbeat. Will Asher be upset if I disturb him?

A flicker of movement in the shadows causes me to take action. I don't want to stand in this hallway by myself any longer.

The moment I set my hand on the doorknob, the music stops. The silence is so abrupt that it takes me a moment to find my bearings and make sense of the new sound coming from inside Asher's room. A sound that reminds me of the time my father took me hunting, and he didn't get a clean shot on a bear. It howled in anguish until he was able to put it out of its misery.

I push open the doors to find the room dark. Fumbling for a light, I finally find a switch that turns on a lamp in the far corner. It's not much, but it's enough for me to see Asher thrashing in his sheets, shouting.

"No! No! Stop!" He must have been screaming for some time, because his voice is hoarse.

With no regard for my safety and whether it's a good idea to wake him in the middle of what I assume is a nightmare or night terror, I rush over to the bed. "Asher! Asher!"

He doesn't hear me. The sheets are twisted in his hands, and his face is crumpled in pain. "No, stop. Please, stop. I promise I won't do it again!"

Tears prick my eyes. "Asher." I touch his shoulder. When he still doesn't wake up, I shake him. "Asher, wake up. You're having a bad dream." I shake him harder, letting my fingernails dig into his skin. "Asher!"

His eyes snap open, and he startles me when he bolts into a sitting position, and his hand wraps around my neck.

Oh, god. This is why they tell you not to wake someone.

My hands grab his wrists. "Asher, it's Anabelle," I manage to say before he squeezes too hard.

He blinks a few times, his eyes clearing from the grips of his nightmare. "Anabelle?"

His brow furrows. Then he notices that he has me by the throat, and his face crumples as he drops his hand to the bed, fisting the sheets. Seeing him so forlorn and desolate makes something snap in my chest. There's no trace of the powerful, hard-as-steel man I'm used to.

"Are you okay?" I cup his face. I don't care if he doesn't want me to show him any affection or comfort.

But he doesn't push me away. Instead, he hauls me onto the bed with him, wrapping his arms around me and squeezing. He dips his head into my neck, sucking in air.

"It's okay, you're okay." My hands run up and down his bare back, his skin hot and moist with sweat. "It was just a dream."

"No, it wasn't," he whispers into my throat.

I stiffen then relax into his hold. Obviously whatever he was dreaming wasn't his imagination, but the replay of something terrible that has happened to him.

We stay like that for a few minutes until Asher's breathing returns to normal. When he pulls away, and I meet his gaze, the air rushes from his lungs. I see the extent of his pain. I don't know what happened to him, but it must have been bad to still haunt him to this day.

"Are you all right?" I ask, taking his hand.

He nods then clears his throat. "Yeah. Thanks for waking me."

I nod. "Of course. Sorry I barged in here."

He doesn't ask why I was even down at his end of the wing, and I don't offer the information about the song. I'm not sure he'd believe me anyway.

"It's fine." He pulls his hand away from me and pushes it through his hair.

"Okay well, I'm going to head back to my room and try to get back to sleep."

I move to push off the bed, but he grips my wrist, keeping me in place.

"Will you stay?" His voice is a near whisper.

Part of me thinks that he hates himself for asking, but a warm sensation blooms in my chest, like a rose just loosening its petals. "Of course. Yes." I nod.

His shoulders relax in relief.

"Just let me turn the light off." I motion to the small lamp in the corner.

"I'll do it." He shifts his legs to the side and gets out of bed wearing only a pair of relaxed gray lounge pants.

I climb in and go to the far side of the mattress, sitting up and watching as he walks across the expansive room. I try not to focus on the way the muscles in his back bunch and flex with every stride. Now is not the time to be getting turned on.

When he clicks the light off, I ease down in the bed, pull the sheet up over myself, and turn on my side so that I'm facing away from him. I know he wants the comfort of someone sharing his bed after whatever trauma he just relived, but I want him to know I'm not going to read anything into his request or try to take advantage of his situation.

The mattress dips behind me. Though I'm not facing him, and it's nearly pitch black in this room, I somehow *feel* him. As though my body is acutely aware of his presence and every atom in my body is straining toward his. I close my eyes and try to relax enough to fall asleep again, but it feels impossible knowing he's so near and yet not near enough.

It's not until a few minutes later when the bed shifts, and Asher's hand slides around my waist, hauling me back into his chest, that I'm finally able to drift off.

CHAPTER
TWENTY-NINE

ANABELLE

I wake up, daylight filtering in through my closed eyelids, and I blink awake. It takes me a moment to remember where I am and exactly whose chest I'm sprawled across.

Asher's.

I recall the music, the nightmare, and the way he held me as though he was afraid I would disappear as I drifted off to sleep.

When I move to roll off him, his hand—I just realize now—is on my ass, preventing me from doing so.

"I'm sorry, I must have draped myself all over you when I was sleeping."

A deep chuckle rumbles in his chest against my ear. "You say that as if I would complain."

"Won't you?" I tilt my face to look at him. He drops his hand off my butt and gives me room to move, so I roll over onto my back.

"No complaints." He rolls to his side and looks at me with his head propped on his hand.

Asher Voss in the morning is a sight to behold. His hair is disheveled and the wavy strands hang down on the sides and over his forehead. There's no trace of the tortured man who lay in this bed last night.

"How are you this morning?" Does he even remember having the nightmare?

The sparkle in his blue eyes dims. "Fine. Thanks again for waking me up."

I nod. "Of course. I wasn't sure if I should or not."

"You did the right thing. What were you doing down at this end of the wing? Was I so loud that I woke you up in your room?" His eyes fill with concern.

"No, I didn't hear you until I was outside your door. I..." Do I tell him about the music? This is the second time it's happened, and I have no explanation for either time.

"You what?" He frowns and brushes a stray section of my hair away from my face.

"I heard this music. It was the same music that drew me to the library the first time you found me there..."

"What kind of music?" All right. At least he doesn't seem to think I'm crazy.

"Opera maybe? It's hard to say really. I thought maybe you were listening to it."

He shakes his head against his hand. "Nope. I don't know what that was."

Asher doesn't seem particularly concerned about it. I wonder whether he's seen his fair share of strange things around Midnight Manor over the years.

"You're really okay?"

He looks okay right now, but when I think back to last night... god, he seemed so gutted. How can he so quickly brush it off?

"I'm usually a little out of sorts the day after, but I'm used to it by now."

I hesitate for a moment before I ask my next question. It's fine if he doesn't want to share, but I also want him to know that he can open up if he feels the need to.

"What was your dream about? It's fine if you don't want to talk about it," I quickly add.

The pain returns to his eyes and regret slashes me. But to my surprise, he speaks. "When I was growing up, my father used to beat me for anything he thought was a transgression—big or small. Sometimes my mother would try to stop him, and he'd hurt her. I've been thinking about my mother a lot lately, so I guess I shouldn't be surprised that I dreamed one of those times she tried to step in to protect me." He frowns.

"Asher, I'm so sorry." I trail my fingers down his face.

He turns his head and kisses the inside of my hand. "There's no reason for you to be sorry. It's my father who was the massive prick."

"Still, I can't imagine what that's like—to watch your mother be hurt like that..."

He looks over my head, and his eyes become haunted, almost as though he's reliving it all over again. "After this one particular time when I was ten, I made her promise not to try to intervene anymore. She wasn't having any of it, but I told her it hurt me more to watch my father beat her than it did to feel his fists against my face. I remember she wept that day and wouldn't stop."

The pain and anger in my chest feel near impossible to control. If his father were still alive today, I'd want to take my fists to his face. "That's terrible that you felt like you had to protect her. No child should feel that way."

He gives a sad sort of chuckle. "I tried to protect everyone—my mom, my brothers, myself. For all the good it did."

"Did your brothers suffer the same fate you did?"

His gaze meets mine again. "Those stories are for my brothers to tell, not me."

I nod in understanding.

What kind of man beats his wife and four children? A sociopath, that's who.

"I don't know what to say, Asher. I'm sorry you had to endure that."

He brushes his thumb over my bottom lip. "There's nothing to be done about it now."

"Didn't anyone try to step in? Surely other people must've known."

Asher threads his fingers into the hair at the side of my head. "You grew up with money, Anabelle, but you didn't grow up with the kind of money my family has. The kind of influence and power to ruin generations of a family. People who worked on the estate knew, but they would never say anything. The only ones who did are the ones who are still employed here from back then—Marcel and Mr. and Mrs. Potter."

That makes sense, I realize. They always seem to look at Asher through eyes more akin to a parental figure, rather than an employee.

"Once, when I was probably around eleven or twelve, my dad beat me so badly that both my eyes swelled shut. In the week it took for the swelling to come down enough that I could see again, my mom read me books by my bedside all day to keep me from getting bored, and Mrs. Potter made me homemade ice cream every day."

I don't bother asking why his mother didn't take her children and leave. She was a victim too. Leaving any man when you're in a situation like that is difficult, but leaving a man with the wealth and power of Asher's father? It must have seemed insurmountable.

A tear slips down my face as I picture a young Asher with a bruised face, relegated to staying in bed to heal rather than running around and exploring the massive estate as any child should.

"Hey, why are you crying?" Asher's voice is softer than I've ever heard it. He swipes away the lone tear with the pad of his thumb.

"I just can't imagine growing up like that. Always afraid of the man who's supposed to love you. I was so close to my father. I just... I feel bad that you never got to know that feeling."

He gives me a sad sort of smile. "I'm glad you had that at least, even if you lost it too soon."

I nod, trying to push away all thoughts of my dad because I can't handle anything more right now.

"What about your mom? Are you close with her?" he asks.

My chest tightens. "I was close with her too."

Asher frowns. "Was?"

"Since my dad died, she's been... depressed. Hardly speaks or eats, and rarely gets out of bed. Physically she's still here, but it's like I've lost her too."

"I'm sorry, I didn't know."

"I feel guilty because sometimes I'm glad I'm living here so that I don't have to see her waste away every day. Does that make me a terrible daughter?"

He shakes his head. "No, it makes you human. I know first-hand how hard it is to watch someone you love suffer. I don't blame you for wanting to escape it. Do you visit her when you leave here on Saturday nights?"

I sigh. "Usually. Sometimes I just go to Black Magic to pass the time and have a drink because I don't think I can face her."

"I'm sorry."

I only smile at him. It's not his fault, and there's nothing he can do, so I change the subject.

"Can I ask about the bear tattoo?"

He stares down at his hand, spreading his fingers and flexing his fist. "My mom compared each one of us to an animal. She said I was strong, but thoughtful. Protective of her and my brothers. She called me her little bear for a long time."

I put my hand over his and squeeze. "I love that."

His eyes lock with mine, and there's a heavy want.

"Do you have the nightmares often?"

His eyes grow haunted again, and I regret my words. "Enough, but I've been having them more often lately."

I wonder why, but I don't ask. "Is there anything I can do to help?"

Instantly his demeanor changes. He looks as if he wants to say something, but he presses his lips together.

"Asher, what is it?"

"It doesn't matter."

I move to sit up, and he rolls from his side onto his back and sits up. "It does matter. Tell me what I can do. Anything." I stare at him, willing him to keep being open with me. To tell me what I can do.

"My past... I think it's the reason I value control so much..."

"Asher, tell me what you need." I don't drop his gaze.

"I need to be in control right now. I need to know that I still have some control in my life, that I'm still the one in charge. It's the only thing that pushes the dreams away, the memories."

I move so that I'm sitting on my knees, and I place my hands on either side of his face. "Then control me, sir."

A rush of air leaves him, and his body grows rigid, his eyes hard. I know I don't have to ask him again. The man who wants to direct things is here, even if it isn't Saturday night, and we're not in the basement.

"Take your clothes off."

"Yes, sir."

I scoot to the edge of the bed and step onto the floor, turning to face him. Then I slowly lift the cami top over my head and slide down my sleep shorts until they rest on the floor. Asher licks his lips and peruses my body slowly from head to toe. It's difficult not to cover myself. I feel so exposed in the dim morning light. But I stand my ground, knowing this is what I can do to pull him back from the brink of his nightmares.

"Do you have any idea how fucking gorgeous you are, Anabelle? So young, too young for me. You have no idea the things I want to do to you. If you did, you'd probably run."

I want to open my mouth and argue with him, but that's not the role I'm playing here, so I remain quiet.

He stands from the bed, and my nipples pebble in anticipation. I thought I was going to have to wait until the next sex club night for this.

"Go wait in the ensuite. Stand in front of the mirror and take in how beautiful you are."

"Yes, sir."

The way his eyelids dip in response every time I call him sir makes my core ache.

I do as he says, standing in front of the mirror. I'm not certain what he's doing, but I think I can hear him opening and closing drawers in his closet. When I hear him walk into the bathroom, my instinct is to turn and look at him, but I force myself to remain eyes forward. He told me to look at myself in the mirror, and I want to please him, so that's what I'll do.

Asher stands behind me, and because of our height difference, I can clearly see his face over mine in the mirror. It's not until this moment that I see what seems to have been so obvious to him from the beginning—our age difference.

He is every part the mature, virile man. With no makeup on and having just woken up, I look like a child in comparison.

I watch as he takes the weight of my breasts in his hands, squeezing gently. Then he uses each thumb and forefinger to pinch my nipples, pulling them out from my body, and I moan. It's impossible not to, the sensation is so seductive.

Letting one hand drop, he reaches into the pocket of his lounge pants and pulls out something. He holds on to one end while the other dangles, and I realize it's a pair of nipple clamps joined together by a chain.

"Do you want me to put these on you, Anabelle?"

I nod and lick my lips. "Yes, sir." My voice is breathy and wanton, nearly desperate.

Jesus, he's barely laid a hand on me, and already I'm like a cat in heat.

Using the mirror as his guide, as well as looking over my shoulder, he attaches the first clamp to my right nipple. I groan deep in my throat. It's a weird mixture of pleasure and pain, discomfort and relief. When he attaches the clamp to my left nipple, my breathing picks up.

Asher leans in, running his tongue up the column of my neck and biting lightly on my earlobe before he tugs on the chain dangling between my breasts. I cry out—not from pain, but because the sensation is overwhelming.

"I'm gonna ride you hard. You okay with that?" he says into my ear.

"Yes, sir." *Just do it already*, I want to scream. The space between my thighs is buzzing, and I'm desperate for relief.

"I might fill you full of my seed, or I might come all over your ass. Any preference?" He tugs on the chain again, a little harder now, and sensation zips through me like a lightning bolt.

"No, sir. No preference."

"Get up on the counter. Kneel on it facing the mirror. We're both going to watch while I pound into you."

I have to bite back a groan.

The expanse of the counter is long, so I don't have an issue finding space to fit me, but I have to bite back a cry due to how cold it is against the front of my shins.

Asher yanks my hips back until my ass is perched over the edge, and my feet hang over the lip of the counter. "I want your eyes on us the entire time. Got it? You look away or close your eyes, and I stop."

I nod. "Yes, sir."

"Don't disappoint me." Then he plunges inside me in one solid stroke.

CHAPTER
THIRTY

ASHER

Those first few seconds after I slip inside Anabelle's pussy must be what heaven feels like. That's the only thought running through my mind as I rut into her like a wild beast.

Gone are the lingering shadows from my nightmares last night. Gone are the tendrils of the past trying to wrap around me. In their place is Anabelle, who is full of life and light and everything I'll never be and will never deserve.

And I'm a selfish enough bastard to take what I can get while I can.

She does as instructed, keeping her gaze steady on the two of us. Her tits bounce with every thrust inside her body, the chain between the clamps dangling. I know that by now her nipples will be somewhat numb, so I tug on the chain again. She cries out and looks as though she might close her eyes but stops herself at the last second.

Her ass looks so perfect hanging over the edge of the counter. Like an offering just for me.

"Next time I'm going to fuck your ass like this. Would you like that, pet?"

"Ah, yes, sir."

I glance down between us and harden even further at the evidence of her arousal coating my cock. This woman has me so twisted up inside. It's invigorating and frustrating all at once, and I take it out on her body as I set a punishing pace, not easing up in the least. She takes it all with no complaint, watching in the mirror.

It's impossible not to look down again and watch her pussy stretch around my girth. The feeling of ownership that I have over her when I'm inside her is concerning, but I can't stop. I can't. Anabelle is as necessary as air to me now.

Knowing I can't hold out much longer, I bring both hands around her body and unclip the nipple clamps. Now that the blood is rushing back into them, I twist her nipples between my thumbs and fingers.

Her back arches, and she cries out in pleasure. I keep it up, wanting her to experience as much pleasure as possible because she's close. When I twist a little harder, I feel the first flutter of her womb around my cock. Then her back arches even more, and she's unable to keep her eyes open any longer, closing them as she comes.

Her pussy tries to milk my cock, vibrating around it, and I'm done for. After a few more thrusts, I pull out, fisting the base. I jerk my cock until her lower back and ass is coated in my cum. And then, because she makes me feel proprietary as fuck, I wipe it into her skin as though in doing so, I'm claiming her as mine.

Leaning in, I pull her hair off to one side and kiss the top of her spine, savoring the taste of her skin. "Are you okay?" I murmur against her heated skin.

She nods. "Yeah. That was... intense."

I raise my head and grin at her in the mirror. "That's a yes to nipple clamps then."

Anabelle has the gall to look embarrassed, which is ridiculous after all we've done.

I help her up off the counter and turn her to face me. "Come on, let's have a shower."

Then I kiss the corner of her brow and take her hand, leading her to the walk-in shower that could easily fit fifteen people. Once the water is up to temperature, I pull her in under the spray. She moans when the warm water hits her skin, and my dick twitches, ready for another round. But her pussy must be sore after that pounding, so it'll just have to calm the fuck down.

Reaching for the shampoo, I tell her, "Turn around."

Even though we're done playing, she does as I say, ever obedient when it comes to me. I squirt some shampoo in my hand and lather it in her hair, rubbing her scalp and making sure I get it all the way down the length of her hair.

She looks at me over her shoulder. "I'm going to smell like you now."

I arch an eyebrow. "Is that a bad thing?"

She shakes her head. "I like the way you smell."

Anabelle says the sweetest, most innocent things sometimes. She's too honest for her own good. It's going to get her in trouble or put her at risk someday.

"Rinse out now."

She goes back under the spray until the water runs clear around our feet. I repeat the exercise with conditioner, finger combing it through.

"Thank you for sharing everything you did with me." Her voice is quieter than normal, as though she's hoping maybe I can't hear her, but she can't go without telling me because it means a lot to her.

I still for a beat, pausing before I resume combing through her hair. "I've never spoken to anyone about it. Even my brothers and I rarely speak of what happened growing up."

There's really no explanation for why I told Anabelle, other than it felt like the right thing to do. I trust her, I suppose.

"Do you think that's healthy? Maybe you guys should discuss it more. Bring it into the light rather than letting it fester in the shadows. Perhaps it would help you guys heal."

I don't think there is any healing from what we went through, but I don't tell Anabelle that. I don't ever want her to know how dark the world can be. She may not have had a perfect life, but she's untarnished compared to me.

"Perhaps," is all I say on that subject. "How do you feel about playing hooky today?"

She spins around to face me. "Really?"

I chuckle. "Really. I know the boss and can probably swing it."

She smiles wide. Just the reaction I was looking for. "What would we do?"

"Have you ever been horseback riding?"

"I'm no expert, but I can hold my own if you put me on a gentle horse."

I twist the ends of her long hair in my hand then lean in for a kiss. "Let's finish this and get you saddled up then."

MRS. POTTER OUTDID HERSELF. I survey the food spread over the blanket where we stopped to let the horses graze while we eat the picnic I had asked her to prepare under the shade of a tree. I saw the gleam in Mrs. Potter's eye when I told her what I needed it for, but I ignored it.

She's about the only person I would tolerate telling me I need to find someone special, and she thinks that Anabelle is going to be it, but that's not what this is. I might have already crossed some lines with her—fucking her outside of the sex club nights, inviting her into my bed—but there will be no fairy tale happy ever after for us.

"Have you been riding ever since you were a little boy?" Anabelle asks before popping a grape into her mouth.

"Yeah, I've always been pretty solitary. I liked riding far from the manor and exploring the grounds when I was younger. Until I was shipped off to boarding school as a teen."

"Did you spend all of high school there?"

I nod, still chewing some of the bean salad Mrs. Potter packed for us. "In Europe. I hated having to go, having to leave my brothers and my mom to fend for themselves against my father, but at the same time, a part of me was happy to be away from him. I felt guilty about that."

She takes my hand. "You shouldn't. You were a child, and I think that's a normal reaction."

I tug on the end of her ponytail. "Are you sure you're only twenty-two? So wise beyond your years."

She tosses a grape at me, and I duck so it hits the grass behind us. "It really bothers you, doesn't it?"

My forehead creases. "What does?"

"The difference in our ages."

"Doesn't it bother you?"

She shakes her head. "Not at all. It's just a number. Who cares?"

"Me apparently." I bring the fork to my mouth and take another bite of the salad.

"What bothers you so much about it?" Her head tilts.

"Do you ever stop asking questions?" My hands pull at a blade of grass.

"Nope." She pops the P.

"I already have control issues around sex. The fact that I find someone so much younger than I am to be such a turn-on makes me feel a little like a dirty old man. There, happy now?" I arch an eyebrow, trying to whistle the blade of grass.

"Maybe I like dirty old men." She drops her voice and says it in a way that makes me think she just might.

"Don't start." I narrow my eyes.

"What, I'm just saying." She bats her eyelashes as though she's so fucking innocent.

"You know exactly what you're doing, and unless you want to end up over my lap with me smacking your bare ass for all of mother nature to see, you'll stop."

She grins then bites a grape. "Maybe that's exactly what I'm hoping for."

I shake my head at her, amused. "You're relentless."

"Relentless is what you were when you were pounding into me earlier."

"Jesus Christ. Let's talk about something else." I toss the blade of grass and set the salad aside, no longer hungry because right now, it's taking everything in me not to pounce on her and make her scream my name by way of my cock.

"All right. There is something I want to talk to you about, but I don't want you to think I'm pressuring you or that I expect something."

I nod for her to continue. "Go on."

"What does this mean for us? You said we were only going to have sex in the basement, but that's obviously not the case now. Does that mean it's open season?"

At least she didn't ask me what it means for us as far as a relationship goes. Being each other's fuck buddies and sometimes-confidants is one thing, but a relationship... no. It's too risky.

"What do you want it to mean?" I may be the one who controls the scene while we're fucking, but it's not like she gets no say.

"You know what I want. I want to be able to sleep with you whenever and wherever we want."

I hold back a laugh because she doesn't want to say the word fuck, though she says worse when she's heated. "Just sleep?"

She throws her hands in the air. "Fine, I want you to *fuck* me. I want you to tell me what you want me to do, and I want to please you by doing it. I want to be your little pet."

It takes every bit of my restraint not to lunge at her and take her right here after that statement, and based on the grin on her face, she knows what she did.

"Fine then. Our physical relationship is no longer just for the basement. Satisfied?"

She sets her food aside and crawls toward me. "Not yet, but you can help with that."

This woman will be the death of me. I'm going to become an addict if I don't practice some restraint.

I gently push her back with a hand to her shoulder. "Eat. There'll be plenty of time for that later."

She pouts but does as I ask.

While we eat in silence for a few moments, I ponder the change in the rules and wonder if I'm making a mistake. We're already fucking, so what's the big deal if we do it more than we planned? It's not as if we'll be spending every night in each other's bed.

Sleeping together feels too intimate. It implies more than I want this to be. Sure, she slept in my bed last night, but that was due to extenuating circumstances. It can't become a regular thing.

The lines are already blurry enough. I don't need to take an eraser to them.

CHAPTER
THIRTY-ONE

ANABELLE

I never would have thought that a nightmare would bring Asher and me closer together, but ever since that night, he's been impossible to resist.

We've been fooling around in his room, in mine, in the library—wherever the mood strikes us—but we never spend the night together. Not since the night I found him in the throes of a nightmare and woke him. When he confessed the hell he'd been through as a child.

I tell myself it's fine for us to sleep apart, that I knew what I was getting into, but my heart doesn't seem to get the message.

There's so much more to the man than the front he puts on for the world. I hear him on the phone when he's doing business, and he's every bit the hardened billionaire encased in a fortress of steel. But there's so much pain underneath, a drive to protect those he cares for, a thoughtful and considerate man. Just last night, he took me around the library and showed me where some of the books he thought I might really enjoy are. When he fucked me up against one of the bookshelves, it was just an added bonus.

Today he had to take his private plane to Voss Enterprises's head office. I guess something was going down that he needed to be present for. No big deal. Except that it feels like it is.

I miss him, and I feel miserable and alone here without him. Which is not good. Because I cannot get attached to this man. He's become the only thing that brings me happiness here at Midnight Manor, and when I'm apart from him, the minutes feel like hours.

I need to get my head right because I'll either be leaving here when my contract is up or when he tires of fucking me and sends me packing back to the staff quarters. Either of those outcomes will be unbearable if I allow myself to develop feelings for him.

Perhaps a little distance is a good thing. I'd considered not leaving the manor on Saturday night to visit my family because Asher is due back around dinner time, but I think maybe now it's better if I do.

Friday evening, I venture to the kitchen where the homemade fertilizer I found in Asher's mother's book has been sitting for a day as her handwritten note in the margins instructed. Mrs. Potter thought I was mad when I asked for all the ingredients to concoct it, including apple cider vinegar and a copper penny.

But I'll try anything. I really want to bring this rose back to life for Asher.

Once I've borrowed a watering can from the grounds crew, I venture into the maze. I don't know the way to the center by heart, but I can find my way there—eventually. The same with the way out.

It takes me the longest it ever has tonight, though, because I'm carrying this heavy watering can. When I reach the center, I set down the can to catch my breath. The sticky summer heat clings to my exposed skin, and I take the elastic band from around my wrist and pull my hair back into a ponytail.

Then I walk over to the bush to water the plant using what I hope will act like a magic potion. While I do, I talk to the plant because that's another thing that was written in the book.

The first time I talked to it, I felt silly. But I swear the rose bush has new buds forming, and the existing roses aren't as weary as they were.

"I'm worried I'm setting myself up for heartbreak. Not because Asher's done anything wrong, but because he does everything right. To everyone else, he's an enigma, but the more I learn about him, the more I know what he's been through and how strong he is because he survived it, the more I want to wrap him in my arms and try to convince him to just let me love him."

I sigh. The bush doesn't answer of course, but I'd be lying if I said that, in some weird way, it doesn't feel good to say the words out loud.

"I've decided I'm going to go see my family tomorrow night rather than stay here and wait for him to return. It's not healthy to base my entire life around him when a year from now, I won't even be here anymore."

That thought gives me a sick feeling in the pit of my stomach.

"Anyway, hopefully this little concoction will help you grow strong again. I think it would make him really happy."

The last drips come out of the watering can, and I take a step back from the plant, studying it. Usually, I would've brought my book so that I can read on one of the benches, but I didn't bother tonight, knowing I wasn't in the mood.

While I find my way out of the maze, I think of all the things Asher confessed to me about his father. What a horrible man he was. My father had his faults, but I cannot imagine him ever doing anything like what Asher's father did to his family. Good riddance.

I feel guilty for thinking it, but not that guilty.

I'm so wrapped up in my thoughts that when I pop out of the maze, I don't see Jack Potter until he calls my name.

I turn and face him. "Hi, Jack. Headed back to the staff quarters?"

"Yep, just finished up for the day. What are you up to?" He nods at the empty watering can in my hand.

"Oh." My cheeks heat in embarrassment though I don't know why. Mrs. Potter already knows what I'm up to, and she's probably told her husband. "I'm trying to bring that rose bush in the maze back to life."

He nods knowingly. "How's it going?"

I frown. "Not bad. Not great."

Jack chuckles. "Well, stick with it. It would mean a lot to Mr. Voss." There's a twinkle in his eye that makes me think he may believe there's more between Asher and me than there is.

"Thanks, I will." The caw of some kind of bird sounds from overhead. "Jack, can I ask you something?"

He shoves his hands in his pockets. "Sure, what's up?"

"You've worked here for a long time, right?"

His eyebrows creep up, and he nods.

"How did Asher's parents die?"

It's a chicken-shit question to ask Jack. I could just as easily ask Asher the same thing, but I can't be sure he'd tell me. Lots of rumors claim that they were killed but offer little to no concrete details. I've heard everything from witchcraft gone wrong to suicide.

Jack gives me a sympathetic look. I get the feeling he's trying to soften the blow. "You're gonna need to ask Mr. Voss about that, Anabelle."

I nod. "I figured as much."

"It's not that I don't want to tell you. It's just Mr. Voss's story to tell, not mine."

"I respect that. Sorry to put you in an uncomfortable spot by asking." I move past him.

"Want me to return that watering can for you? I'm going right by there," he says.

"That would be great, thanks." I hold out the can.

He takes it but settles his hand on my shoulder. "Just ask him."

I nod in affirmation, but when I walk away, I'm not sure I will. Asher's answer might make me fall harder for him than I already have.

SATURDAY NIGHT when I swing by the house is a bust. My mother is much the same as she has been over the past weeks. Her doctor says there's not much more we can do unless we want to move her into a facility for more extensive treatment.

I don't know if that's the right call, and even if I did, it's not as though we have the money for it. According to Luke, he's keeping the business afloat but just barely. Our father drained the coffers, and Luke is trying to rebuild them at the moment, though I have no doubt he will.

He was headed out on a date shortly after I arrived, so I wasn't able to visit with him. My grandmother retired early for the evening, saying she was tired.

I could go back to Midnight Manor and see if Asher has returned yet, but that's exactly what I'm trying to avoid doing. I want to prove to myself that I don't need him, that I haven't fallen for him, so instead, I head to Black Magic.

I'm surprised I don't find Sawyer behind the bar when I take a seat on one of the bar stools. Instead, there's a well-endowed woman with a tight T-shirt, daisy dukes, and long blonde hair.

"Hey, what can I get you?" she asks with a smile.

"I'll just have a beer. Whatever's on special." I have to drive back to the manor, so I don't plan on getting shit-faced. I just plan on staying here long enough to prove to myself that I'm not racing back to Midnight Manor because I'm desperate to see Asher.

"Coming right up." She opens the beer fridge and pulls out a bottle, then grabs the bottle opener from the waist of her jean shorts.

"I was surprised not to see Sawyer when I walked in."

"He's moving to days. I guess the owner doesn't want to work as much anymore, so she was looking for someone to work some nights. So here I am." She tosses the beer cap in the garbage behind her and slides the bottle over to me.

"Thanks." I tip the nose at her before I take a sip. I don't think I've ever seen her before, and with a town as small as ours, I'm sure I would have. She's stunning, and I don't think I'd forget her. "Are you from around here?"

But when I ask, she seems to get a little uncomfortable. She shifts in place, and the corners of her mouth tighten.

"You don't have to tell me if you don't want to. Sorry, I wasn't trying to pry."

She waves me off. "Sorry, no, it's fine. I live about fifteen minutes from here, but I don't get out much. I'm Cinder." She stretches her hand across the bar, and I take it.

"Anabelle, nice to meet you."

"Boudreaux?"

My forehead wrinkles. "Do we know each other?"

Again, she looks uncomfortable. "Oh no, your brother has been in here a couple of times, that's all, and he mentioned he had a sister named Anabelle."

I nod and smile again. No doubt Luke would be chatting up this beautiful woman when he comes in here.

Cinder and I chat periodically when she isn't busy helping customers. When she is, I just read the book I brought with me.

It's busier than normal in here tonight, and I recognize most of the people, though I'm not really friendly with any of them. They're all older than I am. All my high school friends booked it out of town as soon as graduation was done.

The patrons keep Cinder fairly busy, and it's clear to me that she's used to working hard. She doesn't get flustered at all when some of the local drunks pester her.

I decide I like her, and her presence here makes me look forward to coming in on Saturday nights. Maybe the two of us could even form a friendship of sorts.

The two of us are chatting over the music when the voice behind me makes me still.

"Anabelle, it's been a while. You're a hard woman to track down these days."

I turn to see Galen. He's dressed in his sheriff's uniform, so he must be on shift tonight. I do not feel like dealing with his bullshit. Why will this man not take a hint?

"Hi, Galen." I give him a small smile, then turn back around to Cinder and continue our conversation.

Before I can say a word, he sidles up beside me, leaning his side on the bar and invading my space. "Where have you been? Every time I swing by your place, your brother says you're out, but he won't tell me where."

"Well, maybe you should take that as a hint that it's none of your business." I give him a saccharine smile then lift my beer to my lips.

"Excuse me for a second." Cinder walks to the far corner of the bar and pulls her phone out of her purse.

Really? She's leaving me now to text a friend?

Galen chuckles as I figured he would, still too dense to see an insult for what it is. "Come on, Anabelle. When are you going to stop fighting this thing between us and admit that we should be together?"

The idea of being with Galen makes my skin crawl. I could never make myself vulnerable to him the way I do with Asher.

I spin on my seat to face him, hating how close to him I am. "Let me make it clear once and for all for you. We are never getting back together. Ever. I'm not pretending to not want to be with you to be coy. I don't want to be with you. I never will. You should move on and find someone who does want to be with you because it will never be me."

His eyes narrow, and I think that maybe, for the first time, he's really *heard* me. "Is there someone else? Is that it? That where you been every time I go to your place?"

I sigh and close my eyes, praying for patience. Maybe I should just tell him where I am. Maybe that will make him back off. "I'm working at Midnight Manor. That's where I am. And as for whether there's someone else, that's not the point. I don't want to be with you. *That's* the point."

His eyes widen and alarm flashes across his face. "You can't be there. What the hell are you thinking even stepping foot on that property, let alone working there. Did they force you?" He grips my wrist as if he's about to yank me off the stool and run out of here with me.

Cinder comes back over to us. "I think she's made it clear that she's not interested, Sheriff."

Galen directs his glare at her but doesn't let my wrist go. "If I want your lip, I'll rattle my zipper."

Cinder blinks a couple of times, seeming surprised.

"Yeah, that's right. I remember you from T&Ts," he sneers.

T&Ts stands for tits and tassels, and it's the nickname for the strip club just over the county line.

Cinder's cheeks turn red and shame coats her features.

"Why are you such an asshole?" I say to him, trying to rip my hand from his grip to no avail.

"You can't go back to that place, Anabelle. This explains why you've been acting so weird with me. What are they feeding into your head up there?"

"If you want to keep that hand, you'll remove it from Miss Boudreaux right now."

My head whips to the side, and I see Asher looking as if it's taking everything in him not to pounce on Galen and attack. He's a feral beast looking for any excuse to maim.

"Asher." His name comes out breathy, but he doesn't glance my way at all. He keeps his eyes on Galen.

"You have two seconds. Be thankful I granted you those."

It's then I realize that the murmuring in the bar has died down, and everyone is watching this exchange.

Galen lets my wrist go, and I pull back my hand. He saunters toward Asher, chest puffed out, hands on his service belt. "Not sure it's wise for you to be sticking your nose into things that don't concern you, Voss."

Asher doesn't move his eyes from Galen when he says, "Get your things together, Anabelle. We're going home."

Home. I hate that my chest warms when he refers to the place that is only a temporary refuge for me as home.

Grabbing my book off the bar top, I look at Cinder. "Thank you. It was nice to meet you."

"You too," she says in a low voice as though if we speak too loudly, we may set off the powder keg between Galen and Asher.

I slip off the stool and walk over to Asher's side.

"If I see you touch her again, you're going to lose that hand. Got it?" Asher arches an eyebrow.

"Not smart to threaten the sheriff in front of a bar full of people." Galen smirks.

"Try your worst, LeBlanc." Then Asher gently squeezes the back of my neck. "Got all your stuff?"

I nod. His gaze roams my face for a bit before he dips down and places a chaste kiss on my lips.

"You're fucking him?" Galen booms. "Are you serious? How fucking stupid can you be? Didn't take you for a slut."

There's no warning as Asher pulls away from the kiss and, in one fluid motion, cocks his fist back and punches Galen square in the jaw.

Galen stumbles back and ends up on his ass on the floor.

"Consider that a warning. Next time, there won't be one." Then Asher takes my free hand. "Let's go."

He leads me out the door, leaving behind a roomful of people gaping at our backs.

CHAPTER
THIRTY-TWO

ASHER

When Cinder texted me to tell me some guy was bothering Anabelle at the bar, I couldn't get there fast enough. I was already worked up on the short drive there. But when I walked in and saw him gripping her wrist, I just about lost it.

I wanted to race across the bar and pummel him into sawdust. I knew if I did, I would probably black out in my rage as I had once before in my life. And I didn't want Anabelle to witness that. That was the only thing that prevented me from crossing the distance between us.

But when he called her a slut? Fuck. There was no way I was letting that go.

That piece of shit can try his worst, I don't care. I have enough money and influence to make myself untouchable. Something he should already know.

Once I have Anabelle safely in the car beside me, I sit with my hands on the steering wheel, knuckles white while I try to control my breathing and slow my heart rate. I need to calm down before I can speak rationally with Anabelle.

She seems to instinctively know this, because she doesn't say a word.

Once I've gathered myself, I turn my head and look at her. "Are you okay?"

She nods. "How did you know where I was?"

"After you mentioned that you go there sometimes on Saturday nights, I called the owner and told her that if there were ever any problems for you, I was to be notified right away. She told her workers. Put your seat belt on."

Anabelle does as I said without argument. Perfect. She's always so perfect.

"Are you upset that I did?" I don't care if she is. I'll do what I have to in order to protect her.

"I probably should be, but no, I'm not."

The sensation in my chest from her words has me rubbing it after I slide on my seat belt. I pull out of the parking lot, anxious to get her back to Midnight Manor. Not seeing her for two days was fucking torture.

"My car is here." She looks out the window as we move farther away from it.

"I'll send someone to pick up your car. Give me the keys."

She pulls them from her purse and passes them to me. I slide them in my pocket.

"Given that you were at the bar, I take it your visit with your mother didn't go well?"

I hear her sigh, and I glance at her again. Pain coats her features like paint.

"No, same as last time. No change."

After I press the button for the gates to the manor, I squeeze her hand. "I'm sorry."

The vehicle moves through the low-level fog on the grounds tonight. It's not common this time of year in general, but it's not uncommon here at Midnight Manor all year. It's just another one of the unexplainable things that add to the manor's lore.

I have to take the road slowly because I can't see more than five or six feet in front of me. She's quiet and contemplative during the ride, and I don't bring up any of the questions I have for her. They can wait until we're safely ensconced inside.

Once I've parked, I lead her to the front door with a hand on her back, then take her to the library. I could have chosen either of our bedrooms, but as much as I want to be buried inside her, we have things to discuss.

Rather than turning on the overhead lights, I flick on one of the lamps on the table in the sitting area and lead her to the couch. The room is dim, and the shadows play on her face, making her look even more young and innocent than she already does.

I need to voice the question that's been burning in my throat from not asking it on the drive over here.

"Who is LeBlanc to you?" I attempt to keep my voice even, but I'm not sure how successful I am when she blinks rapidly at me.

"You know him?" Her head tilts.

"Not exactly. He's tried to make trouble for my family a few times since he's become sheriff. I've had to make a few phone calls to the governor and a senator to put him in his place."

"Oh. I didn't know that." She frowns. "Galen and I dated back in high school. Ever since I returned to Magnolia Bend, he's been intent on getting me back. He seems to think we're the perfect couple and should be married and raising babies together."

Anger, swift and stinging like a slap to the face, lashes me. "You can do better than him."

She holds my gaze and nods. "I know."

That was a stupid thing for me to say. She can do better than me too. A man who's unwilling to commit or have a serious relationship and get married. Anabelle deserves to have someone who wants all those things with her.

But no matter. I'm not giving her up. Not yet anyway.

"Why is he so persistent?" I narrow my eyes. Could she have given him reason to be?

She shrugs. "I have no idea. I've made it abundantly clear that I want no part of him. He's like the Teflon man, and the insults I hurl at him just bounce away. Though I think you made your point. Thank you for defending me."

I cup her chin. "I will always defend you, remember that."

She nods, and I drop my hand. "I suspect he will leave me alone now that you've intervened, though I hope you don't get in trouble for hitting a police officer."

"Don't worry about me, Anabelle. I'll be fine." Something about that statement shifts something in her body language. "What?"

She opens her mouth, looks hesitant for a moment and closes it, then opens it again. "I wanted to ask you something."

"Ask then." She bites her bottom lip, and I pluck it out with my thumb and forefinger. "Speak, Anabelle."

"How did your parents die? I'm sure you're aware that rumors have swirled around for years, but I don't actually know what happened."

My shoulders drop, and I push a hand through my hair, gripping the base of my neck. Not the topic I had hoped to cover tonight. I'd planned on my cock getting reacquainted with her pussy.

At my hesitation, she says, "If it's too painful, we don't have to talk about it. I just... I can't help but wonder after all we've talked about."

"My mother was murdered by one of my father's enemies, and my father was murdered by someone else."

Her hands fly to her mouth. "I'm so sorry, Asher."

It's been so long since I've talked to anyone about this. As far as my mother is concerned, I've only ever talked to my brothers about it, and as for my dad, my brothers and I steer clear of that conversation for our own reasons.

"I'm not sorry about my father, which you can probably guess, but my mother..." I rub at the pain in my chest, at the pain on Kol's face when he told me he'd found her. I have to squeeze my eyes shut to remove the image of my mother's bloodied body.

Fuck, I don't want to talk about this. Not at all.

But maybe it will be like when I spoke to Anabelle about my father's beatings... maybe I'll find some sense of peace from it.

"My mother was very unhappy in her marriage to my father, for obvious reasons. He had a business associate, someone who used to come around the manor a lot. They weren't friends, more like adversaries, but they spent time together because they enjoyed one-upping each other and taunting the other." My voice is monotone as I continue. "From what I understand, at some point, he and my mother began an affair. She was planning to leave my father, but when it came down to it, she told the man she couldn't do it. I don't know why. Maybe if she'd left and taken us with her, we all could have been happy somewhere else. But for her own reasons, she wouldn't leave my father. When the man confronted her about it, he stabbed her through the heart with her garden shears. Whether it was a jealous rage, or he was just so incensed he wouldn't have the *coup* of stealing Ramsey Voss's wife, I don't know. Kol found her out in one of the gardens. He was only ten."

I blink out of the memory and look at Anabelle, who has tears streaking down her face. My sweet, sweet Anabelle who feels so much. Using both hands, I swipe away her tears.

"That's so sad. Your poor mother. You poor boys."

More tears drip over my thumb, and I bring it to my lips, tasting her saltwater tears.

"What happened to him? The man who killed your mother?"

"He was arrested and held for trial. Didn't make it, though. He was stabbed to death in jail while he was awaiting trial. The killer left the shiv in his chest, right where his heart is. Just like he did with my mother." A low chuckle escapes. "That might be the only thing in my life I ever felt thankful to my father for."

Anabelle slides over and pulls me into a hug, pushing her hand into the hair at my nape. At first, it feels foreign, allowing someone to try to comfort me physically. But after a few heartbeats, I let myself sink into her comfort and surround her with my hands, accepting her offering.

She pulls away and places a palm to my cheek. "That's so tragic, Asher. I'm sorry. What happened to your father?"

I place a finger over her mouth. "No more talking. All you need to know is that this land is soaked with the blood of many people, and he's one of them. That's all I can tell you."

Anabelle studies me for a moment then nods, leaning in to kiss me. When our tongues meet, I feel the horrible memories float to the recesses of my mind and disappear like the mist on a lake when the sun comes out.

Too soon, she pulls away and stands from the couch. I'm going to protest, but without a word, she lifts her tank top over her head, toes off her shoes, slides her shorts and panties down her legs, then finally removes her bra. When I reach for her, she bats away my hand and leans in to undo my shorts. With my help, she splays them open and gets my boxer briefs down under my ass.

She straddles me, and I take a nipple into my mouth, swirling my tongue around then nibbling with my teeth as she sinks down on me until I'm fully seated inside her. Anabelle groans and threads her hands through my hair as she circles her hips.

I lose myself in her body as she rides me. And for tonight, I don't worry about controlling the scene or having her do my bidding. I just let her offer me the comfort of her body.

Later that night, after tossing and turning for an hour in my room, I sneak into hers, slide into her bed, pull her close, and finally fall into a deep sleep.

CHAPTER
THIRTY-THREE

ANABELLE

My nerves make me feel as if a confetti bomb went off in my stomach. It's the night of the sex club, and the theme for tonight is ancient Rome, so I'm dressed in a gauzy white dress with gold straps. It's more like two pieces of fabric that hang in front and behind with a gold belt to cinch them in. Beneath, I wear white lace panties, and I have a gold leaf crown on my head.

I give myself one last check in the mirror before turning around. "Who decides what the theme will be?" I ask Asher, who's still getting changed in his closet.

"The director of the night." He steps out, and I have to stop my mouth from falling open.

Asher is dressed like a Spartan and reminds me of Gerard Butler in the movie *300*. He's lucky I don't strip him right here and now because he looks that damn good with the red cape and his chest on display.

He pauses when he sees me. "You look like a goddess."

My cheeks heat. "Thank you." I stand there for a beat while he looks as if he wants to devour me. I need to change the subject because it's clear to me that we won't make it down to the basement if I don't. "So what's the director?"

He clears his throat. "Prior to the party, someone from the club is sent an invitation to be the director. That person gets to choose the theme."

"How do you decide who to send it to?"

He shrugs. "It's random for the most part, though if there's an agenda to be achieved and we can use it as leverage, that may be a deciding factor."

I step toward him. "It's that big of deal?"

"Just think if you had a specific sexual fantasy you wanted to live out. This would help you do it."

"Makes sense." I wonder what I would choose as a theme if given the chance.

Asher wraps his arms around my waist. "Are you nervous?"

"A little... will we... last time we did stuff in front of every-one. Is that what it will be like this time?"

His gaze becomes intense, and he trails a finger down my jawline. "I have no plans to share you with anyone, and that includes having you be anyone's viewing pleasure. From now on, everything that happens will be behind closed doors in my private room."

"I wasn't sure if that was your room last time or not."

"My brothers and I each have our own private rooms. Part of the perks of hosting the parties." He grins at me.

"What are all the other rooms?" His and his brother's rooms would only account for four of the doors I'd seen, and I knew there had to be nearly twenty or so besides the main room.

"Something for everyone. Some are designed as certain configurations like an office, a bathroom, or a locker room so people can play out their fantasies. Others have specific equipment in them depending on what you're into—BDSM, shibari, voyeurism."

The idea of all that makes the space between my legs hum. "Will we ever go into those rooms?"

His eyelids dip a bit. "If you like, though I already told you I'm not sharing you. But if it turns you on to watch others, if you want to see what you might want to explore between the two of us, that's fine."

I nod. "I'll think about it."

"I have something for you." Asher walks over to his night-stand and opens the top drawer, then pulls out a gold mask with diamonds surrounding the outer edge and a gold fili-gree detail. He holds it out to me. "For you."

"It's beautiful." I step back over to the mirror and slide it onto my face.

Asher steps up behind me and kisses the top of my shoulder. "Perfect fit. You ready?"

After taking a deep breath, I nod again. "Yep. Let's go have some fun." ˉ

~

SINCE LAST TIME was different because of my initiation, I wasn't sure what to expect tonight. But we've been here for forty-five minutes, and so far it's just been people standing around having drinks and chatting as they would at any other party. That's if they were all dressed like ancient Romans with masks.

I lean into Asher and ask about something I noticed. "How come my mask is different from everyone else's?"

Everyone else has on either a black, white, or red mask, while Asher, his brothers, and I all have on custom gold ones. It's easy to spot his brothers. Nero has on a raven's mask, Kol has on a lion's mask, and Sid is wearing a wolf's mask.

"You have that one on because you're mine."

I should probably hate the way he phrases it, but I don't. Not even a little. I want to be his.

"For everyone else, the colors signify what they're looking for tonight."

My forehead wrinkles, and I glance around the dim cavern-like room. When I spot Kol getting sucked off by some woman, I turn around and face Asher. "How so?"

Asher bends to speak directly into my ear. "White is a watcher, red is a waiter, and black is a doer."

"Okay, the watcher one seems self-explanatory, as does the doer. What's a waiter?"

"It basically means they're not sure what they're in the mood for this evening. But they're open. So, if someone wanted to play with them, they could suggest it, and they might decide to join in, maybe not. The people in black masks are down for anything tonight—it means you don't have to get their consent for each and every thing. If you wanted to go up to one of the men in a black mask and get on your knees in front of him and start sucking him off, there'd be no objections and no recourse for him."

"Kinda like how I am with you then," I say and give him a cheeky grin.

Asher slides his hand around my back and takes my ass in his grip. I arch my back, wanting more. He glances over my shoulder toward the hallway that leads to his private room, and his eyes light with recognition. He drops his hand and straightens, sticking his hand out as a man with dark hair and a white mask comes over.

"Good to see you. It's been a while," Asher says to him.

The man smiles. I can't see his entire face, but he's clearly attractive. His dark brown eyes settle on me once they're done their handshake. "And who do we have here?"

Asher's hand settles on my lower back. "This is Anabelle. Anabelle, this is Mr. Smith."

He puts his hand out, so I take it. "Nice to meet you, Mr. Smith."

"Likewise." He turns his attention back to Asher.

"How have things been? I wasn't sure. It's been a while since we saw you at one of these," Asher says.

"You know how it is..."

Asher nods and turns to me, saying directly into my ear, "Why don't you go to my private room, and I'll meet you there in a minute? You remember where it is?"

I nod.

"Okay, take off your underwear and leave it on the bed."

"Yes, sir," I say before walking away.

I go into the room, which looks much the same as it did before, and do as he says, removing my panties and leaving them on the mattress. I take a seat on the edge of the bed and wait. As the minutes tick by, the anticipation rises and I grow wet.

Finally, the door opens, and Asher walks in. His gaze diverts to the bed, where he sees my white lace panties. He smirks, and it's such a sexy smirk that I want it between my thighs.

"Stand up." His voice is sharp, like a knife's edge.

I bolt up from the mattress.

"Go stand at the corner at the foot of the bed."

I do, and he moves over to the chest of drawers and grabs a pair of handcuffs with a chain between them. My nipples pebble under the thin fabric of my dress.

He must notice, because his gaze dips, and he licks his lips. "Put your hands above your head."

I raise my hands, and he positions me so that my spine is lined up with the post at the corner of the four-poster bed. Because of my position, my chest sticks out, and when he puts the handcuffs on my right wrist, our chests brush. It's the slightest of touches, but it makes my breath catch.

I can't see what he's doing, but I hear the chain moving against metal. Then the other handcuff is fastened around my left wrist. On instinct, I try to pull my hands down but find that I'm not able to.

I really am at Asher's mercy. Why does that make me so hot?

He leans in and gently removes my mask. "It's just us. I want to be able to see all of you."

Asher probably didn't mean for it to come off as sweet, but it does.

Then he lifts his mask so it sits on top of his head, and he leans in and kisses me. It's drugging and makes my legs feel wobbly. When he pulls away, I make a small sound of protest in the back of my throat, and he chuckles against my neck.

Trailing his tongue down, he eventually reaches my breasts. He tongues my nipple over the fabric then sucks it into his mouth. When he pulls away, the fabric is wet, and I can see my nipple through it. He repeats the motion on my other breast until both my nipples are turgid peaks.

I rub my thighs together, desperate to relieve some of the pressure building there. He chuckles and leans in, taking my nipple in his warm mouth again and trailing his fingers down between the pieces of fabric and delving into my folds. He lightly runs them over my clit, and I arch my hips, greedy for more. He doesn't say anything, keeping his fingers still and letting me set the pace with the movement of my hips. My breathing picks up, and I increase my pace, getting close, but then he pulls his fingers away.

I cry out.

"Spread your legs." He doesn't miss a beat, and his voice leaves zero room for argument, so I do what he says even though right now, I want to squeeze my legs together.

He drops to his knees in front of me and leans in, centering his nose at the apex of my thighs and inhaling deep.

God, it's so dirty, but somehow I love it.

"Have you ever heard of orgasm control?" He looks up at me from below.

I shake my head, though I can infer what it means by the name.

"I'm not going to let you come until I want you to. It might seem frustrating, but trust me when I tell you that the payoff will be worth it."

I watch as he spreads my legs even farther, hiking one leg over his shoulder, and leans in to lick me. He sucks on my clit and fucks my opening with his tongue, but he doesn't use his hands. It's enough to drive me mad because while it feels phenomenal, he's being sure not to give me enough to get me there. Just when I'm about ready to beg, he stands up and walks back over to the chest of drawers.

Panting, I watch as he opens the second one down and pulls something from it, then he walks it over to me. When he gets closer, and I can make it out in the dim light, I see that it's a leather collar with a stainless steel ring in the middle.

"Do you know what this is?" he asks.

"Yes." I've read enough BDSM to know.

"This is a play collar." His eyes seem to darken, turning the color of a stormy ocean.

"It means that I'll be your sub tonight."

He nods. "I want to collar you, Anabelle, but I need to know that you want it too."

I nod vigorously. "I want it."

His smile screams satisfaction. "Turn around."

I try to turn in place, expecting some resistance from the handcuffs, but I'm able to turn without a problem. I look up and see that the chain between the handcuffs is linked through an iron ring at the top of the bedpost. There's enough slack that I can turn all the way around if I want.

There's movement behind me, then the shuffling of material. When Asher steps up behind me, it's clear he's taken off the bottom half of his costume because the hard press of his cock presses against my back. He slides my hair over one shoulder, then his hands come around and wrap the collar around my neck, fastening it at the back. There's an intimacy I wasn't expecting.

"There," he says into my ear. "Now you're mine."

He smacks my ass hard, and I yelp at the pain but then hum in my chest as he rubs his hand over it. The pain settles into a warm sensation radiating out.

"Step away from the bedpost and arch your back with your ass out," he says.

I stand in the position and he slides the two bits of fabric to the side, so it drapes by my hips. I'm totally exposed to him. I have no idea if he's looking, where he's looking, or what he's seeing as I stand there for long seconds.

Then his large hands are on my ass cheeks, and he's spreading them. I want to be embarrassed, but then his tongue is on my puckered hole, and my head dips down. Oh god, it feels so good. I've never had anyone do this to me before. As he swirls his tongue, his finger pushes into my entrance, pumping at a slow and steady pace. My need to come ratchets up higher and higher, and when he curves his fingers inside me and hits me at just the right spot, I buck my hips, unable to help myself.

The smack on my ass vibrates through my core, and I'm so... close. My core tightens, ready to release, and then, he's gone.

"No!" I cry out, starting to turn back around to face him, beg, anything, but he stops me with his hands on my hips.

Then he's surging inside me, stretching me. Every nerve ending in my body fires up, and he pulls the hair at the back of my head so that my neck arches back. My hands grip the bed post so that I can stay in place, and I arch my back even further. I'm so primed and ready that it doesn't take long for my climax to build again. When I feel the first flutterings in my womb, Asher pulls out of me.

Frustration wells inside me, and I swear I could cry.

Without a word, he turns me around and picks me up by the backs of my thighs then pushes into me. The mask is back on his face, and it's like watching myself getting fucked by a beast.

My back is against the bedpost as he rides me hard. His cape is still on, as is my dress, and something about the fact that we're fucking and aren't totally naked really turns me on.

I haven't even come, and yet I feel spent, happy to let him have his way with me. When he changes the angle so that his pelvis grinds against my clit every time he drives into me, I start panting.

"Oh god, Asher. Please don't stop. Please let me come."

Again, I tighten around him, and he's gone, setting my feet on the floor. He undoes the handcuffs in record time and lifts me by the waist, tossing me on my back so my pelvis is at the edge of the bed. He positions my feet so they lay flat on his pecs, then he spreads my knees wider, pushing back into me.

My back arches because nothing has ever felt so good, yet at the same time, I've never had to come so badly.

"I wish you could see what you look like when I'm fucking you, pet. The way your pussy swallows me up. Never getting enough of this cock."

His words drive me higher, make my climax move that much closer. My hands slide over my breasts, squeezing. Asher gently massages my clit. Not enough to make me come, and I know that's by design. Just enough to make me a writhing mess with tears in her eyes, desperate for relief.

"You are a goddess. *My* goddess." Asher draws his hand up and smacks my clit.

I cry out as pain lashes through me, followed by the deepest pleasure I've known.

"Please let me come, sir. Please." I'm begging, and I don't care. There is no personal pride here at this moment. "Please, sir."

"As you wish." He pinches my clit—hard—and I spontaneously combust.

At least that's what it feels like. I shatter into a million pieces that somehow ricochet back together. My core pulses around him, and my orgasm keeps going and going and going.

Finally, once my body has settled, and I've come back to myself, Asher pulls out of me. He spreads the two pieces of fabric on my chest then grips his cock, stroking it until he comes all over my breasts with a deep guttural groan.

When he's done, he stares at his work. "Rub it in," he says and moans low in his throat when I do.

He leans over me, bringing his mouth to mine. I loop my handcuffed hands around his neck and return the kiss. After he pulls away, he helps me up off the bed. My legs are wobbly at first.

"Are you okay?" he asks.

I grin at him. "When can we do that again?"

CHAPTER
THIRTY-FOUR

ASHER

I'm falling for her.

That's the only explanation for why I asked her earlier this week to join me on a date tonight.

Because I don't *date*.

I fuck women in the sex club. And when I have to, I'll have some high society woman accompany me to some event, and sometimes I'll fuck her too.

But I don't date. I don't woo. I don't try to make a good impression to get in some woman's good graces. But that's exactly what I'm doing tonight.

I wait near the front door for Anabelle, my heart in my throat and constricting my airway. All the old fears rise to the surface—that I can't afford to care about anyone because they'll end up leaving me like my mother did, that anyone who cares for me will be taken from me, that the person who is supposed to care the most for me will be the one who inflicts the most pain.

But when I hear the click of heels on the floor and turn and see Anabelle making her way to me, all those fears evaporate.

I left the dress for her in her room earlier today, and I knew it would look gorgeous on her, but I had no idea it would be this. She looks like a fucking goddess, and I want to bow down and worship at her altar.

She's wearing an off-the-shoulder gold satin gown that reaches the floor. The fabric of the skirt wraps from one side to the other toward her hip, causing it to pleat, and on the other side, a long slit reaches three-quarters of the way up her thigh. Her hair is pulled back into a sleek ponytail with waves, highlighting the column of her neck and one of her favorite places for me to lick—besides her pussy.

Every step she takes is a tease of her shapely leg and the apex of her thighs. I have to adjust myself in my tuxedo pants to make room for my growing erection.

"You take my breath away, Anabelle."

She looks a little embarrassed by my praise, glancing at the floor. "Thanks. You look really good as well."

I lift her chin with my thumb and forefinger. "Don't look away from me. Own it. I'm a lucky man to have you on my arm tonight."

"Yes, sir," she says in a soft voice, and my dick twitches.

I give her a grin. She knows exactly what she's doing. I take her hand. "Let's go. We need to get to the plane."

"Plane?"

I haven't told her where we're going tonight, opting to keep it a surprise. "You didn't think we were heading down to Black Magic in this, did you?"

She laughs and follows me out the door.

We arrive in the city, and the car I arranged to take us to the symphony drops us in front of the theater.

Anabelle looks at the banners hanging on either side of the entryway. "I've never been to the symphony before."

"I'm honored to be your first then." I take her hand and kiss her knuckles, guiding her through the entryway and up the stairs of the building.

There's a red carpet here tonight because we're attending a large fundraiser for some local charities that one celebrity or another is the spokesperson for. Normally I skip these things and very often I make my driver drop me at the back so I can't be photographed, but on a whim, I decide that I want a picture of the two of us.

This might be the only chance I have to get a picture of us together before we part. I'm certainly not going to pull out my phone and take a selfie of us. What kind of message would that send to Anabelle? That I plan to have it printed and put in a frame on my desk?

"Let's get a quick picture," I say and steer her toward the step with my hand on her back.

She seems surprised but pleased by my request.

When the press call my name and demand to know who I'm with and what she is to me, I ignore them. Satisfied that

I'll be able to steal a picture of the two of us off the internet tomorrow, I lead us inside and up the stairs where we can gain access to our private balcony seats.

Heads turn as we pass through the crowd. I knew they would. Not only is Anabelle stunning, but she's an unknown. She may have come from money, but she's not a socialite someone would expect to find on my arm for an event. People will be wondering who she is and what she is to me.

Let them. She's mine, and mine she'll stay.

"Would you like something to drink before we go to our seats?" I ask.

She twists her lips for a moment, giving it a thought. "Maybe some champagne to celebrate my first time here?"

God, she is so fucking cute and charming when she's not even trying to be.

"Coming right up. Give me a minute."

Anabelle stands off to the side while I go grab us two glasses of champagne. It doesn't take long since the one bar is reserved for those with private balconies.

When I return, I hand her a glass and hold my arm out for her. "Shall we?"

She slides her arm through mine, and I lead us to our seats.

"Wow, this is really something. Thank you for bringing me, Asher." She takes her seat and looks at me.

I hold out my champagne flute. "To all the firsts."

She smiles and clinks my glass. "To all the firsts."

I'm sure she thinks I'm thinking of things like the sex club and the symphony, but really, I'm thinking of her being the first woman to make me feel... hell, anything.

We sip our champagne, and a few minutes later, the show starts.

I'm enraptured watching her take in the music—eyes wide with a serene smile on her face as though the sound is filling her.

When the first notes of "Dies Irae" begin and the choir sings, there's a stabbing sensation in my heart. Anabelle seems to still when she registers the song, and I frown.

I lean into her. "What's wrong?"

She turns her head, eyes wide with what now looks like concern. "This song..."

I nod at her to go on.

"This is the song I told you about, the one that led me to the library that day and the one I heard playing from your room the night you were having a nightmare."

Now my eyes are wide. "This was my mother's favorite. She used to play it for us all the time."

Anabelle's mouth drops open. "How is that possible?"

The truth is, I have no idea. I've seen some weird shit over the years at Midnight Manor, but this...

It almost feels like a sign... from my mother. Is it possible?

I can't listen to this song without thinking of her and how she used to play it all the time for us boys. It's Latin and translates to Day of Wrath. She told us she loved it because the poem itself was all about Judgment Day and how the repentant would be forgiven and find their place in heaven. Set to music, it gave her hope. That there was always hope that people could repent.

I don't know if she was hoping my father would be the one to repent or if it was her hope for herself. She always said that even though there was fear and dread, there was still always hope, and this piece of music reminded her of that.

"I don't know how it's possible," I finally say to Anabelle.

She gives me a sad, hopeful smile. I take her hand and thread her fingers through mine.

"If I hadn't heard that music, we might not be here like this now," she says into my ear.

Maybe my mother is trying to give me a sign that I'm on the right path. A piece of me hates the hope that thought gives me. But maybe that's just what's left of my father, and I need to let it go. Maybe it's time to do things differently.

CHAPTER
THIRTY-FIVE

ANABELLE

Ever since the night Asher punched Galen at the bar, we've been sharing a bed. He slipped into my bed sometime in the middle of the night that night, and we've been sleeping in his room every night since then.

Last night after we returned from the symphony was no exception. Usually after we wake up and fool around, I'll retreat to my bedroom to get ready for the day and meet him in the office later on. This morning though, he surprises me when—despite the fact we wake up late because we got in so late—he tugs me back to his chest when I roll over to get out of bed and start to get ready.

"You're not going anywhere," he says into the crook of my neck.

I laugh. "We're already behind. You've missed your swim, and I have to start getting ready."

"You're coming to breakfast with me this morning." He kisses the back of my head and hops out of bed to make his way to the ensuite.

"Okay, let me get dressed, then we can figure out which restaurant you want to go to," I call out behind him.

"No restaurant."

I sit up in bed and watch as he makes his way to a dresser and pulls out a T-shirt.

"I'm confused," I say.

"We're going to eat in the dining room with my brothers. I want them to get to know you better."

My eyes widen, but there's a giddy feeling in my stomach. "Well then I definitely need to go make myself presentable."

He pulls the T-shirt on over his head and goes into the closet. "Nope. You just need to put this on." He comes out with my robe and walks over to the bed. "Here."

"Asher, I cannot go have breakfast like this." I motion to the tank and booty shorts I wore to bed last night.

He shrugs. "Why not? I am."

My head tilts. "Because I've never really met them before, at least not since we were...whatever we are. I'll feel like an idiot."

He leans over on the mattress and presses a kiss to the corner of my eyebrow. "It doesn't matter what they think. I'm doing it as a courtesy to them. Now put that on, and let's go."

His voice changes on the last sentence as he shifts more into his dominant persona. It's subtle, but I can always tell. And like always, it makes me want to do what he says.

I scoot to the edge of the bed and slide down so my feet hit the floor. I pull the robe on, tying it at my waist. "Can I at least brush my hair or something?"

"No." He places a chaste kiss on my mouth, then takes my hand and leads me from the room.

At least I still have my hair elastic on my wrist, so I pull my hair up into a messy bun. It's not much, but it's better than bed head, I guess.

As I step inside the dining room and all three brothers stop what they're doing and turn to stare at the two of us, I'm so nervous. Especially because last week, I literally saw a couple of these men fornicating with women in front of me. Asher holds my hand at the far end of the table, glaring at his brothers.

Nero, who I know from Asher is the youngest of them at thirty years old, pushes away from the table and makes his way over to us. He has the same deep blue eyes as Asher, but he keeps his hair shorter on the sides.

"Hi, Anabelle,. I don't think we've been properly introduced yet. I'm Nero." He holds out his hand, and I take it, relaxing a bit when he gives me a warm smile.

"It's nice to meet you, Nero."

Asher relaxes a bit at my side, then leads me down toward his seat at the table.

"And since these two pricks are too lazy to get up and introduce themselves, allow me." Asher glares at them both. "This is Kol."

He motions to the man with dark hair that's buzzed close to his scalp and caramel-colored eyes fringed with thick lashes. Kol doesn't say anything, but he raises the arm that has a giant lion tattoo covering it, then shoves his fork in his mouth.

I return the wave. "Hi."

"And this is Obsidian, but we call him Sid." Asher points at the man with a wolf tattoo on his neck, dressed in an expensive suit.

"Hello, Anabelle." His smile is charming enough, but there's a predator's gleam to his eyes. His hair is dark and wavy, much like Asher's, and his eyes are such a deep brown that they almost look black.

"Anabelle will be joining us for breakfast in the mornings from now on," Asher says.

Kol raises his eyebrows at him but says nothing while Asher pulls out my chair for me.

"Thank you," I say quietly, sitting down.

Nero, who was sitting to my right, slides his things down one more spot so that Asher can take his seat.

Is this all because of the song "Dies Irae"?

Ever since I confessed to Asher last night about hearing that song in the manor, it feels as if something has shifted in him. I'm not complaining, I like the change, but I'm not sure I understand where it's coming from, and I want to make sure it's not a temporary thing.

"Help yourself to whatever you want," Asher says to me, taking the plate from one of the house staff who clearly saw me come in.

"Thank you." I serve myself some eggs, fruit salad, and toast.

The five of us eat in silence for a couple of minutes. Probably able to tell that I'm growing more uncomfortable, Asher speaks up.

"Sid, where are we with the EPA thing on the East Coast?"

Sid swallows his coffee and sets down his cup. "Everything's been resolved. Our guy made sure of it."

"Good." Asher nods and pours himself coffee, offering me some, which I accept.

"So, Anabelle. What did you think of the symphony last night?" Nero asks.

I look down the table at him and smile. "I've never been before, but I loved it. I didn't realize how much different it is listening to it live. It's like it fills you up or something." My cheeks heat. "Sorry, that probably sounds really cheesy."

"Not at all. I get what you mean."

"How did you know we went to the symphony?" Asher asks.

"Mrs. Potter told him," Sid says with a grin.

"Jesus, that old woman is the biggest gossip in this place." Asher shakes his head.

"Who are you calling an old woman?" Mrs. Potter walks into the dining room, looking nonplussed at finding me here. In her hand is something I recognize well—Asher's green drink.

"Forgive me," Asher says with a smile I haven't seen him direct at anyone but me.

She shakes her head and sets it on the table between us. "Since you missed your swim, I didn't know if you'd still want this."

"Thank you," he says, bringing it to his lips for a sip.

"You're welcome." She squeezes my shoulder. "Good to see you, Anabelle."

I feel a little uncomfortable at having jumped sides and give her an awkward smile. "You too."

She barrels out of the room much like she barreled in.

"Don't do that," Asher says to me in a commanding voice.

Everyone at the table stills, including me.

I turn my head and look at him. "Don't do what?"

"Don't be uncomfortable because you're sitting here at the table eating rather than serving us." He spreads some honey on his toast.

"You can't just command me not to be uncomfortable, Asher."

I hear a snort across the table and look over to see Sid with his fist to his mouth, trying not to laugh. Kol is watching our interaction intently.

"There's no reason for you to feel weird."

I have no problem with Asher bossing me around and being domineering in the bedroom, but he can't control my feelings. I set down my cutlery. "That's not how it works. You don't just decree something, and people suddenly change how they feel about it."

"Why should you feel weird about it? You're here because I want you here."

I huff. "Did you forget that not that long ago you were treating me like shit and doing everything in your power to embarrass and humiliate me, and everyone in this manor knows it?"

"She's got you there," Sid says.

Asher whips his head in his direction and glares at him for a beat, then returns his attention to me.

"There are lots of ways you can dominate me, Asher, but emotions won't be one of them. I'm going to feel what I'm going to feel, and you can have an opinion on it, but you can't order me to change it and expect it to miraculously happen."

He frowns and takes my hand. "I just want you to feel like you belong at this table."

My head tilts. "I'm sure in time I will. Today is just not that day, okay?"

His jaw hardens for a beat, then he nods. "Okay. I'm sorry." He brings our joined hands to his lips and kisses my knuckles.

"All is forgiven." I give him a smile, then turn toward the sound of laughter across the table.

"Never thought I'd see the day," Sid says, shaking his head at us.

"What?" Asher drops my hand and goes back to eating his breakfast.

"The day you listened to a woman," Sid says. "Hell, anyone for that matter."

"Must be one helluva voodoo pussy," Kol says.

"Don't." Asher whips up out of his chair and pins Kol with a stare.

Kol raises his hands in front of himself.

"I have some news," Nero says, and I can tell he's trying to change the subject.

I shoot him a grateful smile as Asher slowly sits back down.

"You're all going to get to meet Maude at the masquerade ball, then I'm going to ask her to marry me."

I smile wide at Nero, but I'm the only one around the table who seems happy about this news.

"What's the hurry?" Kol asks. "She knocked up?"

Nero glares at him. "No, she's not knocked up. I love her, that's the hurry."

I smile at Nero, and he seems to look grateful for it when he notices. He then looks at Asher. "I know her background check came back clean, otherwise you would've already told me to stop seeing her." It's clear that he wants the approval of his eldest brother.

Asher sips his coffee. "How do you know I ran a background check on her?"

Nero scoffs. "Because I know you."

Asher shrugs. "Just because it came back clean doesn't mean there aren't any skeletons in her closet that wouldn't show up on a background check."

He rolls his eyes. "Well, she and her mom and sister will be at the ball as my guests, so you can make your determination there. But unless there's a major red flag, I'm asking her."

I don't know what masquerade ball he's talking about. Asher hasn't mentioned anything about it to me. If he were planning to take me, wouldn't he have mentioned something by now?

Asher doesn't say anything, instead finishing his green juice before looking at me. "You done? I need to get ready for the day and get into my office. It's an exciting day for me today."

"What have you got going on?" Sid asks.

Asher grins at me when he says, "Today is the day I get to fire Preston Wallace from the board of his own company."

CHAPTER
THIRTY-SIX

ASHER

I close the office door behind Anabelle. "If you hated eating with my brothers that much, we can have breakfast in my room from now on."

She's been quiet since we left breakfast, and I can't figure out why. Did my brothers make her uncomfortable? Was it the little tiff we had about me trying to control her emotions? I can't be sure.

A crease forms between her eyebrows. "What? No, it was fine. A little uncomfortable at first, but it got better."

"What's going on then?" I take her waist and pull her toward me. She's wearing a navy blue dress with white polka dots that flares out at the waist and ends at her knees.

"Nothing, what do you mean?" Her lips say that, but the way she's ever so subtly pulling away from my embrace tells me I'm not imagining things.

"You've been quiet since we left the dining room."

She rolls her eyes at me, and it makes me want to drag her over my knee and spank her ass until it turns red. "You've barely seen me. I went to my room after we ate so I could get ready. We've walked through the manor, and here we are."

"Doesn't matter, I can tell something is running through this gorgeous head of yours." I tap her temple with my finger. "Now what is it?"

She sighs and pulls away from me. "It's silly. Or maybe it's not, I don't know. I don't know what this is, so maybe that's the real issue."

I frown. "Keep going."

Anabelle bites her bottom lip. "Nero mentioned something about a masquerade ball. It seemed like it's a big deal."

I push my hands into my pockets to keep from reaching for her. "It is, I guess. It's an annual event that Voss Enterprises holds to raise money for the charitable portion of our business, but why would that make you want to pull away from me?"

She fists her hands at her sides. "Are you going with Madeline Ridgeway? I know you took her to some other event not that long ago."

"Why would you think I'm bringing Madeline?" My head tilts as I study her shifting in place, seeming less sure of herself.

"I don't know... you haven't mentioned anything to me about the ball, and I assume you would have if you wanted me to go with you. You just said yourself that it's a big deal... maybe you want to bring her. She's a big deal in social circles. Maybe the two of you... you know." Her arms flail wildly in front of her.

It's then I realize that she doesn't get it. I step up to her and take her chin, forcing her to look up at me. "I will not be taking Madeline. I'll be taking you. I haven't mentioned it for no other reason than I have a thousand other things going on that need my attention, and the fact that you even think I might take another woman tells me you don't understand that since the second you walked into my office and insisted there was something you could do to keep your family estate, I've been obsessed with you."

She swallows hard, looking up at me with wide eyes.

"And not the boyish kind of obsession where I think about you as I lie in bed at night. The kind of obsession that permeates my thoughts all day. The kind of obsession that won't even let me think of being intimate with another woman." I let my hand drop from her face and push it through my hair. "Do you know why I was drunk the day you ran into me on the path near the family graveyard? Besides it being the anniversary of my bastard father's death?"

She shakes her head. "No."

"Because it was a sex club night, and I had no interest in fucking anyone. No one. On the night that I was looking to find a distraction in anyone's body, all I could think about was you. You and what a fucking temptation you are. You and how young you are and how I should just send you home to your estate and call off our whole deal. You and how no matter what, I couldn't stop thinking about you, wanting to know more about you, wanting to fuck that sweet cunt of yours."

Her mouth falls open, and I don't miss the way she presses her thighs together.

"The only reason I asked Madeline to that event was to try to push you away. Nothing happened between us, and nothing will ever again." I push my hands into her hair on either side of her face. "You have ruined me for anyone else, Anabelle Boudreaux. It's you or no one."

She sucks in a breath and tears glisten in her eyes. Happy tears, I hope. I press my lips to hers, and the feeling of rightness, of coming home settles into my bones.

Before we can get too carried away, the phone on her desk rings. She pulls away, and I settle my forehead on hers.

"I should get that," she whispers.

I pull back and stare at her. "Not until I know that you get it."

She smiles at me. "I get it, Asher. And I feel the same."

Christ, this woman. She'll be the death of me.

I sit in my chair and dial up Preston Wallace. This is the first time I've ever been happy about firing someone.

"Preston Wallace," he answers.

"It's Asher," I announce myself, although he already knows it's me.

"What do you want?"

"Well, I wanted to inform you that your services are no longer needed." I tap my fingers along the desk like they're doing a happy dance.

"What? You have no authority." His tone is bitter, and I knew he never did keep track of his shit. The man thought he was golden sitting at the top of his company, ready to reign when his old man died.

"Oh I do. I own over half the company now. We're making some cuts so apologies, but the first one is to you."

"You can't do that!"

"I just did," I say, the smile growing the angrier he becomes.

"My dad will never allow—."

"Has no control over it. I have all the control now Preston. So be a good boy and pack your cardboard box. Security is waiting outside the door for you." Something hard smashes against the wall. "I hope that was a personal item. I'd hate to bill you for destruction." Keeping my voice even-keeled is hard when I want to tell him exactly why he's getting what he deserves.

"You're an asshole."

"I know."

"This isn't going to stand! There's no way!"

I shrug although he doesn't see me. "Don't make this harder than it needs to be for yourself."

"You'll get yours, Voss, just wait."

"I don't think so." There's a knock on his door echoing through the receiver. "Now answer that and be civil so they don't have to throw you out on your ass. Have a nice life, Preston."

"Fuck off, Voss."

I laugh and hang up the phone with a grin. Anabelle swings around in her seat on the other side of the office, looking at me with concern.

"Why are you looking at me like that? You should feel as jubilant as I do right now. Preston Wallace finally got what was coming to him."

"I'm glad about that," she says. "I'm just worried there will be some kind of backlash for you, and it will all be because of me."

"There's no backlash, Anabelle. What I did was legal, and even if it weren't, let's be honest, I could make any problems go away."

"If you're sure..."

"I'm sure."

"Okay, fuck Preston Wallace then."

I chuckle. I love Anabelle's dirty mouth on the rare occasion it makes an appearance. My dick stirs in my pants. "I have a video conference call in five minutes. What do you say we celebrate?"

One of the other great things about Anabelle is that she can always tell when I'm slipping into dominant mode. I don't even have to tell her, she just seems to know. And it's obvious to me that she can tell now too, with the way her back arches a bit.

"What did you have in mind, sir?"

I grin at her. "Crawl over to me."

As I knew would be the case, there's zero hesitation from her. She simply slides off her chair onto all fours and crawls across the large room to me. I watch her every movement the way a lion might watch a zebra while stalking it.

By the time she's near my desk, my cock is rock-hard and straining the fabric of my pants. I use my feet to roll my chair back a bit.

"Now get under the desk."

"Yes, sir." She crawls into the space between my desk and me and settles on her knees, awaiting further instructions.

I reach down and run my hand over her head a few times as I might praise a pet. "Now take out my cock."

She licks her lips. "Yes, sir."

She undoes my belt, then the button on my dress pants before she slides down the zipper. It takes some work, but she manages to get my boxers down enough to rest under my balls. I'm sure she's expecting me to order her to give me head, but instead I let her sit there for a few minutes while I pull up the email on my computer that has the link to the meeting I'm due in.

Her breathing picks up, and the scent of her arousal fills my nostrils. My dick twitches, and she makes a small noise in the back of her throat. I grin as I click the link to enter the video chat.

We all say a brief hello, then I get things started. "Joseph, why don't you start us off and go through the pertinent parts of the latest report?"

"Sure thing." He starts his monologue.

I hit the mute button. I keep my gaze on the computer screen pretending to be completely enthralled by the fourth quarter forecasts. "Now suck my cock, pet."

"Yes, sir."

Her tiny hand wraps around the base of my cock, though not all the way around, and her lips slide over the head. I groan as the wet heat seeps in, and she uses her tongue to increase the sensation.

The background noise of Anabelle's slurping and choking on my cock has me hard as steel while attempting to keep my face impassive.

When Joseph is finished with his report, I place my hand on the top of Anabelle's head while she's on a downstroke. She understands that means she has to stop for a moment and be quiet.

I unmute myself. "Thanks, Joseph. Those forecasts look good. Sam, what do you have?" I mute myself again as Sam starts his report on the risk assessment of another company we're thinking of taking over.

I'm not in the mood to prolong things anymore. With my eyes still on the screen, I say, "Make me come, Anabelle. And if you do it quickly, I'll reward you when I'm off this call."

She knows just what to do. She sucks on my balls while twisting her fist on the end of my dick. It doesn't take long before I'm teetering on the edge of explosion.

"Fuck, I'm gonna come."

Anabelle returns her mouth to the head of my cock, and her hand jerks my shaft. It's a Herculean effort to keep my face passive, but if anyone else in the meeting suspects something, they don't let on.

I groan and buck my hips, emptying myself down her throat. Chancing a glance, I watch as she licks her lips and wipes her chin with the back of her hand.

She'll be rewarded greatly.

The moment the conference call is done, I close out of the video chat, hoist her up onto my desk, and eat her pussy until her voice is hoarse from screaming my name.

CHAPTER
THIRTY-SEVEN

ANABELLE

Every day with Asher just gets better and better. And though I try to stop myself from falling for him, it's impossible at this point. After his speech in his office last week, I was a goner. Sometimes late at night, I lay awake and wonder, could this really be our happily ever after? Can two people so opposite from one another find love so true? Time will tell, I suppose.

We spend our days working side by side and our nights tangled up in the sheets. The only downside has been that I've had to lie and tell him I'm going for a run when really what I'm doing is running through the maze to try to tend to the rose bush. I think I'm really making progress. There are new buds, and the roses look healthier and more vibrant.

Lately I've been talking to the roses as though they're Asher's deceased mother, telling the plant how I'm falling for Asher and all the things he makes me feel. It's silly, but it's working, so I keep doing it.

Tomorrow night is the masquerade ball, and I'm as nervous as I am excited. Asher bought me a gorgeous yellow ball gown to wear, and I can't wait to spend the night on his arm.

I'm reading in Asher's bed when he comes out of the ensuite, having just had a shower. He doesn't bother putting anything on before he slides under the covers. I love his confidence as much as I love his body.

He picks up his own book from the nightstand, as has become our routine over the past week, and we read in silence for a bit. But as always, he proves distracting.

I shut my book and set it on the nightstand. "Can I ask you something that's been niggling on my mind?"

He gives me an amused grin and arches a brow. "Niggling?"

"It's a word." I swat his chest.

He uses the opportunity to tug me closer to him. "By all means. Ask away."

I trail a finger down his hard chest. "Why were you so mean to me at first? You said that you were into me the first day I came here, but you were so mean. Not just that day, but for many days after that."

It's the one thing I keep running through my mind, the only reason I've held myself back from completely and utterly falling for him.

Asher frowns, running the pad of his thumb over my bottom lip. "Because I knew you were special the moment I laid eyes on you, and you represented everything I couldn't ever have."

My chest tightens. "Why would you assume you couldn't ever have me?"

"Because you're too young. Because I'm not deserving. I'm not what you'd call a good man. I'm damaged. But when I'm with you... you give me hope that I can be more than just those things. At least with you."

He cups my face and kisses me. His pace is languid and thorough and doesn't feel like any other kiss we've shared. I pour all my emotions into the kiss, hoping that he can feel how much I care for him, how much he means to me.

Asher trails kisses down the line of my jaw, softly, sweetly. This is a side I haven't seen from him in bed yet, and I savor every second of it. His hands drift down to the hem of my tank, and he pulls it up and over my head, tossing it somewhere on the floor beside the bed. Then his lips find my nipple, and he sucks it, twirling his tongue around the peak. My breath hitches in my throat, and my hand dives into his mop of hair, threading through the tussled strands.

He worships my breasts for what feels like hours, unhurried and content. When he turns me so my back hits the mattress, he trails his tongue on the underside of my breast while he tugs my sleep shorts down my legs.

"I'm so happy I found you," he says as he dips lower until his tongue sweeps between my folds.

He brings me to the brink of orgasm with his mouth before he's moving back up my body and sliding inside me. Our gazes lock and hold as the slow, steady roll of his hips pushes me higher and higher.

My arms are wrapped around his neck, and I play with the hair at the back of his head. Neither of us looks away from the other, and it feels like so much more than our bodies are joined. It feels as though our souls are entwined, braided together, never to be torn apart.

My climax builds, brick upon brick, layer upon layer, until my orgasm rolls through me like a thundercloud, crackling with power. Asher comes at the same time as I do, pressing his lips to mine to swallow my moan until the rhythm of his hips slows to nothing.

He pulls back a bit and gazes at me, brushing the hair off my temple. There's so much in his eyes that when he places a chaste kiss on my lips and pulls out of me to roll off the bed, I'm surprised. After what we just shared, I thought we'd bask in the afterglow a little longer.

He doesn't say anything as he heads to his walk-in closet, still nude. I can't help but admire the bunching and flexing of his ass, even if I did just have an orgasm. When he returns, he's holding a white box. I know it's not a ring, and quite frankly I'd be shocked if it were.

"What's this?" I ask.

"I bought you something. I was going to give it to you tomorrow night before the ball, but I want you to have time to think about it. It needs to be your decision."

My forehead wrinkles. "I don't understand."

He takes the lid off the box and inside, nestled in black velvet, is a thick diamond choker necklace. My hand flies up to my mouth.

"You remember the collar you wore in the sex club?"

I nod, my gaze flicking from him to the necklace.

"This is a day collar. Something you can wear in front of others, outside of the club. It's a symbol of our connection and of our Dom/Sub relationship. Think of it as a promise or a contract between us, that there will be no other, that we are committed."

My heart swells in my chest, and I can't help smiling. "I don't have to think about it, Asher. I accept."

The twinkle in his eyes when he smiles at me is more beautiful than the necklace. I can't imagine how much this exquisite piece of jewelry must have cost him.

"Thank you." He kisses me. When he pulls away, he takes the collar from the box and sets it aside. He nods toward my neck. "May I?"

I turn and hold my hair up so that he can fasten the collar. Once he does, I let my hair fall down and turn back to him. "I want to see what it looks like."

His deep blue eyes shine like the sun glinting off the ocean. "It looks perfect."

I leap off the bed and rush over to the standing full-length mirror, gasping when I see the collar on me. I'm still naked and somehow that suits it. My hand trails up to my neck. The collar is thick enough that it covers almost the entirety of my neck, and the diamonds glisten in the dim light of his room. "It's beautiful."

Asher comes up behind me in the mirror and sets his hands on my shoulders. "I realize you won't wear this for everyday life. I'll get you another single strand of diamonds for that. But I thought this would be perfect for tomorrow night, and other nights like it in the future."

The mention of a future makes my stomach feel as if it's full of champagne bubbles.

"I love it. Thank you." I turn and wrap my arms around his neck, drawing him down for a kiss.

It doesn't take long for the press of our naked bodies to register and for things to become heated. Unlike our first joining tonight, Asher reminds me who's in charge when he draws two more orgasms out of me.

CHAPTER
THIRTY-EIGHT

ASHER

I wave off the driver and help Anabelle from the back of the limo myself when we arrive at the venue the night of the masquerade ball. It's overcast and drizzling this evening, but thankfully, the drop-off space is under a large portico to keep us dry.

Anabelle looks unbelievable in her yellow gown. It's off-the-shoulder with large puffy sleeves that start halfway down her upper arm. The front dips just enough to hint at her cleavage, and the bottom half of the dress is form-fitting with a large slit up the front, but she still looks classy and refined. And the best part is the diamond collar around her neck. The one she accepted from me.

You'd have thought it was an engagement ring for how nervous I was before I asked her to wear it. When she accepted, I felt lighter somehow, as though everything was falling into place. Places in my soul I didn't even know were empty gaping wounds, she's filled up and healed.

"You ready to do this?" I ask her.

She looks up at me through the gold mask I had made for her. It doesn't go as low on her face as mine does, but the outer edge is surrounded in diamonds, and the mask itself has swirls and filigree on it. I'm wearing my golden mask that resembles a bear. Maybe slightly too ferocious for an event such as this one, but it's what I'm most comfortable in.

"Still nervous. But ready."

I trace the bottom edge of her mask with my forefinger. "You'll be fine. Just stick with me."

She nods, and I hold my elbow out for her so she can loop her arm through. When we enter the building, there's a red carpet with a backdrop for the charity. There's no press here. Only our own photographers so that we can control which pictures are released.

"Let's get our picture taken." I lead her over, and we pose for the photographer.

Once we're done there, I lead us into the ballroom.

"Oh wow," Anabelle says with wonder in her voice.

My chest puffs out a bit over the fact that she's obviously impressed by how things have been put together here tonight. The décor is on par with any top celebrity or multi-millionaire's wedding, only my brothers and I have used our own money for this purpose. We want everything raised here tonight to go directly to our charitable efforts.

I hate when I go to an event, and they've clearly spent a third of what they're bringing in to wine and dine money from the attendees.

"What kind of charity work does your organization do?" Anabelle asks, turning to me.

"We try to spread the wealth around, so each year we have a different focus. Over the last couple of years, we've worked with organizations who help the homeless, some that have to do with illiteracy, and a few that run breakfast programs in schools. But we always include women's shelters and some organizations that help abused children."

Anabelle gives me a sad smile and squeezes my hand. "Will we have the opportunity to dance tonight, or will you have to make the rounds the entire night?"

I turn her toward me. "Do you really think I'm not going to take the opportunity to dance with you this evening when you look like that?"

Though I can only see part of her cheeks because of the mask, I'm pretty sure they pinken.

"Good. I've been looking forward to dancing with you."

"And I'm the only one you'll be dancing with tonight. Remember that."

She rolls her eyes. "Should we go find Nero? Meet his potential fiancée?"

I huff out a long breath. "Don't remind me of his insane intentions for tonight."

Anabelle sets her hand on my chest. "Asher, give the woman the benefit of the doubt, at least until you meet her."

"She probably doesn't deserve it," I grumble.

Anabelle's hands move to her hips. "What would you say to your brothers if they said something similar about me?"

"I'd tell them to mind their own fucking business."

"So maybe you need to take your own advice." She pins me with a stare.

I know she's right, though I don't want to concede. "I've been looking out for my brothers since we were kids."

Anabelle's face softens, and she traces my jawline with her finger. "But you're all adults now, and your father is long gone. Maybe it's time to let the reins go just a little."

It's a hard habit to break.

When we were kids, and my father got angry, I'd often take the blame for things my brothers had done so that they wouldn't have to deal with his form of corporal punishment. As it was with my mother, taking his fists myself was easier than watching him hurt the ones I love. That only worked until my brothers got old enough to understand what I was doing, though.

The instinct to protect them is as strong today as it was when we were children. But Anabelle's right. Nero's a smart man, the most intelligent of the four of us, and I have to trust that if he sees something good in this girl, it's for good reason.

"All right, fine. If we must. Let's head over to our table. They're probably somewhere over there."

She nods and loops her arm through mine again. We make our way through the crowd, and despite my mask, we have to stop a few times in order to say hello to people. I introduce Anabelle simply by her name, unsure whether to refer to her as my girlfriend or what.

What we have feels like so much more than that, especially now that she's wearing my collar.

When we finally get to the other side of the ballroom where the tables are set up, I spot Nero standing near our table with a red-haired woman in a navy blue dress and a silver mask.

I take a deep breath and prepare myself, remembering what Anabelle said. "Nero."

He turns and smiles. He has his raven's mask on that he uses at the club. I realize for the first time since he first mentioned Maude that she may change things for him. Will he invite her to join the fun—that would certainly be his style—or is she the kind of woman who would be appalled by such a thing?

Nero was still partaking in the fun at the club when he first mentioned her, but he wasn't at the last event for anything other than observing. Something I didn't give too much thought to at the time since that's his kink, but maybe there was more to it.

He smiles and shakes my hand, then directs his attention to Anabelle, moving in for a hug. "You look beautiful, Anabelle."

When my mood sours at the sight of another man's hands on her, I have to remind myself that he's my brother. Unlike him, I'm not fond of sharing.

"Thanks, Nero. You look very handsome." They separate, and Anabelle sticks her hand out toward the woman beside him. "You must be Maude. It's great to finally meet you."

She smiles and shakes Anabelle's hand. "Thank you. Great to meet you as well."

"Maude, this is my brother Asher." Nero gestures to me.

I nod and reluctantly stick out my own hand. "Pleasure."

"Likewise," she says as she takes my hand.

There's a beat of awkward silence before Anabelle rescues us. "So, Maude, are you used to these kinds of big events?"

"I've been to some before, but nothing this extravagant." She glances around. I don't like the way her eyes gleam, as though she's tallying everything up and figuring out what it might cost.

"Me either. It's a little overwhelming." Anabelle laughs, and Maude just gives her a small smile.

My eyes narrow. I don't care if it will piss Nero off, but if this woman gives Anabelle attitude, I'm going to say something.

"So what do you do for a living, Anabelle?" Maude asks.

"Oh..." She glances at me. "Well at the moment, I'm actually working as Asher's assistant."

It's clear to me Anabelle's a little embarrassed to admit that, probably wondering how it will look since we're here together.

"I see." Maude looks between the two of us. "Well, you're still young. Plenty of time to find yourself." Again with that small smirk.

"And what do you do, Maude?" I ask.

Nero must sense my irritation because I notice his knuckles whiten around his drink.

"I went to Harvard and earned my degree in economics, and I work for the state now."

So she's smart. That might explain one reason Nero is so head over heels for her.

"Very impressive," Anabelle says because that's the type of person she is, happy for other people's success. I get the distinct feeling that Maude is not that kind of person.

"Where are Sid and Kol?" I ask, changing the subject.

"They went to get a drink before we had to sit for dinner." Nero sips his cocktail, seeming to relax a bit. "Actually, here they come."

Sid and Kol join our group. Neither of them has brought a date tonight, which isn't surprising to me.

"Anabelle, you look lovely tonight," Sid says, leaning in to give her a hug.

Kol simply nods in her direction, acknowledging her presence. That's about all I'd expect from him. "I fucking hate these things." He pulls at the collar of his tuxedo and takes a drink from his glass.

Obviously they've already met Maude, because Nero doesn't do any introductions. I'll have to ask later what their impressions of her are.

The six of us make conversation for a while. I swear I spot Maude checking out Kol a few times from behind her mask, but there's no way that can be right.

Eventually, I turn to Anabelle. "Let's go grab a drink from the bar."

"Okay. It was good to meet you, Maude. See you guys in a bit."

I don't waste any time pulling her away from the group.

"See, that wasn't too bad, was it?" Anabelle says as we move through the crowd.

"Speak for yourself. I don't like her."

She sighs. "Asher..."

"I said *I* didn't like her. I didn't say *he* couldn't like her."

She smiles and pushes up on her tiptoes to kiss my jawline. "That's more like it. Now let's go enjoy our evening."

I plan to do just that because I can already tell that tonight is just further confirmation of how well Anabelle fits into my life.

CHAPTER
THIRTY-NINE

ANABELLE

Though I was really nervous about tonight, I'm having a great time.

I was worried that people would look at me and wonder why Asher is with me or think our age difference is inappropriate, but everyone has been really nice. The fact that we're all wearing masks helps, I think, because it's difficult to tell my age, but nonetheless, I don't feel completely out of place, which was my worry.

Kol even says a few words to me throughout the dinner. I have to count that as a win. Sid is his usual charming self, and Nero does his best to include me in the conversation.

Asher doesn't say much unless he's spoken to directly, but he's constantly touching my leg under the table or putting his arm around my shoulders. I know his silence probably has more to do with him getting used to the idea that he has to let Nero live his life and less to do with me.

Near the end of the dinner, the event planner comes to the table and tells Asher that it's time for him to deliver his speech.

Asher nods and turns to me. "I'll be back in a bit. Stay with my brothers."

I nod.

"Wish me luck?"

"He doesn't need luck. He's done about a thousand of these since the old man died," Sid says.

It's jarring to hear their father mentioned so casually. I try to keep my face blank, so as not to let on that I know anything about what went on when they were children.

Asher steps up on the stage and takes the mic, introducing himself. He starts in about why we're all here tonight and the importance of the work that the charities who will benefit from the fundraising efforts tonight are doing.

It's a side of him I rarely see. He's charming yet powerful, persuasive yet not heavy-handed. Everyone in the large ballroom hangs on his every word, and when the speech concludes, everyone applauds loudly.

I realize that the feeling in my chest is pride at what this man overcame that hardly anyone in this room knows about. Sure, it informs who he is, but he wasn't crippled by his past. He rose above. And pride at the fact that he's mine.

As soon as he's close to returning to our table, I pop up from my seat, embracing him once he makes it over to me. "That was a wonderful speech."

He pulls back and kisses me. "Do you want to go share that dance now?"

I look behind us and see that indeed, people are making their way onto the dance floor. "Absolutely."

Neither of us bids goodbye to anyone at the table as I let him lead me onto the dance floor. When Asher takes me in his arms, I realize there's nowhere else I'd rather be. I have fallen for this man despite my best efforts, but I think that perhaps he's fallen for me too.

He glides me around the dance floor, and even though we're in a room filled with people, it feels intimate somehow. The heat of his hand on my back through the fabric of my dress permeates my entire body. We spin and rotate, maintaining eye contact, and it almost feels as though we're having a conversation without speaking.

The music swells, and I feel it in my chest, as though my heart is near to bursting as I realize how much this man means to me. How the idea of the two of us not being together isn't something I can comprehend any longer.

The song ends, and we stand in place, staring at each other.

Asher gently slides my mask up so that it sits on my hairline and cups my face with one hand. "Anabelle, I—"

"Asher!" Nero comes up behind him and stands at our side. "Shit, sorry for interrupting."

Oh my god, I think he was about to tell me he loves me.

Asher's jaw tightens, and he glares at Nero. "What is it?" he says, his voice as sharp as the lash of a whip.

"I need to know what you think of Maude. I'm nervous as hell about later, and I need to know you're okay with it and have no real objections."

Some of the tension eases out of Asher's body. "I think you should do whatever you think is right. You're a grown man and can make that decision for yourself."

Nero's smile is nearly blinding. This feels like a moment that should be between the two of them.

"I'm going to run to the ladies' room and let you two talk. I'll meet you back at the table?"

Asher places a chaste kiss on my lips, then leans in to whisper thank you in my ear.

I pull my mask back into place and give him a smile before making my way off the dance floor. I find the bathroom easily enough, and when I come back out, one of the event workers is lingering in the hallway and smiles when she sees me.

"Excuse me, miss? There's a gentleman who asked to see you. He's down the hall and take a left."

"Oh, okay, thank you." I smile at her, then glance to my left down the hall and my right toward the ballroom.

What is Asher getting at? Is this some surprise he has planned? Or maybe we can slip away already?

With anticipation making my tummy fizz, I head down the long hallway that runs the length of the ballroom and turn left like she said. I frown when I don't see Asher. In fact, this end of the hall is much narrower, and there's no one down here that I can see.

"Hello?" I walk down the hallway. Maybe he's in one of the smaller rooms that runs off this hallway? "Asher?"

But all the doors are closed. Until I reach the last one, and I see light escaping out from under the bottom.

With a smile, I gently push open the door. "Asher, what's going—"

A rush of air leaves my mouth as I'm yanked inside and pushed up against the wall.

"Shut up, bitch. It's not your precious Asher."

I have to blink several times to make sure I'm seeing what I think I'm seeing. A man dressed in a tuxedo has one hand pressed across my sternum and in the other is a gun that he has pressed at my temple. It takes me a moment to realize that he looks familiar, even with his black mask on, and ice travels through my veins, freezing me in place.

Preston Wallace.

A cold, calculated gleam fills his eyes. "I see you've realized who I am, Anabelle." He says my name with a sneer.

"What are you doing?" I manage to say past my throat that feels as if it's closing up.

"The mighty Asher Voss thought he could just fuck me over, and there would be no consequences?" His head arches back as he laughs.

I use the opportunity to glance behind him and see that we're in a small meeting room. There's a long conference table in the center of the room with chairs around it and another door at the far end of the room.

I don't know how, but I have to get out of here.

"There will be consequences all right. He thinks he can take over and kick me out of my own company?" He's shouting in my face now, clearly unhinged. "He'll pay. He took what was mine, and now I'm taking what's his."

He presses harder against my sternum and up into the base of my neck, constricting my airway. Gasping, I pull at his forearm to no avail. He seems to enjoy the fact that I'm fighting him, based on the expression on his face.

He's not budging so I do the only think I can think of—I bring my knee up and hit him in the groin. The impact is dulled because of the ball gown I'm wearing, but I manage to make contact enough that he folds over with a grunt.

When I push, he stumbles back enough that I'm able to run around him, bounding toward the door that leads out into the hallway since it's the closest. I'm about to grasp for the handle when his hand is in my hair, yanking me back. I cry out at the pain in my scalp and stumble backward into his chest.

He wraps an arm around my waist, holding me there. "You're going to pay for that. Maybe I'll keep you awake rather than knock you out when I have my way with you."

I swallow back the bile traveling up my throat.

"Let's go. You're going to be a good girl and walk with me out to the limo. I'll have this gun pointed at you under my jacket, so don't even think about trying anything. You'll bleed out before anyone can save you."

Tears prick my eyes, but I nod frantically.

Preston forces me to walk with him, my arm wrapped around his, away from the direction we came in. He must be parked in the back.

When we get outside, it's raining harder, and I'm soaked in seconds. He rushes me toward a waiting limo, and when he uses one hand to open the door, I struggle a bit in his hold. It's not enough to really try to get away—I don't stand a chance since he has a gun. It's just enough to be difficult and slip the mask off my face so it lands on the ground. I have no doubt that Asher will be looking for me soon. If I can leave him any small clue as to my whereabouts, I'm going to do it.

Preston pushes me inside the limo, and I slide as far over as I can toward the opposite door.

I just have to survive this. No matter what he does, I have to survive so I can make it back to Asher. I can deal with the fallout of whatever sick things Preston has planned after.

Survival. That's all that matters.

Preston gets in and slams the door closed, then presses a button I assume must let him communicate with the driver since the partition is up between us. "Let's head to the airport."

The vehicle moves, and I look out through the back window, tears in my eyes as the distance between the danger I'm presently in and the safety Asher provides increases.

"Trying for one last look?" Preston's caustic laugh grates at my nerves, and there's nothing I'd rather do than launch myself at him and claw out his eyes. "Maybe if I'm feeling generous, I'll tape it when I fuck you before I kill you and send him a copy." A self-satisfied gleam fills his eyes, and he leans back in his seat with a grin. "Yeah, I think that sounds like the perfect idea. Something to remember you by."

"You're never going to get away with this. Why would you throw your life away for revenge?"

His eyes narrow on me, and he shoves the gun up under my chin, gripping my one hand in his other hand so hard that I cry out. I suck in a breath and hold it, squeezing my eyes shut.

"You should have told me you were his! I would've just knocked you out and fucked you in the back of my car. You're not worth the trouble you've caused me."

It takes me a moment to register that the sudden sting of pain in my temple is because he's pistol-whipped me. I feel something trickle down my face and assume it must be blood.

"But I'll get my revenge. Oh yes, I'm sure he'll love that tape I'll send him, and when he's never able to find you again, it'll drive him mad. Meanwhile, I'll just disappear, never to be seen or heard from again. That's the benefit of having endless wealth."

Tears track down my face, and my chest constricts. It's hard to breathe as I think of what it would do to Asher to see a tape like that. I don't know that he'd ever recover. Would he just become vengeful and eventually let his despair and hatred eat away at him from the inside?

I can't let that happen. No matter what, I can't let that happen.

Cowering in the corner, I try to get my bearings. That knock to the head still has me seeing stars.

The limo moves along for a while, then it comes to a stop. I can tell from the window that it looks like we're on a highway and stuck in a traffic jam. Maybe this will buy me some time to figure something out or for Asher to find me.

I could try to jump out the door now that we're not moving. But Preston is unhinged, and I have no doubt that he might jump out behind me and still try to shoot me. He seems like a man who has nothing left to lose.

I can tell that he's getting aggravated by the delay. He keeps shifting in his seat until he finally punches the intercom button with his finger. "What's going on?"

The driver's voice comes over the speaker. "I think it's some kind of accident, sir. I can see lights ahead, and no one is moving."

It wouldn't surprise me with how hard it's raining now. Maybe this is the opening I need.

CHAPTER
FORTY

ASHER

Nero is smiling and looking about as genuinely happy as I can recall ever seeing him.

Anabelle is right—I can't take this from him. Even if I am right, and there's something shady about Maude, I have to trust he'll figure it out in time. And if he doesn't... well, that's what a good prenup is for.

"I promise you this is the right decision." Nero clamps me on the shoulder.

I nod, not willing to go as far as to agree with him. "Do you know what you're going to do?"

He grins. "I got a room for us nearby. I've arranged for the suite to be filled with flowers and some desserts. I plan to share a bubble bath with her and surprise her there and ask her to marry me."

"You're a regular Prince Charming."

He rolls his eyes. "I have a feeling you'd do the same for Anabelle."

I don't tell him that I think he might be right. The idea of making a lasting commitment with her has crossed my mind more than once lately. But I don't want to scare her off. She's fourteen years younger than I am. She still has so much more of life to discover and live. I've already had the benefit of doing all that. I'd hate for her to ever think I held her back because she committed to me too soon, for her to end up resenting me.

The collar is a step in that direction. Maybe in a couple of years, I'll broach the subject of marriage.

"Well, good luck." I shake Nero's hand and clamp him on the shoulder.

"Thanks, big brother. Listen, if you don't mind, I'm going to take off now. I'm so nervous I just want to get this thing going."

"Sure thing. The rest of us can handle things here."

"Awesome." He doesn't wait a beat, heading off the dance floor to go find Maude.

With mixed feelings, I head back to the table to wait for Anabelle to return from the bathroom. Sid and Kol are still there.

I'm not surprised that Kol is at the table. He hates these things, hates having to have mindlessly chitchat. But Sid would usually be making the rounds by now, using his charm to get people to part with their money.

A lot of people view Sid as the tamest of us all, but sometimes I think they have it all wrong—that he might actually be the most dangerous of the four of us. The true essence of a wolf in sheep's clothing.

"Little brother find you to get your blessing?" Sid says, then sips his drink.

I take a seat beside him. "He did."

"You give it to him?" Kol asks.

"I did."

Kol's eyebrows raise up to his hairline.

"I don't feel right about it, but he can make decisions for himself. He's an adult," I say.

Sid laughs. "This must be the Anabelle effect we're seeing."

"Guess so. Who knew some good pussy could act like a Valium?" Kol says with a smirk because he knows his statement will piss me off.

I narrow my eyes at him. "Don't start."

"I'm just busting your balls. To be honest, I like her. She doesn't take your shit," Kol says.

Not unless we're in a scene. I smirk.

Speaking of Anabelle, she should have been back by now. I frown and look over the crowd.

"Anabelle didn't come by here while I was talking to Nero, did she?" I ask my brothers.

They both shake their heads.

"Huh." I stand. "I'm going to go check the bar. If she comes back, tell her to wait here for me, okay?"

Kol gives me a salute as if I'm a drill sergeant because he's an asshole, but Sid simply nods, a look of concern on his face.

When I reach the bar, I don't see her there, so I do a quick sweep of the ballroom and don't find her, though it's possible I just missed her. I decide to check the bathroom.

I don't see her anywhere in the hallway, so I make my way into the ladies' room. A few of the women at the sinks give me a funny look, but when they realize it's me, they scurry out.

"Anabelle? You in here?"

There's no answer.

My heart rate speeds up as I step back out of the bathroom, whipping my head in both directions of the hallway. There's another ladies' washroom farther down and around the corner, and I decide to check that before I really start to panic. She's not there either.

Pulling my phone out of my pocket, I text Kol and Sid to meet me in the hallway. Nero is probably already gone, and there's no sense bothering him when I'm likely panicking for nothing.

Except deep down, I know I'm not.

I spy Kol and Sid running down the hall toward me, leaving people staring after them.

"What's going on?" Kol asks, and I see some of his military training kick in.

"Anabelle went to the bathroom, and she hasn't returned. I checked the ballroom and both bathrooms out here, and she's gone." I push a hand through my hair and grip the strands hard.

"Okay, first... there's no chance she just ran out on you? Did you guys have a fight or a disagreement? Did she seem off at all earlier tonight?" Kol asks.

I step toward him. "She didn't run off and leave me. Something's happened."

Sid steps between us. "Okay, if she's nowhere to be found, we have to assume that someone has taken her or hurt her, that it's not a medical emergency or something."

My chest squeezes at the idea of someone kidnapping her to do her harm.

"Let's split up and have one more look for her before we hit the panic button," Sid says. "Kol and I will look in here, and you check outside. Maybe she went to get some air."

We all glance at the pouring rain and know that's not likely, but it's the one place I haven't looked yet.

"Text if you guys find anything." I run toward the door as though my life depends on it, and in some ways, it feels like it does. Because if something has happened to Anabelle, I don't know how I would move on.

I push that thought from my head as I race out the entryway and under the portico. The two greeters are chatting and look startled when they see me. I probably look like a rabid animal.

"Have you seen a woman with a yellow dress come out here some time in the last twenty-five minutes?" I ask.

They shake their heads in unison.

"No, sorry," the one says.

I don't waste another word on them, running out from under the portico into the driving rain. "Anabelle!"

I don't know exactly what I'm looking for, but I keep shouting her name, running around the building. It's not until I'm on the opposite side of the building that I spot something gold on the walkway near where the driveway meets the curb—Anabelle's mask.

I'm soaked through as I pick it up, feeling as if someone has stuck an ice pick in my heart. Though I want to crumble and fall apart worrying about what might be happening to Anabelle, I can't allow that to happen. Instead, I let the rage take over.

How dare someone try to take what is mine?

I pull my phone from my pocket and fill Kol in on what I found. He tells me to meet him in the security office. I don't know where that is, but I'll find it.

I tug on the closest doors, finding them locked. They must be exit-only. In frustration, I let out a roar toward the sky, intent on destruction, then run around to the front of the building with the mask in hand. If this is the last piece of her I ever hold, I will rain down hellfire on whoever has hurt her.

The same two guys are standing at the entrance, looking at me wide-eyed as I approach.

"Where's the security office?" I demand.

"Um... I'll show you to it."

"Hurry."

I follow him there, and when I get inside, I find my two brothers already standing around a desk with a few monitors across it.

"Anything?" I push my way between them.

"He's just pulling it up for us based on where you found the mask," Kol says.

It takes another couple minutes for the security guy to find what we want. I spend the time pacing and dripping onto the floor, my hand pulling my hair tightly.

"Got it," the guy says, and I rush back over to stand behind him and watch.

My entire body goes numb as I watch a masked man I know is Preston Wallace drag Anabelle down the walkway. She struggles a bit before they reach the limo, and it seems as though she purposely dislodges her mask.

She did. For me to find.

"Good girl," I whisper.

Preston pushes her into the limo, and it drives away.

"How long ago was that?" Kol asks.

"About twenty-five minutes ago," the guy says.

My stomach sinks and leaches out onto the floor. Twenty-five minutes is plenty of time to kill someone, to rape them, to do any number of unspeakable things to them. My brothers and I share a look because we all know it firsthand.

"Hallway. Now." I don't bother looking to see if they follow me. I know they will. Outside the office, I whip around to face them both. "Where could he have taken her?"

Kol looks me dead in the eye. "If you were Preston, what would you do?"

I think about it for a moment. "Fly in and out of here. It's the fastest way to get the hell out of here and away from us because he has to know I'm coming after her."

"I'll call the airport we came into and see if his plane is there," Sid says, pulling his phone from his pocket and stepping off to the side.

"It could be a trap to get you to just do that. Maybe you're his real target for what you did to him," Kol says.

I have his tuxedo jacket in my hands and have him pressed up against the wall before I know it. Because he's said out loud what I've known all along. This is my fault. I couldn't leave it at just kicking the shit out of him, I had to humiliate him as well.

"I don't fucking care if it's a trap for me. He has Anabelle! I'm going to rip him to shreds, and I'm going to enjoy every moment. If he does anything to harm a hair on her head, I'll make it slow. He'll wish he never heard the last name Voss."

Kol, to his credit, doesn't fight me. "I'm just saying you need to go in there prepared, that's all."

I give him a small shove and let my hands drop. There's no way I can stand here any longer doing nothing while Anabelle is out there alone and afraid.

"His plane is there. I just talked to my pilot," Sid says, walking back over to us.

I nod. "Sid, you stay here and make sure he doesn't say a word about what he saw on that tape. Pay him whatever you need to. Get a copy of the video, then have the original destroyed. Then get back to the party and make the rounds. Make sure people see you. Kol, you're with me."

I know Kol has a gun on him—he always has a gun on him, and he's a good shot because of his time in the military.

They both nod.

"Let me know as soon as you locate her. I'll fill Nero in," Sid says.

I shake my head. "Don't. Let him have his night. If we really need him, then we'll call."

Sid's lips press together. I'm assuming he doesn't like my call, but he nods in agreement.

Thankfully, Kol has a place in the city, so he drove here rather than taking a limo like Anabelle and I did. He climbs in the driver's seat, and we're racing away within minutes.

"Put the airport in the GPS," he says, whipping out of the parking lot.

"You don't know how to fucking get there?" I glare at him.

"The weather is shit. That means slow-downs at best, accidents at worst. I want to see what the fastest route there is."

399

"Oh, okay. Good idea." I punch in the name of the private airport, and a bunch of potential routes come up.

The most direct route down the freeway is almost all marked in red.

Kol glances at it. "Must be an accident. Let's hope that's the route they took."

He selects the fastest route, which goes around the highway all together, and punches the gas.

WHEN WE REACH THE AIRPORT, Preston's plane is still there. I honestly don't know if it's a good or a bad thing.

"What if they're not headed here? What if he..." I can't even finish the words.

"He's coming here. He probably got stuck on the freeway. No way he'd kidnap her and leave his plane waiting for you to discover. He has to know you would find out it was him right away. It's not like you wouldn't have noticed that Anabelle disappeared. This plane is the only head start that he has."

He's right. Knowing that makes me feel a little better. Not a lot, but a little.

"What's the plan?" I ask Kol when he parks around the back of one of the hangars.

"Depends on what you want to do with Preston. You plan on calling the authorities on him?" Kol looks across the dim car at me.

I arch an eyebrow and give him a look that gets across my intentions.

"All right then. He'll have staff on his plane. Unless we plan on taking them all out, we need to ambush him before they get that far."

"What about the single lane in?" I say.

He nods. "That's our best bet. If I park my car on an angle there and lift the hood like it's broken down, the driver will have to stop because he won't be able to get past. You and I can wait in the ditches on either side of the road. As soon as the limo stops, we hop up, open the doors, and hope the element of surprise is in our favor."

Fuck. I squeeze my eyes shut for a moment. So much could go wrong with this plan. But what option do we have?

"If the doors are locked, which they probably will be, hit the window hard with the butt of this." He opens the glove box and pulls out a gun. "Don't shoot it. The windows will be blacked out, and we have no idea where Anabelle is sitting."

I nod, taking the gun from him. "You have one of these for yourself?"

He grins. "Of course." Then he reaches down near his ankle and pulls a gun from a holster there.

Kol puts the car back in drive and drives to where we talked about, parking it so that it's blocking the entrance.

"Ready?" he asks.

"More than," I say and push open the door.

401

Fear threatens to overtake me as I lie stomach-down in the ditch at the side of the road, half covered with muddy water and rain pelting my face. Not fear for myself, but for what Anabelle might be experiencing right now.

I force it away in favor of the rage that's like a hot coal in my abdomen.

Enough time passes that I wonder if we got it wrong, if Preston isn't coming back here. Just when I begin to give up hope, I hear the hum of a vehicle engine over the sound of the rain.

I don't dare peek to see if I'm right, instead waiting until it gets closer. When I hear the car approach, then the slight whine of brakes and the sound of the engine running changes, only then do I raise my head to make sure it's a limo.

It is.

Like a shot, I burst up out of the ditch. One quick tug on the door handle of the car tells me it's locked. With every bit of strength I have, I smash the butt of the gun against the window, and it shatters. I hear the window on the other side of the vehicle do the same.

Preston is on my side, and before he can turn the gun on his lap in my direction, I reach in and smash his head against the door. It stuns him enough that I can hit the unlock button, then swing the door open.

I yank him out and throw him on the pavement. He's still stunned, blinking up at the rain and probably wondering what the hell just happened. I'm on him in an instant. My hand is at his throat, the gun at his temple.

"You dare to touch what's mine!" I shout over the rain. I fist his collar, pull him up, and pummel the back of his head against the road.

I want to draw this out, make him pay, but I know that I'll never be able to. I have to settle for my face being the final thing he sees before he dies.

"You're going to rot in hell, and if I find out that you laid even a finger on her, I'm going to drag you back out of there myself and kill you all over again." In my fury, I lift him again and smash his head down. Blood trickles out from under him and quickly disperses in the rain.

I need to get to Anabelle. I need to see if she's okay. I didn't even chance a look at her in the limo because all I could think about was making this piece of shit pay.

Removing my hand from his collar, I press the gun to his temple again and press the trigger. A sick sense of satisfaction courses through me at the bloody trail that runs from the road down into the ditch.

I push the gun into my waistband and pop up. "Anabelle!"

Frantic, I rush to the other side of the limo and find Kol there with one arm wrapped around a weeping Anabelle. The other is pointed at the driver, who's standing beside the driver's side door with his hands raised.

"Anabelle, are you okay?" I rush to her, pulling her away from Kol and letting my hands skim gently over her face.

She has a cut over her eyebrow and a bruise already forming there. There's also a bruise blooming on her collarbone. I'm sure there are more I can't see right now.

"Asher," she weeps, crashing into my chest and wrapping her arms around me.

I hold her but not too tightly because I don't want to hurt her. "Are you okay?"

"I am now," she says.

"You two take off. I assume your jet is here?" Kol says, and I nod. "I'll take care of this mess. You get Anabelle home."

I glance in the direction of Preston's body. "You sure?"

"I got this."

I nod and pull Anabelle around the limo and Kol's car and through the airport's entrance. "Don't look behind you."

I don't want her even more traumatized from seeing Preston's body.

The rain beats down as I pull my phone from my pocket and hit the pilot's contact, telling him to ready the jet ASAP. The stairs on my jet are down by the time we reach it, and Millie, the flight attendant I've employed for years, looks at us wide-eyed. I'm not worried about her telling anyone what she sees. I pay all my employees well enough to prevent that from ever happening.

"Tell Ralph we need to leave as soon as possible."

She nods and takes off in the direction of the cockpit while I bring a trembling Anabelle to the back of the plane where my bedroom is. I lead her to the end of the bed and force her to sit down before I take a seat beside her.

"Are you okay?"

She nods, squeezing her eyes shut. "I was so scared, Asher. Thank you for coming for me."

She hugs me, and I take her in my arms, running my hand up and down her back, so grateful that she's okay. When she pulls away with tears in her eyes, my gaze snags on the injury on her head.

"I'll have the doctor meet us at Midnight Manor to have a look at you. Did he..." I gulp hard, unable to say the words.

If Preston sexually assaulted Anabelle, I swear I'll figure out some way to make him pay, even in death.

She shakes her head. "No, no, you found me before he could... but he said he was going to. He was going to do it and send you a tape of it." Her face crumples, and she cries again.

That cuts like a blade over my skin, bleeding me out because it's all my fault. If it weren't for me, she wouldn't be traumatized like this.

I draw her into me until she settles, then I ask if she wants to take a shower. "I have some spare clothes I keep in the plane that you can change into."

She nods. "Will you come in the bathroom with me, though? I don't want to be alone."

I cup the uninjured side of her face. "Of course."

Once we're in the air, I help Anabelle out of her dress. When I spot another bruise developing on her arm to match the one on her head and her collarbone, I feel as though I might be sick. If I'd been a few minutes later...

It's then I know what I have to do. It will kill me to do it. I'll never be the same.

But I love her too much to let her be in harm's way because of me. I can't let her be in danger because of me, the same way my mother was. That would make me just like my father.

CHAPTER
FORTY-ONE

ANABELLE

When we arrived home last night, the doctor was there to meet us. He didn't think I had a concussion, but I did need stitches on my forehead. My injuries gutted Asher. The expression on his face as the doctor sewed up the gash on my forehead was so tortured it's embedded into my memory.

Asher undressed me, helping me into a silk nightgown, pulling back the covers and tucking me in. Sleep came quickly, but for how long I'm not sure. I wake up stiff and achy, darkness descending. Confused, I roll over to feel the bed empty beside me. Searching the room, I find him sitting in the same chair he was the night he found me in the basement.

"What are you doing all the way over there?" I ask, my hand stretched out for him to take.

"I didn't want to wake you." His voice is gravelly and heavy bags sit under his eyes showing he hasn't slept at all.

"What time is it?" I yawn even though I slept the day away.

"Just after seven in the evening."

I nod and stretch but wince from the bruise on my arm. Asher cringes and glances away from me.

"Are you hungry? I can have Mrs. Potter make you something." There's no love in his voice. It's monotone and devoid of emotion.

"A little maybe."

He stands and starts for the door without a word. What has happened to the man I love?

"Asher, wait." My own voice barely a whisper in the big room.

He stops but doesn't turn around.

Having no choice, I ask his back, "What's going on? Why are you being different?"

At first, he doesn't look like he's going to respond, but he slowly circles around, and I gasp seeing the water filling his eyes. "You could have died, Anabelle," he croaks.

I frown. "But I didn't. You made sure of that."

His face transforms to wrath, all hard lines and sharp edges, and he strides toward the bed. Resembling nothing like the man I know. "You would have died because of me!" His fingers jam into his chest, his eyes lighting with fury.

410

My head rocks back. "I have you to thank for still being alive."

"Thank me?" He spits the words out with disgust. "You wouldn't be in this position if it weren't for me." He pushes a hand through his hair, his calming mechanism.

I stand from the bed and pad over to him. "Asher..." I gently pull his hand out from his hair. "Preston made the decision to take me, not you. That's on him."

He shakes his head. "No, it's on me because I couldn't leave well enough alone. I had to stick it to him and embarrass and shame him publicly. If I hadn't taken his company away from him, he never would have kidnapped you."

"That's not true." I shake my head, attempting at every angle for him to look at me. See the truth in my eyes.

"It is!" he bellows.

I step back from his anger, and he sighs.

"It is," he says softer this time and places each of his hands on either side of my face, cradling it. "I can't do this to you. I can't let your fate end up like my mother's." Then he releases me and turns his back to me.

I still, my stomach drops, and my body shakes. Tears well up threatening to fall. "What do you mean?"

"You need to leave."

"What?" I place my hands on his back, lowering my head to lie at the strength that lies underneath. "You can't mean that."

He turns, taking my wrists in his, holding them suspended in the air. "Now. Tonight. Your estate is yours. I've wiped the debt clean. You need to get far away from me."

Tears sting my eyes, and I shake my head, wringing my wrists to get free. "No. No, I'm not going anywhere. You're just upset—"

"You're leaving, Anabelle." He releases my wrists and the voice that comes out of his mouth is the same cold, calculating one he used when we first met. "Grab your things and leave. It's for the best. This was never going to be a happy ever after anyway, and if you thought it was, you were as delusional as I was."

My mouth opens and closes like hungry fish in a pond. "You don't mean it."

"Every word."

Despite my best effort to not show emotion, a single tear tracks down my cheek. "I thought you cared about me." If he did, there's no way he could send me packing just because he's scared, right?

"It doesn't matter how I feel. The fact is I will not let you pay for my sins." His voice is hard and unwavering.

"So you're just going to push me away? And what, go back to fucking random women in the basement?" The thought of him with someone else makes me sick, and I press my hand against my stomach praying I don't throw up all over him.

"I'll go on with my life, and you'll go on with yours. Move back to Nashville, the further away from me the better. Go do whatever it is you want to with your life. You're young, you still have lots of time to figure it out. I made arrangements for your mother to be checked into the Briarwood Mental Health Facility. All the costs have been taken care of. You just have to call them up."

I shake my head still lost on how we got to this place. We were so happy. "I can't believe you're doing this," I whisper.

"It's what has to be done. I'll get out of your hair so you can gather your things. I expect you not to be here when I return." He stalks toward the door.

The agony of heartbreak is replaced with a vengeance of anger roaring inside of me. How dare he cast me away like this? Did he never care for me? Was I not enough for him?

"I hate you!" I shout, grabbing the first thing off the nightstand and throwing it as hard as I can at him.

The item shatters, and I see the necklace he gave me only two nights ago in a million pieces.

Asher pauses with his hand on the door and takes one last look over his shoulder. He looks resolved, which somehow only makes me feel worse. I crumple to the floor, sobbing, not knowing what to do with myself until my anguish gives way to anger.

Screw this. If he wants to toss me aside like I'm nothing to him, I can do the same. I rush out of his room and into my own, grabbing my purse, and taking only that with me. I don't want to take anything that garners any memories of him with me.

Within minutes, I'm driving through the iron gates of Midnight Manor for the last time. I'm sobbing again, the anger dissipating now that I'm off the property.

Where am I going to go? I don't want to go home, not yet. Not until I have a handle on my emotions. I don't want to have to explain to my brother and grandmother why I have stitches on my head and why I'm home for good.

I find myself in town and park in the lot beside Black Magic Bar. Numbing myself with alcohol sounds good. I'll worry about how to make it home later. Maybe if I call my brother from the bar phone, he'll pick me up. Asher never did return my cell phone.

Sawyer is bartending when I go in, which is a bit of a bummer. I was hoping it would be Cinder. Surely some guy has screwed her over in the past, and we could commiserate together.

"Two tequila shots and three fingers of bourbon," I tell him as soon as I sit at the bar.

"Going a little heavy to kick things off, don't you think?" Sawyer says, eyeing the bruises and the stitches on my face.

"Shut up and just get me the drinks."

He raises his hands in a placating gesture and goes about putting my order together. I knock back the first shot without a chaser, then the second and slide the empty shot glasses his way before taking a hefty sip of bourbon.

An hour later, I have a good buzz on. While I'm still wallowing, the pain has dulled somewhat.

That is, until the biggest pain in the ass known to man pulls up the stool beside me.

"Can't believe he let you out for the night," Galen says.

I turn my head to glare at him, ready to give him the what for when the shock on his face registers. It takes me a moment to understand what it's about, but when he opens his mouth to speak, I know.

"Did Asher Voss do this?" He stands, towering over me, his eyes and finger pointed to my forehead.

"Of course not." I roll my eyes at Galen and take another sip of my drink.

"What happened then?" Anger rolls off him like a tumbleweed.

I press my lips together. I can't tell him what happened to Preston. That Asher killed him. I might be pissed as hell at Asher right now, but I would never let him go down for protecting me from a predator like Preston Wallace.

Time runs too short, and my mind too occupied with what just happened that I'm unable to come up with a convincing lie.

"That's what I thought." He slams his hand on the bar top, and I flinch. "I've had enough of the Vosses thinking they can do whatever the hell they want around here. One little call from Asher to my boss, and I'm shut down from pursuing anything against them. They're not above the law. But this." He stares at my forehead again. "This is where their privilege ends." He stalks toward the door.

I grab my purse off the bar top and race after him. "Galen! Galen, wait!"

He ignores me and pushes the door open. He's not in uniform, but he has his police cruiser with him, parked at the side of the building.

"Wait!"

"I should've done this a long time ago," he says as he whips open the driver's door. "All those mystery cars coming and going. The parties that no one knows what's happening up there. I'm done letting them take what's mine—my authority, my town, my woman."

"Galen, wait!" I come up behind him, pulling on his arm to get him to turn around. "Asher didn't do this to me, I swear."

"Sure he didn't." He wrenches his arm out from my grip.

"I promise you it's the truth." I grow frantic, and panic courses through me.

Galen pats my shoulder. "Okay, okay, Anabelle. Relax, okay?"

Thankfully, he seems calmer, so I shake my head, ready to convince him further.

"You've been drinking. Do you want me to drop you off back at Oak Haven?" he asks.

If it means getting him to give up on going up to Midnight Manor, then yeah, I do. "That would be great."

"No problem. You'll have to sit in the back though. I'm not allowed to have anyone ride up front with me."

"Sure, whatever." I mindlessly wait for him to open the back door. As long as I get him to my estate, he'll forget this whole thing with Asher.

He opens the back door for me, and I slide in. Once both feet are in, Galen rips my purse from my hand and slams the door shut. I lunge for the door handle, but there isn't one, and the locks click into place in the front.

"What the hell?" I bang on the window with my fists.

Galen bends down so his face is on the other side of the glass. "I won't let you screw this up for me." He fishes my keys out of my purse and stalks over to my car. He gets in and drives away.

No, no, no!

I bang on the window until my hand aches and try unsuccessfully to get the door open, but there's no way to unlock it from back here. Standing between the front seats and me is a black metal cage-like partition.

I have to stop Galen. He's on a mission, and I just know it's not going to end well.

After banging some more on the window and getting nothing but an aching hand, I lie down on my back and start kicking the glass. It doesn't budge, but I keep trying.

After about a minute or so, I hear, "Anabelle?"

I whip up to see Cinder staring at me with wide eyes. She must be coming in to start her shift.

"Cinder! Oh thank god. You have to get me out of here."

"What are you doing back there?" She tries the door, but it won't open from the outside either.

"Galen trapped me back here. He's off to hurt Asher!" At least that's what I'm assuming. He definitely seemed like he was in a 'shoot first, ask questions later' mood.

"Okay, hang on." Cinder disappears from view and returns a few minutes later with a car jack in her hands. "Back up!"

I move to the far side of the car and tuck my head down with my hands over my head, then hear *bang, bang* and finally the splintering of glass. Two days and two broken windows.

"Thank you!"

She helps me out through the window, and I narrowly miss face-planting in the dirt parking lot.

"Are you okay?" Her gaze snags on the cut on my forehead.

"Yes! I just have to get up to Midnight Manor."

"Here, take my car." She shoves her keys at me and points in the direction she's parked. "The blue Toyota."

I give her a quick hug. "Thank you, I promise I'll bring it back in one piece."

Without waiting for her to say anything, I rush over to the car, start it, and race out of the parking lot.

CHAPTER
FORTY-TWO

ASHER

Sending Anabelle away was the hardest thing I've ever had to do. I almost couldn't do it. Once I left that room, I almost raced back there a hundred times to take it all back. But then I'd think of my mother and her fate because of the man she was married to, and I'd stop myself. I can't be the reason for Anabelle's demise.

I've been wallowing and drinking since she left, trying to relive the memories so I don't ever forget them. They're all I have left of her, and I couldn't bear if they too disappeared one day.

I'm still wallowing when my cell phone rings. I know it's not Anabelle because she doesn't even have my number. I confiscated her phone as soon as she arrived here. That's the only reason I bother to pull it from my pocket.

"What?" I say by way of answering.

"Mr. Voss, it's Philip from the front gate. We've just had a breach, sir."

I sit up straight in my chair. "What happened?"

"The car just careened right through them, sir. It was Miss Boudreaux's car, sir, but—"

I hang up, standing and rushing out of the room.

What the hell is Anabelle thinking? She could have been hurt. I know she's pissed at me, but she can't put herself in danger.

I run through the house, both desperate to see her and afraid to. Afraid I'll be too weak to send her away again now that I know what it feels like without her, even if it was only for a few hours.

When I burst through the front door, her car comes to a screeching halt nearby. But instead of Anabelle getting out of the car, it's that asshole Galen.

"What the fuck do you think you're doing?" I stalk over to him, and I'd love nothing more to flatten him.

"I saw what you did to her. You Vosses think you can get away with anything."

"I would never raise a hand to her. She'd tell you the same." My hands form into fists at my side.

"She did tell me. She confirmed for me that you're the one who hit her and put those bruises on her. That you're the one who hurt her."

His words make me stumble back. Anabelle might be mad at me, but would she really falsely accuse me of something she knows I loathe my father for doing to me?

"I'm here to arrest you, and this time, all the money in the world won't save you, Voss."

"I'm not going anywhere. Get off my property before I call the feds and have you arrested." I turn and make my way back into the house when I hear the cocking of a gun.

I slow, circling around to Galen.

"Make your way toward me slowly so I can put the cuffs on you."

"Get off my property. I'm not going to ask you again," I growl.

He laughs, and he sounds a little unhinged. "You're not in control. Not this time anyway. Now do what I told you."

"Not a chance."

"As much as you'd like to think you're above the law, you're not. You and your entire family are a menace to this town. Doing God knows what up here in this place. Do you know how many investigations I've tried to open only to be shut down by a phone call from the higher-ups? Even Anabelle's dad's death never got a proper investigation because of your interference. Why wasn't I called to the scene to see the body? You four have always thought you were above the law, but not anymore. Everyone knows your dad was fucked up. Who knows what your mother was like? It's probably good she was murdered so that she's not here to see how you four turned out. Don't worry, I'll take gooood care of Anabelle once you're charged."

At the mention of Anabelle and my mother in the same sentence, I lunge at him, uncaring that he's holding a gun.

The sound of a gunshot ricochets from both in front of me and behind me, then it feels as if someone has punched me in the chest. I suck air for a second and stumble before falling to the ground. Then I'm looking at the starry night sky.

There's some kind of commotion going on around me— screaming and yelling maybe? I'm not sure. Then she's there. My angel. My Anabelle. Her face is over mine, blocking out the sky, but that's okay because she's more beautiful than the night sky could ever be.

But she's crying for some reason. I frown and try to say something to her.

"Shhh, no, don't say anything." She pushes on my chest, and that's when I feel it. My shirt is wet and pain sears through me like a branding iron.

Anabelle keeps crying and saying she's sorry, but why?

"I love you," she says when she presses her forehead to mine.

I swear I hear "Dies Irae" before everything goes black.

AT FIRST, I'm afraid when I wake up to darkness, but then I see a pinprick of light in the distance, and I walk toward it. I keep walking, and at first it feels as if I'm making no progress, but finally the light gets bigger, and I can feel the warmth radiating off of it.

"Asher, you're going the wrong way."

The voice startles me for a moment, its familiarity. It's been so long since I've heard it. "Mom?"

"Asher, turn back."

I frown, then race toward the light, race toward her. "Mom!"

When the light is so big it almost fills my entire vision, I see her, and tears leak out of my eyes. She looks so beautiful. Just like I remember from when I was a child. Unlike when I was a child though, she looks at peace, happy.

"Mom, you're okay."

She smiles serenely, dressed in an iridescent white gown. "You have to go back, son. It's not your time."

Why would she try to send me away? I haven't seen her in so long.

"But I want to be with you, Mom. I miss you." My breathing is ragged.

She touches my cheek the way she used to do, and a feeling of peace washes through me. "We'll be together again eventually. But not now. I sent her to you. You must go back to her."

My thoughts are slow like molasses. "Who?"

"Anabelle. You have to go back to her, son. She needs you."

Anabelle.

Everything rushes back to me at once. Galen showing up at the manor, Anabelle crying over me, the pain I felt when I sent her away.

I look at my mother, tears cascading down my face because I know she's right. I need to be with Anabelle, and that means saying goodbye to my mother—again.

"It's okay, son. I'll be here when it's your time. Go, be happy. You deserve it." She lets her hand drop from my face.

"I love you," I tell her.

The moment the words leave my lips, I feel as if I'm being sucked backward through a tunnel.

"I love you too, son" sounds from everywhere and nowhere all at once.

And then once again, there's nothingness.

CHAPTER
FORTY-THREE

ANABELLE

Sitting beside his hospital bed, I clutch Asher's hand. I haven't left him since they wheeled him in here three days ago.

The horror I felt when I saw him bleeding out on the ground still haunts me. I don't think it's an image I'll ever get out of my head. All I could think of was that he was going to die without knowing I loved him. I never had the courage to tell him.

They had to restart his heart twice when he was on the operating table, and the first twenty-four hours after surgery were harrowing. I made a promise to myself that if he made it out of this alive, I would tell him exactly how I feel about him, no matter if I'm scared that he doesn't feel the same or that he'll still want to send me away.

I hear the door creak open behind me, then Sid's voice. "Anabelle, you should really go home. Get some rest, shower."

I shake my head as he comes around to the other side of the bed. "Is that your way of telling me I stink?"

He eyes me with pity. "That's my way of saying you need to take care of yourself too. Whether you're here or not won't change the outcome. Let me take over for a bit."

Asher's brothers have been surprisingly kind and supportive over the past few days. Even Kol, who I have to thank for the fact that Galen is dead.

Apparently, security called Kol after Asher hung up on them before they could tell him it wasn't me driving my vehicle when it burst through the gates. Kol saw that Galen had been about to pull the trigger and shot too, hitting him between the eyes and killing him instantly.

It took Kol a day to show up at the hospital because he was questioned by police. Sid told me what story to tell about my injuries when they came to speak to me at the hospital —I had fallen down the stairs. The doctor who had stitched me up backed up my story. Everything that had happened with Galen at the bar, I told the truth about.

Kol was released and not charged. I don't know if that's because they worked some billionaire voodoo magic or what, and I don't care. No one should pay the price for killing a piece of shit like Galen LeBlanc.

I squeeze Asher's hand and push the hair off his forehead. "I'm not going anywhere, Sid."

He nods, accepting that he's not going to get anywhere with me on this subject. Nero and Kol have already tried and given up.

We're both quiet, gazing down at Asher. His skin is still a sickly gray color, nothing close to its usual olive tone.

"Do you think he's going to wake up?" I ask in a low voice.

"The doctor says there's no reason he shouldn't."

I wish his words inspired confidence. "I know, but it's been three days."

"His body has gone through a lot of trauma. It needs to heal." Sid gives me a wan smile, and I nod.

"Any change?"

I turn and see Kol walk into the room.

I frown. "No change. Not yet."

He nods and stands beside me, squeezing my shoulder. It's obvious to me that this past week has really shaken him.

I turn and look up at Kol. "I never got to thank you for what you did the night of the gala. And for shooting Galen."

We haven't really broached either subject. When I asked once what became of Preston and the driver, Kol shut me down right away, telling me that the less I knew, the better.

Kol squeezes my shoulder again before letting his hand drop.

I'm not surprised he doesn't say anything. He's a man of few words.

It's weird, but over the past few days, I've come to feel as close to Kol, Sid, and Nero as I do my own brother. I suppose going through trauma together will do that.

Luke stopped by yesterday to see me after he heard through some people in town what had happened. He wasn't pleased that he had to hear it from other people, but once I explained that my entire focus is on Asher, he seemed to come around.

"Where's Nero?" I ask to fill the silence.

"With his irritating fiancée," Kol says.

I shake my head. "Try to be nice."

"He said they'll be by this afternoon," Sid says.

I nod and stare back down at Asher. "I just want him to wake up." I stand and hover over Asher, bringing my lips to his forehead. "I love you. Please come back to me."

When I pull away, I gasp when I see his deep blue eyes gazing up at me.

"Either I died and am in heaven, or I'm dreaming and when I blink, you'll be in some naughty nurse's outfit."

"Asher!" I hug him on instinct but pull away when I hear him groan. "I'm sorry."

"I'll get the doctor." Sid rushes from the room.

"Asher, you're awake. Oh thank god, I was so scared."

"Good to see you on the right side of the sod, brother," Kol says from behind me.

Asher chuckles but cringes in pain. "Thanks. What happened after I was shot?"

"Don't you worry about that. There will be lots of time to talk about that. We're just all so glad that you're okay."

The doctor rushes in with Sid at his heels and demands that we all back up and give him some room to examine Asher.

I move to the corner, biting my lip and anxious for the moment the doctor says everything checks out. And then it hits me—what if Asher still sends me away once the fog of his recovery wears off? What if he still doesn't want to be with me?

No. I don't care what I have to do to convince him. I'm not going anywhere.

The doctor does his thing, and when he's finished, he turns to us. "Everything looks good. Assuming there are no setbacks, he should be able to go home in a couple of days." He turns to look at Asher. "You'll need to come back for some follow-ups, but you can recover at home and have a nurse come in everyday to check on your progress."

When Asher doesn't respond because he's staring across the room at me, Sid steps in. "Thank you, doctor. We appreciate all you've done for us."

The doctor says his goodbyes and leaves the room. Asher is still staring at me.

"We'll give you two some time alone." Sid looks at Kol and nods toward the door.

The door closes behind them as I walk over to the bed, unsure what to expect from Asher. Will he be happy that

I'm here? I take the seat I was in before, and he reaches for me. I take his hand and clutch it as though he might disappear.

"Anabelle, I'm sorry for the things I said. For sending you away like I did."

The anxiety rushes from my body, replaced by elation. Tears swim in my eyes. "I was so scared when I found you."

"I was so afraid I was going to die before I could tell you I love you," he says.

I blink, and the first tears fall.

"I've never loved anyone like I love you, Anabelle, and I refuse to be away from you again. I want you to be a part of my life forever. Whatever that means to you, I don't care. We can live together, be a Dom and Sub, get married... I just know that living without you isn't an option."

I let my head drop and bring his hand to my forehead while I cry in relief. Once I've composed myself, I look back up at him. "I was prepared to fight you and tell you that I'm not going anywhere. Thank you for saving me the trouble."

He chuckles and cringes again.

"I love you, Asher Voss. All the parts of you. The damaged ones, the healing ones, and the perfect ones. I never want to be without you again." I stand and lean over him, pressing my lips to his.

"Forever," he says.

"Forever."

❧

ASHER HAS BEEN RECOVERING at home for a couple weeks now and is finally able to get out of bed and walk around a bit. He certainly hasn't been the easiest of patients, but I'm not complaining. I'm just happy that he's here for me to fuss over.

Today, I'm taking him to see his surprise as part of his daily walk. We move slowly through the house because I don't want him to overdo it, and when we reach the entrance to the maze, I turn to him.

"You sure you're up for this? If not, it can wait for another day."

"Stop worrying about me. Let's go." He starts in ahead of me.

I roll my eyes and follow him. Because I've been in and out of this maze so many times, it doesn't take long for us to approach the center square.

"I've been working on this for a while," I say as we get close. "I wanted to do this for you because I could tell it was special to you."

He takes my hand and squeezes, giving me a quizzical look. "I'm intrigued."

We walk into the open square, and he sees his surprise right away. I know because he stops walking, and when I look up at him, his eyes are glassy with tears.

"How..."

I let go of his hand and walk over to the rose bush that's in full bloom and healthier than ever. Plump red roses cover the bush, and gone are the dying leaves and the overabundance of thorns. "I found a book of your mom's in the library, and she had a bunch of notes in it on how she cared for it. I just followed her instructions."

"My mother..." he whispers and steps up beside me. "Anabelle, I..."

He doesn't finish his sentence, instead bending down and kissing me thoroughly. Joy fills in my chest. His reaction is all I could have hoped for.

He pulls away and cups my face. "Marry me."

I blink several times and let out a nervous chuckle. "What?"

We haven't discussed what he said to me in the hospital bed. It didn't seem right to talk about when he was still bedridden and recovering.

"I'm not prepared. I don't have a ring or anything with me, but I'll get you whatever you want. Just please, be my wife. I won't live without you, and I want to be as committed to you, to us, as I can be."

Maybe it makes me crazy, but I don't have to think about my answer. I'm nodding before he's even finished speaking. "Yes, I'll marry you!"

He kisses me again. Eventually we sink down onto the ground, making love among the petals and the thorns.

EPILOGUE
NINE MONTHS LATER...

ASHER

Anabelle and I were married in an intimate springtime ceremony in the center of the maze. It seemed fitting. That's where we first came together, it's where we committed to our lives together, and it's where the symbol of my mother was nursed back into being by the love of my life.

A week after she agreed to marry me, I presented her with a giant rock of an engagement ring as well as another day collar. The single strand of diamonds rests around her neck right now as a symbol of our Dom/Sub relationship while the engagement ring and wedding band serve as signs of our love and commitment to each other.

"I don't know how you're dealing with it all, Nero," Anabelle says from my left. "I'm so thankful we had a small ceremony. I can't imagine having to make all the decisions you guys are making." Then she turns to me. "Can you pass me the bacon?"

Anabelle is now a regular at the breakfast table of course. I didn't think I'd get so much joy from watching her relationship with my brothers grow, but I do. They're about as overprotective of her as I am at this point.

Last week, Anabelle left the manor on her own to visit Oak Haven Estate, and Sid questioned whether I thought that was a good idea or not.

He needn't have worried. I had one of the security personnel tail her to make sure she wasn't in any danger. What she doesn't know won't hurt her. I'm still paranoid about someone who hates me wanting to use her as a pawn.

Her mom has been back home for a few months. The facility they put her in, which I had arranged before I sent Anabelle away, did wonders. Things aren't perfect, but Anabelle's mom has more good days than bad now, and her bad days are nowhere near as bad as they used to be.

It was nice to see that light in Anabelle's eyes when she spoke about her mom when she came back from their visit.

"I just want Maude to be happy. Whatever she wants, she can have," Nero says.

Since Maude accepted Nero's proposal, it's been full steam ahead on the wedding planning. They're having a huge affair this fall. I keep waiting for him to figure out she's not who she says she is, but so far, he's a fool in love. Aren't we all, I suppose? Hell, maybe I'm wrong, and I'm just being overprotective like always. Time will tell.

"Have you settled on the flowers yet?" Anabelle asks.

I think she makes sure to show extra interest because I literally never ask anything.

"Not yet. Still searching for the perfect shade of blush pink, I'm told." He laughs as though it's endearing and not at all idiotic.

I sigh, and Anabelle squeezes my knee under the table. I take it for the warning it is.

"I'm sure it will all come together before the big day." I smile then shove my honey toast in my mouth.

Anabelle squeezes my knee again, and I can tell that this time, it's for a job well done.

I kiss the corner of her eyebrow and murmur against her skin, "You keep doing that, and I'll have you back in bed in under five minutes, wife."

She grins at me when I pull away from her. "Maybe that's my plan."

Pushing my seat back, I look at Nero. "If you see Sid or Kol, tell them to come to my office later. I have a few things to discuss with them."

He nods and doesn't say anything about the fact that I'm cutting breakfast short to go fuck my wife. I'm sure he's used to it by now.

I have no idea where my other two brothers are, nor do I care at this moment.

"Bye, Nero. Have a good day," Anabelle says as I practically drag her from the room.

Once we're in our bedroom, I waste no time undressing my gorgeous wife. The diamond necklace stays on though. It takes me only minutes to divest myself of my own clothes.

I sit on the edge of the bed, leaning back on my palms. "Get over here and get on my lap, wife."

It didn't take long for me to figure out that Anabelle gets off on me calling her wife. It's just another tool in my arsenal to turn her on, though it doesn't take much these days. We're ravenous for each other.

She struts over to the bed and straddles me before sinking down on top of me.

"Fuck, you always feel so good." I lean forward and wrap my arms around her, tugging on her earlobe with my teeth.

Anabelle moans and moves her slick heat up and down my cock.

Since I was shot, the connection we share has only grown—both physically and emotionally. We share everything. I've even opened up to her about specific incidents I had to endure at my father's hands, and she's shared with me the trauma Preston and then Galen were for her.

It makes me feel connected to her on a level I didn't know was even possible. And that connection makes the sex even better than it was to begin with.

Together, we're healing.

I bring my thumb down to where we're joined, and she moans.

"Asher, oh god, don't stop that."

"No plans to, my love."

I work her the way I know she likes, and in less than a minute, she's clenching around me, milking my orgasm from my cock. We both climax on a cry, then wrap each other up while we recover.

A loud, angry knock sounds on the bedroom door. Someone has some fucking nerve.

"Go away!" I shout.

"We have a situation," comes from the other side of the door.

It's Sid.

"What the fuck kind of situation can we have this early in the day?" I grumble to Anabelle. "Come back later," I call to Sid.

"Asher, I wouldn't be standing outside this door having just heard the two of you come if it weren't important."

"Oh my god," Anabelle groans. She gets off of me and rushes to the bathroom.

I stride over to the door buck naked, not giving a fuck. If he wants to interrupt me while I'm fucking my wife, he can deal with it.

I swing the door open. "This better be good. You just embarrassed Anabelle."

Sid's gaze runs up and down my body, and he raises an eyebrow.

"What's so important that it couldn't wait?"

"Kol found Rapsody."

I blink several times. "Why did no one tell me?" My jaw hardens.

"You're in newlywed heaven. You two barely come up for air these days. We didn't want to bother you with it."

"You didn't have any issue bothering me now." I pinch the bridge of my nose. "So what, he went and confronted her?"

Sid shifts in place. Not good. "You could say that..."

My hand drops from my face. "Obsidian, what did he do?"

"Apparently yesterday was her wedding day. He may or may not have kidnapped her from the church."

It's Asher & Anabelle's big day and you're invited to attend!

Download your complimentary Bonus Scene by scanning the QR Code below:

Why is Kol so obsessed with finding Rapsody? Find out in
the next book in the Midnight Manor series,
Shattered Vows, a Rapunzel reimagining.

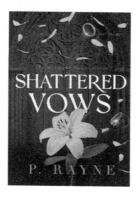

Acknowledgments

We hope you enjoyed diving into this new world we created at the top of the hill in Magnolia Bend!

The Midnight Manor series sort of came out of nowhere. We were finished writing the Mafia Academy series and had to start something new and so began the brainstorming process. It was a lot of... oh, what if we did a fairy tale retelling series... and what if we made them billionaires... and what if it had a gothic vibe to it... and maybe there could be sex parties! LOL Basically we threw a lot of what we love to read into one series to see what might come of it. We're delighted with the final product and how it turned out!

Writing about a brotherhood of billionaires is a lot of fun because they can pretty much have whatever you want. LOL You want a private plane? Done. A hedge maze? Done. A separate residence for the staff? Done. We're excited to explore what other kind of goodies we'll find on the Midnight Manor property in the coming books!

We like to think that while Asher and Anabelle have found their HEA in each other, their story is still evolving. Asher has started healing and Anabelle has her own traumas to deal with and those aren't things that we can put a nice bow on in this story's space of time. BUT, we can make it clear to the reader that they're on the right path and they'll get there eventually, together.

A huge thanks to everyone who helped bring this book to market...

A big thanks to the handful of beta readers we used throughout the process. Thanks for taking the time to read a sloppy copy of this manuscript and give us your thoughts!

Thanks as always to our editor and proofreader for helping us to take this story from a dull shine to a sparkling jewel!

The Valentine PR crew always keeps us in check and follows up and follows up to make sure we're hitting those deadlines. Not only do we need it, but we appreciate it!

A huge hug to every blogger, influencer and reader who was excited about this story as soon as they heard about it and who read, reviewed, shared or made edits. Word of mouth is so hard to come by and we appreciate all your hard work and efforts to help us spread the word about Moonlit Thorns. It does not unnoticed!

And a huge thanks to YOU for taking your precious time to read our story and to escape into our world for a while. We hope you'll return.

Midnight Manor still has a lot of secrets that need to come into the light so be sure to grab the next book in the series, Shattered Vows. It's a Rapunzel retelling between Kol and Rapsody!

xo,

Piper & Rayne

ABOUT P. RAYNE

P. Rayne is the pseudonym for the darker side of the USA Today Bestselling Author duo, Piper Rayne. Under P. Rayne you'll find dark, forbidden and sexy romances.

ALSO BY P. RAYNE

Mafia Academy

Vow of Revenge

Corrupting the Innocent

Corrupting the Mafia King's Sister

Craving My Rival

Standalones

Beautifully Scarred

Midnight Manor

Moonlit Thorns

Shattered Vows

Made in the USA
Monee, IL
30 September 2024